BETWEEN SHADOW AND FLAME

GUTHANDERKAZ BOOK ONE

C.T. BRYCE

ISBN: 9798987815908

FOR FULL CONTENT WARNINGS, PLEASE VISIT
www.guthanderkaz.com

Printed in the United States of America
Second Edition

This book is dedicated to you. Yes, you, the one reading this right now. Thank you for taking a chance with us.

We hope you find meaning in these pages, and enjoy the journey.

Contents

CHAPTER ONE

My childhood was a fairytale. I lived in a literal castle with a mother, father, and brother. Mom bolted when I was seven, taking me with her. I remember only snippets of that night, my confusion, her sobbing in a car. That was the end of the fairytale. She never told me why we left. She refuses to speak of it at all.

We never stopped running. The list of schools I've attended is longer than the average Spotify playlist. But I still haven't seen my Dad or brother since. Well, not in person, anyway.

Mom stashed some photos in a secret scrapbook. She doesn't know I'm aware of it, and I'm careful not to enlighten her. The first day we settle into a rental, she hides it, and I find it again the first chance I get. It's a fun game she has no idea we're playing. We've resided at this cottage for almost a month, and my first opportunity has finally appeared. Mom scheduled an interview marked 'all day.'

I dip from school early. Mom's hiding spot is uninspired (back of the closet, so clichè), and I find it immediately. I sprawl on the floor and flip to the correct page to claim my reward.

There are only a handful of pictures. There are some of those photo strips you get from amusement parks and some pictures with Dad and me, or all three of us. This is it; the only evidence I have that the family I remember even exists. There's nothing else, nothing on her phone, not even her wedding ring.

None of the pictures depict the castle or my brother. Sometimes, I wonder if I just dreamt up a brother so I'd feel like I had a true friend out there somewhere.

I search the photos for bits of myself in my parents' features. Dad's got these deep-set, upturned eyes; mine are the same shape, just more rounded, like Mom's eyes. I have his straight, greek nose… well, except for the tip. It's got a little bump at the end; I blame Mom's button nose. Dad's got these intense cheekbones and a strong jawline, in contrast to Mom's round-cheeked, heart-shaped face. I hope I inherit more of Dad's face shape as I grow older. I've definitely got his intense eyebrows. Even my pigmentation is a blend. Hair lighter than Dad's black, darker than Mom's blond. Dad's got black eyes, Mom's are sky blue, and mine? They're the color of a deep, deep ocean.

Yes, I'm obsessing over a million little details. But memorizing and noticing it all in private means that later, I can look in a mirror and see a shadow of Dad reflected back.

I hear the front door open and the sound of jangling keys. I glance at my phone. All day my ass, it's barely after lunch! I shut the book so softly that the sound's muffled by my exhaling breath and slip it back into its hiding place. My heart's beating as loud as the approaching clopping of her heels. Still, I take the time to move several papers, trying to set it precisely how I found it. If I'm discovered, she might throw out the scrapbook, too. Then I'd have nothing left.

There's only one door to her room. I hold my breath. Her footsteps pause in the kitchen, and I don't waste the opportunity. I dart to the window and squirm out in a flash.

I land as quietly as I can and crouch, tensed. I don't hear anything. I grab my backpack and edge forward, still crouched, to peer around the corner.

I see Mom through the living room window. She's holding the mail, staring at one letter in particular, uncharacteristically still. The address is turned towards her and away from me, not that I could read it from this distance. But it's sealed with a red wax stamp. Mom sinks into the seat, still staring at the letter. I'm torn between curiosity and caution. As usual, curiosity wins.

I burst into the front door without knocking.

"David!" Mom starts, scattering the mail across the floor. She curses softly and scrambles to scoop them up. I'm almost as alarmed as her; I can't remember seeing Mom react like that to anything.

"Sorry," I help her retrieve the mail. Yeah, it worked out for me, but I wasn't trying to scare her. "Are you okay?"

"Fine, I was just lost in thought." Mom smiles. Something's wrong. Mom's got dimples when she smiles and means it; there's no sign of them now.

The texture of one of the envelopes draws my attention. It's a rich toothy velvet, and it's heavier than the others. I look at it. It's the envelope I saw Mom staring at through the window. Up close, I can see an emblem sealed into the wax, a hydra, some mouths roaring, some holding objects. I flip it over, and Mom snatches it from my hands before I can read the address.

"Thank you, David," Mom says with an air of dismissal rather than gratitude.

"What's that? It looks-"

"Shouldn't you be in school?" Mom interrupts. Crap.

Mom reads my guilt before I can think of a defense and points to the door with a hand full of letters. "Room."

"But-"

"Now, David. I need to call the school," She says in that Angry Mom Voice. I retreat to my room. I know better than to argue with that tone.

Mom calls me back to the kitchen a short while later. She sits on one end of the table, hands curled around a teacup. Across from her at my usual spot is a steaming mug of hot chocolate. Oh no. She should be mad; why is she bribing me? It's still bright out, but there's now a crackling fire.

"Have a seat." She gives me a dimple-less smile.

I sit slowly, bracing myself for whatever doom she's clearly about to announce. Mom doesn't continue immediately, drumming her fingers against her teacup. "How much time do you have left in the semester?"

My stomach drops. "Why?" I ask. Mom opens her mouth as if looking for the right words, confirming my fears. "Mom, we just got here a month ago!"

"I know, sweetie; I'm sorry. I know this isn't easy… you know, we can always set you up with homeschooling," she offers, almost hopefully. It's not the first time. I clench my fist.

The only friends, the only social life I have, exists because of school. That's literally the only reason I go at all. I've tried socializing online, but I suck at social media, all of it. I have no problem making friends in person, but I'm miserable over text. "No," I say. It's all I can trust myself to say without involving things that shouldn't be told to a parent.

"If you're sure, I just think it would be easier for you. It would be consistent-"

"Still no. Where are we going?"

Mom hunches over her tea, averting her eyes. "I don't know yet."

"You don't even know? Then why are we leaving?"

"Current story isn't going to work out. You should get started on your homework."

"What the hell is the point of doing my homework?" I demand. "What difference is that going to make if we're going to leave… do you even know when?"

Instead of answering, Mom stands. "I'm sorry, David. You're right, you can stay home. I need to wrap up a few things. Why don't I order us some pizza?"

Another bribe.

I turn away from her to glare at the fire.

I should have gone today. I don't want to go back, but if I'd known, I'd at least have said goodbye. It doesn't matter. The whole class will forget me and the friendships we formed in a few months. They always do.

Red catches my eye. Wax bubbles at the heart of the fireplace, the exact color of the seal on the letter. The void in my stomach gapes further. I'm certain that that bit of wax is all that remains of the letter. And that letter might well involve why we left.

I pick up the hot chocolate and stalk to my room. If Mom isn't going to tell me anything, Fine. I'll just figure out why on my own.

I research dragons in heraldry and coats of arms. Apparently, hydras represent the conquest of a powerful enemy. Luckily for me, they are rare enough that the list of notable coats of arms with hydras takes up less than a page.

I hadn't had a great look at the seal for obvious reasons. Still, the glimpse I saw matches the island country of Fyrnlendh. I know nothing about Fyrnlendh.

I scan Wikipedia, hoping to find something useful. Unfortunately, the article on Fyrnlendh is boring. It's just a brief overview of geography, history, population, political system, and other useless statistics. I'm not sure what I'm looking for, but discovering Fyrnlendh is the leading exporter of gold is not it.

I finish the article and drum my fingers. None of the random trivia will help me figure out why Mom freaked out. I'm going to need something else.

I switch things up and search for Fyrnlendh in the news. The first page includes articles on various topics; civil rights laws, sports, weather, and a museum exhibit. I scan each one diligently, desperate for anything relevant.

A startlingly familiar face stares at me from my screen. I click on the article the photo is attached to without reading the title, scrolling until I see the full-sized, uncropped image. Dark eyes glare out from a scowling face I've stared at too often to confuse with anyone else, though never with this expression. I see in it features I recognize in a mirror. It's the face of my Dad.

I forget how to breathe. I can't so much as twitch my fingers, can't do anything but stare at the photograph. I gulp in air, but I can't get enough, and my heart is pounding in my ears. And it's him, it's him. I have no doubt, not with how long I've spent memorizing him.

I tear my gaze away from his, skimming the caption. "Lord Viktor Guthanderkaz," it begins, and I can't focus on the rest. Viktor. I've seen it before, in the album, scribbled on the back of a photo. I thought it might be his name, but I could never be sure, and I could never ask. Now I know. My Dad's name is Viktor. Viktor... how do you even pronounce the surname?

It doesn't matter. I copy paste the name in an email to myself, just in case. I can barely see the screen and realize that my eyes are blurry with unshed tears. I bite my lip, close my eyes, and press my hands against my face to push the tears away. I'm still shaking, still struggling to breathe normally.

And all the while, the thought repeats like a mantra. I found him. I found Dad. I have a Dad.

Was Dad the one Mom had been running away from? Did he know I was alive? Did he know I existed at all? Was he trying to find me?

I wish I could go back in time and grab the letter from Mom's hand. I would have if I'd known. I wouldn't have cared about the consequences. What punishment could she offer that's worse than burning a letter from Dad?

I need air. I need sun. I need to breathe again. Away from Mom and the cottage, away from everything. I stand on shaky legs and stumble out the window. I don't want Mom to see me like this; I don't want questions. I retreat into the forest. I need music--I don't care what. I shakily put on my earbuds and click at random. I just need to drown out my own thoughts.

An orchestra of strings rolls over me, cushioning me, shifting me one degree from reality. I let out a long slow breath, draw another in. I walk through the forest, watching leaves dance in the foliage above my head, almost in time with the song.

I find a large tree and lean against it, bark biting into my back. I need to find out more about him and then… then find a way to contact him. My legs lose their strength, and I slide to the ground. I pull my legs up, burying my head in them. What can I say? Hi, I'm your estranged son; oh, and by the way, do I have a brother or did I just imagine it?

What if he doesn't want me?

My lungs fill with ice. This time I can't hold back the tears. I rock back and forth, sobbing, hugging myself, submerged in my sorrow. I cry until there's nothing left, and then I just lie there, trying to process everything I learned today in a single day.

If I'm going to find my Dad, I have to face my Mom first. I'm emotionally exhausted. I definitely won't be able to handle it. I doubt I could even manage to explain why my eyes are swollen and red. Wouldn't make a strong statement when facing Mom anyway.

Instead of confronting her, I do a search using Dad's name.

Viktor Guthanderkaz, my Dad, is the head of some sort of royal family, which doesn't make much sense considering Fyrnlendh is listed as a democracy. Maybe they're just figureheads? Was the whole royalty thing why Mom left? Was she some sort of lost princess or something or trying to escape an arranged marriage?

But, no… they looked happy in the pictures. Hell, the fact that Mom kept them at all is telling. Why would she, if she hated him?

I return to the article, desperate for answers.

His wife is listed, and the name isn't Mom's. I shouldn't be surprised, but it still stings. It mentions Dad having two children, but no names are listed. I hope one of them is my brother. I hope my brother still likes me.

There's no mention of anyone else. No sign of Mom anywhere.

In fact, the article itself is ridiculously sparse. Apparently, the royal family keeps to themselves, and Fyrnlendh has extensive privacy laws. It's even a rumored destination for celebrities who want anonymity. (Which can't be confirmed because any confirmation not from the consenting subject is apparently illegal in Fyrnlendh. Talk about intense.)

Still, I have a name. That's more than I had before.

I confront her over breakfast. I don't ease into it; I don't have the energy, and patience has never been a strong suit of mine. And I'll never be able to eat until I do. "Why did you burn a letter from Dad?"

Mom's fork clatters to the table. She stares, ashen-faced. "What?"

I struggle to keep my voice steady. "When were you going to tell me? Were you *ever* going to tell me?"

"David," Mom breathes. She reaches her hand across the table towards mine. I jerk away, but hold eye contact, not about to back down. She lets her arm fall to her side, then presses one hand against her brow, leaning into it as if she has a headache. She starts again. "David, it's not that simple."

"Simplify it."

Mom turns away from me, breaking eye contact first. She stands. "I need tea. Do you want any, or maybe some hot chocolate?"

"I want Dad." I feel like a child saying it, but I don't care.

I hear her pause, and then the clinking of her bustling about the kitchen resumes. "You don't know your father, David."

"I do too," I say stubbornly, turning back to face her. "I remember him. I even remember what he looks like. It's how I figured it out." I don't mention the photos. I don't like the thought that I probably wouldn't have recognized him without them. It feels like a betrayal to admit, even to myself.

Mom stares at me for a long moment. Her brows draw together, and she turns away. "I didn't want this for you." She says, so quiet I can barely hear it.

"What exactly is the 'this?' you didn't want?" I demand. "Constantly moving and never having any real friends? Never knowing my family? My Dad? My brother."

I sound more confident of my brother's existence than I am, but the widening of her eyes confirms it. I do have a brother. The knowledge is immediately dampened. "Half brother."

For a second, I can't seem to process the words. "Half? But…"

"You were too young for us to explain it at the time. And we… we wanted you to be able to bond. Which clearly you did." Another false smile. I don't match it.

"So what happened?" I demand. Half brother… Did Dad cheat on her…? Is that what this is about?

"It wasn't safe," Mom says inscrutably. "For you… ..for any of us."

"What the hell is that supposed to mean?!"

"That those with power are rarely kind. And your paternal great-grandfather was a very powerful man." Mom speaks with a venom I've never heard from her before. She isn't looking at me anymore. Her eyes are distant, haunted.

I hesitate. Mom's clearly distressed, but... But I need to know. "So why isn't the rest of our family with us? Why isn't Dad? Or Basil."

Mom refocuses on me. "...you remember his name?"

I hadn't until I spoke it, but I disguise my surprise with a glare. I don't want to give her any ammunition to claim that whatever connection I have isn't good enough. "He's my brother." And the only genuine friend I've ever had.

"Half-" Mom starts, then sighs. "It doesn't matter. They... couldn't get out. Only we could. But it's what your father wanted too."

"Then what about the letter?! You didn't even read it."

Mom shakes her head, and her eyes are distant once more. "You don't understand. He didn't send that letter. He wouldn't have."

"You can't know that! You didn't even read it!"

"I don't have to," Mom says firmly and places two cups, one in front of herself and one in front of me. "Either way, it's not worth the risk."

"What risk?"

"You don't need to know the details because they will never find us."

"That isn't your choice to make!" I slam my hand against the table so hard tea bounces out of the cups, and I don't even care. "I have a right to know my family!"

"You don't know what you're asking. Your father and I made this decision together." Mom's voice doesn't rise to meet mine. She remains frustratingly calm as she wipes up some spilled tea with a napkin.

"You don't even know the one you're running from is still alive," I snap. "That was ten years ago, and if he's my great-grandfather, he has to be ancient."

Tears burn behind my eyes. "... you're never going to tell me, are you? You've been lying to me this entire time! The article wasn't canceled, was it? This isn't about finances; this is about running away."

"No." Mom takes my hands, staring intently into my eyes. "It's about protecting you."

I yank my hands away, jerking away from the table. Even now, even confronted, she isn't telling me anything. She'll never tell me anything or do anything.

Mom rubs at her forehead. "David… there's a lot about this you don't know and don't understand."

"Then fill me in. I'm not a kid anymore; I'm seventeen-" Mom gives me that infuriating look that tells me she absolutely considers seventeen to be a child, which just makes me angrier. I pretend not to notice and continue "-and for all you know, Dad changed his mind! Doesn't he have a right to?"

"He wouldn't," Mom says firmly, stabbing a piece of bacon with her fork.

"You don't know that! It's been ten years!"

"Eat your food, David," Mom says cooly. I glare at her, but shove some scrambled eggs into my mouth, mainly to avoid distracting the important argument with a stupid one about food. She continues as I eat, "It's my job to keep you safe. It hasn't been an easy task. Look at where we are." She lifted her hands to gesture, one still holding her fork, "and they still found us. This isn't the first time."

I swallow before I finish chewing. "Why burn the letter? Why not even let me see it?"

"It's not safe," Mom says again. She's repeating herself so much it feels halfway like talking to a video game character, the same dialogue on loop.

"Not safe to read?" I challenge.

"Yes." She says. I gawk at her. Mom is not usually like this; she's usually much more reasonable. Mom clearly notices and adds. "Clearly, even seeing it was dangerous."

I glower. "I thought you cared about the truth."

She straightens, voice sharpening. "David Rose."

"David Rose or David Guthanderkaz?" I challenge. I even pronounce it correctly, at least according to the pronunciation videos I found on YouTube.

"Do not say that name!" This time her voice isn't the usual Mom sharpness. She thunders at me like the voice of God echoing from the heavens, and I wilt back a bit, eyes wide. "Not in this house, not ever!"

"Why not?" I demand. "It's the name of my family."

"This is not up for discussion," Mom says, voice infuriatingly calm, picking up her fork again. "We're not going to contact them, and that's final."

"You don't have the right to make that choice for me!" I snap.

"Of course I do. I'm your mother." Mom says.

"You're a terrible mother!" I snap. I regret it immediately. The look of pain Mom is too shocked to hide etches in my memory. I jerk away from the table and flee to my room, ignoring her calling my name. I slam and lock the door, heart pounding. I don't want to hurt her, but she doesn't understand.

I can't remember the last time I cared this much about anything. I can't give it up.

Mom knocks at my door later, but I just put my headphones in and focus on what I'm doing.

I don't find a trace of Dad on social media. Not that I'd expect him to check his own messages if he did, he'd probably have a secretary or something for that.

Luckily, Fyrnlendh has an embassy. That's the good news.

The bad news is it isn't anywhere near here. I can't exactly ask Mom for a ride, not after how she reacted. The cheapest way to get there involves two buses and a train, takes over 40 hours, and costs around $200.

I couldn't pawn everything I own for $200; even if I could, Mom would notice. I'm not thrilled with the alternative.

Look, I'm not precisely the follow-the-rules sort. Rules are arbitrary and pointless, more about ego than ethics. But I still have morality. No amount of anguish or anger is going to make stealing from Mom feel right. I just don't see another option.

Besides, if this works out, surely Dad will pay Mom back, right? Right.

I know where Mom keeps her emergency cash. And this is an emergency, at least for me. The longer I take, the longer Mom has to figure out or try to stop me. She's already made it clear she's not willing to negotiate.

I don't emerge until the afternoon. The house is still as glass. There's a note tucked under the daffodil-filled vase at the table. It's brief.

Leftovers are in the fridge. I also made you some lunch. Please remember to eat. We'll talk more tonight.

I love you.

Mom.

Another pang of guilt pulses in my gut, but I push it aside and slip into her room. I hesitate after pulling out the money. I try to reassure myself by focusing on how much more she has after I take what I need. It doesn't help.

I pocket the money, but guilt still keeps me planted to the floor. I don't want to do this. It feels like a betrayal; I don't want to betray Mom. Why won't she listen? Why won't she talk about anything instead of saying I won't understand again and again like I'm an idiot two-year-old.

I clench and unclench my fists twice, taking in a deep breath. Then I grab a nearby piece of paper and scrawl a quick note.

Be back in a few days. Don't try to find me.

I hesitate, eyeing it, and then add my own

I love you.

I put it on her dresser instead of the kitchen table. I want her to find it, but not right away. Then I pick up my mostly packed backpack and stuff the leftovers inside. I'm just about to leave when another thought strikes me. I turn, return to Mom's room, and dig out the secret album. I scan the contents before making a selection.

It's a picture of my Dad holding me. I'm young in the photo, maybe three; I've never been good at judging the age of kids. Hopefully, old enough that a stranger can see the resemblance. With utmost care, I pull it out of its place and slip it into the back of my phone. It's easier to alter a file than a photo. I hope the authenticity will help.

I arrive at the Fyrnlendh embassy hungry, tired, and in need of a shower. It's a towering gothic building that looks ancient amongst the drab skyscrapers. The national flag flutters from a flagpole, and broad steps lead to a large double door recessed into the classic gothic arch. Dominating the front is an elaborate stone relief of the Fyrnlendh coat of Arms, from which roars the familiar Guthanderkaz Hydra.

I ascend the steps and enter a lush hallway. The walls and ceilings are black with gold trim. In fact, there's gold everything; light fixtures, furniture, art… someone really wants to remind everyone of their main export, I guess. Or has a very gaudy sense of interior design. Or both.

Three people stand at a front desk, and the only other door sits just behind a metal detector flanked by two tall men. Everyone in the room except me is wearing a black suit, and they all turn to face me as I enter.

I clear my throat and walk up to the desk, pretending not to be aware of how much I don't fit in. "Hi," I say as I approach, fiddling with my backpack. I never did come up with that plan.

Three faces stare at me with varying expressions. One looks outright disgusted, which, rude. Another appears to be a mixture between surprised and amused. But the one who speaks is a woman with dark features and a sympathetic smile. "Hey, can I help you? Are you lost?"

"Um, no. Or, I don't think so. Is this, um, the Fyrnlendh embassy?"

"That's right. Are you a Fyrnekh citizen or interested in our visa program?"

"No, um. This is a little complicated, actually. But I think my Dad's from Fyrnlendh." I say. Pretending not to know his status is my best chance at believability. "I have a picture."

"Is there a reason you're not here with your mother?" The woman asks, frowning.

I fidget, but decide to be honest here. "She doesn't want me to see him, but I have a right to at least meet him." I try not to sound defensive.

The woman opens up a notebook. "What's your name?"

"David."

"Last name?"

I bite my lip. "Rose."

The woman takes out a sticker that says 'Guest' in all capital letters, writes 'David' on it, and then hands it to me with a smile.

"Please have a seat, David Rose. I'll speak to one of our consulars, who might be able to help you with this. In the meantime, please wear this sticker for the duration of your visit."

"Thanks," I say, relieved.

I turn and retreat to one of the dark couches. It looks plush, and I expect to sink into it, but a log would be more yielding. Probably chosen for aesthetics instead of comfort. The woman picks up a phone and speaks what I assume is Fyrnekh. The words are a nostalgic jumble, like a childhood lullaby I've forgotten the words to. I shift my backpack into my lap, drumming my fingers.

My phone rings. It's Mom again. She's been calling me pretty non-stop since the first night. I haven't answered beyond texting her that I'm alive and refusing to tell her where I am. I'll let her know when I've actually been seen, I decide. When it's too late for her to interfere.

"David?" I look up.

A tall man with a thick accent regards me through square glasses. "I'll be helping you sort things out today if we can. Please come with me."

I follow him out of the room and through the metal detector into a hallway of dark wood doors, evenly spaced with no markings to differentiate them. Before I can process how easy it would be to get lost, my guide strides down the hall, and I hurry to keep up.

He shows me to a small, windowless office. A dark desk sandwiched by leather chairs takes up most of the room. There's little in the way of decoration, just the Fyrnlendh flag and a framed print featuring a floral painting you might find if you do a serach for 'generic office art.' The most personal thing is a gold nameplate reading "Fyorik Ketheyx." I hope I don't need to pronounce his last name.

"Have a seat," Fyorik says, gesturing to the chair closest to the door as he sits on the opposite side of the desk. I set my backpack down and fall into the chair.

"I hear you're trying to find family?" I nod, and before I can add, Fyorik continues. "What's their name?"

He positions himself in front of the computer, hands poised over the keyboard as he looks at me.

"Viktor..." I say, fidgeting.

"Viktor Rose?" The man asks a reasonable guess. I shake my head.

"Rose is my Mom's maiden name. I… don't know my Dad's. She doesn't talk about him… but I have a picture."

"…a photo may help." He doesn't sound confident. But he waits patiently while I dig out the photo, hesitating before offering it over.

"I was just a baby, but-"

He leans over, glances at it, and does a double-take. I can't blame him; this probably seems ridiculous, which is why my best bet is to play ignorant. "Maybe you could match it up to a driver's license or something? You guys have some form of photo I.D. like that, right?"

Fyorik's gaze flickers between me and the photograph. I keep my expression pleading and guileless.

"Is…that not a thing?" I ask when he doesn't respond immediately, disappointment coloring my voice.

This seems to pull Fyorik out of his stupor, and he hesitates, looking me over critically. "What do you know about Fyrnlendh?" He finally asks.

"Not much," I admit honestly, then eagerly add. "But they were speaking the language out there, I think? It sounds really familiar. I mean, I can't understand, but…." I trail off, flushing.

"If you were a small child, it can hardly be expected." He croons. He sounds sympathetic and seems to believe me, but now he's talking down to me. I'm seventeen, not seven. "May I see that? This… wouldn't be my area of expertise."

I hesitate. "You'll give it back?"

He smiles indulgently. "Of course. I might make a copy, though, if that's alright."

"That's fine," I say, but it still takes a moment of effort to offer him the picture.

He accepts it with surprising delicacy, cradling it as one might an exceptionally fragile flower. His care reassures me more than his words.

"I'll return shortly. Please stay here." He says, then heads out, leaving me alone in the room.

Fyorik returns maybe fifteen minutes later. He pauses, staring. I stare back at his upside-down face from where I've draped myself sideways on the chair. He clears his throat. "It's going to be a while. My… colleague is looking into things. Are you hungry? Thirsty?"

"Yeah, actually," I say, sitting up. My last meal was the day before, and not substantial, just a $3 ham and cheese on the train. "Both."

He looks strangely relieved. "Would you like me to, er, order you some cheeseburgers?"

I tilt my head. Is it common for consulars to order food for people they're helping? Why does he look nervous?

"Sure. Cheeseburgers sound great." I say, feigning ignorance of this strangeness.

He sighs with relief. "I will arrange that right away. Please wait here."

He leaves me alone to get food. If he expects it to take so long, why not just take my contact information and call me back? Especially if there's going to be enough time to get food. I shake my head, trying to dispell the feeling of unease.

My phone rings again. This time, I finally reply.

> *I told you I'm fine. I'm getting a hold of Dad.*

My phone buzzes almost immediately.

Do you have any idea how worried I've been? Where are you? And what do you mean getting a hold of your father?

> *I'm at the Fyrnlendh Embassy.*

There is a long silence, and I feel increasingly nervous, so I add.

> *I didn't want you to try to stop me. I know you would.*
> *This is my choice to make.*

There's an even longer silence. Anxiety and guilt stews in my stomach.

> *I borrowed money for the train. I'll pay you back.*

I'm not worried about the money, David. I just…
I'll be there soon.

The door opens, and I pocket my phone quickly, looking up at Fyorik as he holds out a bag of fast food and a soda. "Is this all right?"

"That looks great," I say eagerly. I'm starving, and I've always loved burgers.

Fyorik offers me the bag and soda and closes the door, reclaiming his seat across the desk from me. Which makes me a little self-conscious as I pull out a burger and take a huge bite. As I eat, I become increasingly aware of him studying my face and pause, looking at him. He averts his eyes quickly, but as soon as I resume eating, I can feel them on me again.

This is definitely unsettling, but pretending not to notice seems the safest way forward. "Um… is there a bathroom I can wash up in?" I ask after I finish.

"Oh! Of course, please, this way."

The restrooms are unexpectedly ostentatious. The whole place is, really. I was expecting a building like the DMV; lots of folding chairs and styrofoam ceilings, everything old, faded, and cheap. This place is more like a blend of the Ritz and the Backrooms.

I finish quickly and head out. Fyorik is waiting outside the door.

"By the way, do you have my picture?" I ask.

"Ah, yes… well, my colleague does. Why don't I bring you to sit, and I'll get it for you."

"Sure."

He leads me off again, but something feels wrong at the first turn. This is definitely not the way we came. I stop and point. "Isn't your office that way?"

Fyorik halts. Something about the set of his shoulders makes me think he was hoping I wouldn't notice. He turns to face me, smiling. "Yes, it's not very comfortable. Since it's a long wait, I thought you might prefer a more comfortable room, maybe with a window?"

Okay, a window does sound nice. I'm going to go crazy in this labyrinth of endless identical doors. "Sure, but can I grab my backpack first?"

"Ah, yes, of course." He turns and gestures, and I follow him.

I study his back for a moment. He's starting to feel less like a guide and more like a guard. I decide to test the theory. "How long is this going to take? Should I leave and have you call me back?"

"No! No, that… won't be necessary." He says. He sounds panicked.

Prisoner it is. I try not to think about what Mom said about things being dangerous and keep my voice light, like I haven't noticed that he's been suspicious. "It's just kind of boring waiting…"

"It shouldn't be much longer." He reassures. It feels like a lie.

"My mom's probably worried," I say in a grand moment of understatement.

He glances back at me, expression guarded, trying to read my face without turning his own towards me. "Did you come here with permission?"

"She knows where I am. She's planning on meeting me later." I'm glad that the texts from earlier add truth to those words. If Mom gets a flight, it should take her hours rather than days. I assume that's her plan, but she didn't go into detail. Which is fair. I didn't communicate either; I'd be a hypocrite if I complained about it.

"What is her name? We can be sure she is shown to you as soon as she arrives." Fyorik says smoothly. "The Surname would be Rose, yes?"

Alarm bells are going off again, but I'm not entirely sure why. I follow my instincts and don't give the full name. "Yeah, same surname. I'll text her once I get settled."

"Please do."

The new room is up an elevator. I can't help but consider the extra steps to leave, though logically, this place must have stairs for emergencies. It's a comfortably furnished lounge. A fire dances behind an old iron gate, blocked by a glass cover. Large bookcases line one wall, and two others are lined with windows. I look out to the city below. High enough that even if the windows opened, it wouldn't be safe to leave unless I was some sort of parkour master, which I unfortunately am not.

Might as well entertain myself while I wait. I check the bookshelves first and am immediately disappointed. It's full of almanacs, encyclopedias and the like, all with embossed leather covers. They look like they've been dusted but never opened, much less read. Like the office, there's nothing that hints at personality. It's all pretension.

I survey the room. That leaves a well-crafted chessboard and a large black piano. Fyorik is nowhere to be seen, and the door I entered is now closed. Definitely not suspicious. Well, I'm not about to play chess with myself.

I sit on the piano bench and pull out my phone, staring at it. I should warn Mom, but I don't want to worry her with my suspicions that they won't let me leave. What do I say? What do I do?

Still haven't heard anything from anyone. They got me some burgers while I wait.

There. Nothing overt, but hopefully, she'll realize how weird that is. (It *is* weird, right?)

She doesn't reply. Maybe she's in the air? I chew my lip, but there's not much I can do now.

I've never had a chance to learn to play piano. Maybe I could look up some tutorials.

The door opens, and a man with short-cropped hair and dark calculating eyes strides inside. His gaze sweeps up and down, scrutinizing me. He's scowling slightly, but that seems to be his resting expression because it doesn't change for better or worse at what he sees.

"I believe this is yours." He says at last. His accent is barely Fyrnekh at all, if that's what Fyorik's was, and more closely resembles an English accent. He glides smoothly over, holding out the picture. I reach to take it eagerly, and he moves his hand back again at the last moment. "But one thing first."

"What do you mean one thing first? That's mine." I say, eyes narrowing. He can't just get away with stealing stuff. Can he…? Is that part of diplomatic immunity?

"Before I hand you anything, tell me…" He pauses briefly for effect. His voice is smooth and sonorous, but his eyes are sharp and cold. "Are you telling the truth?"

Some small voice tells me I should answer quickly, but for a moment,

I'm too shocked to respond. "I'm sorry, what?"

He subtly lifts his chin and steps closer, but he doesn't look angry. He looks more… I don't know. Intrigued? Pleased, even? The reaction is confusing and doesn't leave me less unsettled. "About this? About yourself. Your family… not that I have been told the whole story…"

"Yes, that's my dad; I'm looking for him," I say, glowering. "And that photo is mine; you can't just take it."

"It would be inappropriate to do so," says the man. He offers it back to me with another cold smile. I snatch it, wanting to carefully put it away but wary of taking my eyes off the man. His smile widens, which only pisses me off. "We should make introductions, shouldn't we?"

He sweeps his arm behind him in a graceful bow, but his eyes remain fixed on me the entire time. "I am Nicolae Guthanderkaz, Ambassador from Fyrnlendh."

My eyes widen at the name before I can stop myself, and his sharp eyes clearly catch it. "You know the name. You know more than you let on, don't you?"

I flush, but there's no point in hiding it now. "…I found out his last name, and that's how I knew to come here," I admit. "But I didn't think anyone would believe me if I just said it."

"A reasonable assumption. If I had merely heard someone came claiming to be some long lost member of the royal family, I may well not have looked further." Nicholae admits with a wry smile. Now that I look, his sharp cheekbones and thick eyebrows do remind me of Dad a little. "There was no arguing with the picture, however."

"And?" I ask.

"I spoke with your father." A rush of hope, dread, and a thousand other emotions overwhelm my thoughts and steal my breath. When it's clear I can't answer, he continues. "He's very eager to see you, David."

I swallow, blinking back tears. Mom's wrong; she has to be. I realize my hands are trembling and shove them into my pockets to hide it. "If your last name is Guthanderkaz, does that mean we're related?"

His smile seems just a little warmer this time. "Only distantly. Our family is large with a very well-tracked genealogy. I am much more removed from the direct line than you are."

His expression turns more curious than cold as he looks me over before his gaze flicks back to the piano. "You play?"

I flush. "Oh, no, not really. I was bored, so I thought I'd look up lessons online."

Nicholae makes a thoughtful sound that reveals nothing. Still, at least I finally feel safe enough to tear my eyes away and replace my photo. When I look back up, he's inspecting me.

He opens his mouth. The door slams open, and we both turn to look.

Mom marches into the room in a barely contained blaze of wrath. It's as clear in her eyes as the fire smoldering behind the grate in the room. A distressed-looking man in a suit trails behind her and shoots Nicholae an apologetic look.

I shrink back on instinct. I don't remember the last time I've seen her furious. But even though I deserve it, it's Nicholae she glares at.

"Come on, David. We're leaving." Mom says, holding his gaze. She holds a hand towards me, palm open.

I freeze. Yeah, things have been suspicious, but Dad... Before I can formulate a response, Nicholae smoothly interjects. "Transportation is being arranged. His father is waiting for him."

Mom looks ready to skin him with her teeth. "He is my son. You have no right to kidnap him-"

"On the contrary, you're the one who kidnapped him a decade ago, aren't you, Miss Rose?" Nicholae purrs. Something about how he says it makes me feel sick, even more when I see the hint of fear in Mom's eyes. He continues in the same calm, smooth voice. "If need be, we can extradite you for the crime, but the Lord Guthanderkaz is very forgiving. Seeing David reunited with his family is what he wants, not vengeance."

"You are not taking my son," Mom says, hands clenching. She lifts her chin and takes a murderous step forward, and the dancing light of the fire almost merges with her hair, glowing with her fury.

"You are, of course, welcome to join," Nicholae intones with a sardonic smile. "I'm sure he'd be delighted to see you again as well, and won't it be best for the family to reunite? But he is going home, one way or another. Wouldn't it be easier for you without the legal ramifications? Such offers of pardon are not easy to come by, and who can say if such generosity will last."

Mom's eyes flick to me. I flinch a little, expecting her anger, but I'm not prepared for the despair that fills them instead. I'd rather the anger, any day. I'd rather she ground me for the rest of my life than see that expression on her face. Her shoulders slump, and she closes her eyes, taking and releasing a deep breath. "...fine. We'll go."

"I'll let them know." Says Nicholae, smugness dripping from his voice.

Mom ignores it, instead heading over to me, placing her hands protectively onto my shoulders. She squeezes them gently, and I can't think of a single thing to say, my mouth dry. Nicholae watches her, amused. I really, really don't like the expression and feel another wave of guilt. From behind me, Mom begins speaking again. "We'll need to get back and pack-"

"No." Nicholae interrupts.

Mom's grip on my shoulder tightens, and I wince. I must make some sort of sound because she quickly loosens her grip and rubs at my back with one hand apologetically.

"No, I'm afraid there won't be time for that," Nicholae continues with an expression of mock regret. "You will be escorted to the plane directly as soon as it's made ready. But if you give directions, we will happily send someone to pack your things."

Mom stiffens and doesn't say anything in reply.

I stare at the floor. I don't want this, I don't want Mom to be miserable. I certainly didn't imagine this could result in legal ramifications for her. I just want to see Dad.

Nicholae's phone chirps and he glances at it. "Ah, it seems your ride is here. I do hope you enjoy your trip," Nicholae says, smiling at me. There's an expression in his eyes I can't decipher that feeds my feeling of dread. "It was a pleasure to make your acquaintance, David Rose." His gaze flicks back to Mom. "Your safety is of the utmost importance to the Lord Guthanderkaz. I, of course, will be personally escorting you to your plane."

"Of course." Mom mutters bitterly under her breath. But she doesn't protest further, staying close to me as he leads us out of the embassy and into an awaiting limo. It's my first time in a limo, and I can't even enjoy it.

When Nicholae said plane, he actually meant private jet. We don't go through security or anything; the limo drives right up to the jet. I wonder if it's so we have no chance to leave. Mom strides with grim dignity, I follow, but pause to glance back at Nicholae. He just smiles and waves.

The inside doesn't even resemble an airplane. It's more of a weirdly elongated living dining room combo. Mom sits and folds her hands on her lap. They're trembling.

"Mom-" I start, then stop. What do I even say?

"Get some sleep, David," Mom responds, not looking at me.

I shrink back, feeling another wave of guilt. "...you didn't have to come." It isn't what I mean, but I can't take it back.

"I did," Mom says. I flinch, staring at my shoes, and hear her sigh softly. "I'm sorry, David."

Why is *she* apologizing?

"I really handled this badly. I… should have talked to you about things more. If I had-" Mom stops. "We can't change the past. I'm not angry at you. I love you. I'm just… …concerned." Her voice is strained, and I'm betting she intends stronger words than 'concerned.'

I finally look at her again, but her eyes are distant. "...did you really kidnap me?"

Mom looks at me sharply. "Your father and I were in agreement. It would have been perfectly legal in the US."

"But not there?"

Mom actually shivers and rubs at her shoulders. "...No." She sighs. "It's a long flight, David. You should try to get some sleep."

That's the end of the conversation. I can't make Mom say more, even now. And I'm too tired to try.

CHAPTER TWO

Fog welcomes us off the jet, leaving the rest of the world a muted dream space. I can't perceive more than a shadow of the airport's buildings, but a limo is again waiting. Mom gets in without protest, and I trail after.

It's a long drive, and the fog follows us the entire way. I can't see much of Fyrnlendh. Even the tallest buildings seem to fade like ghosts in the mist… until we reach the castle. I press against the window for a better look, shivering. It towers before us, dark form magnified by the fog, a mountain with painted glass windows.

The car rolls to a stop, and I spring out. Leaves crunch under my feet. I can smell the sea on the fog, heavy with salt and brine. The only thing I can hear is the wind through the trees, the distant cawing of birds, and Mom's footsteps behind me as she follows me out of the car.

I tilt my head to take it all in.

The sun's setting behind the castle and the weight of its shadow makes it take up more space than it should. I don't see any power lines or satellites or cell phone towers. Nothing newer than the spiderweb of ivy that smothers the first five stories. Claustrophobic forests surround us, mutating into English-style gardens as they close in on the castle's perimeter.

"This place is incredible." My breath comes out in a puff that merges with the fog.

I glance at Mom. She's contemplating the castle grimly but squeezes my hand reassuringly. Is she angry? I want to fix things. "...I need to see them."

"I know," Mom says softly. "I just hope-"

She doesn't finish the thought; her words are interrupted when the vast doors groan open, revealing a man standing straight as his tie. He bows.

"Good evening." He says. He speaks slowly, his voice dominated by a Fyrnekh accent. "You come faster than I am expecting you. I apologize. This way, please."

I start forward, only to be halted by Mom's iron grip. "Where is Viktor?" She asks.

The man turned slowly at my father's name, staring at her. "The Lord Guthanderkaz think you will like to refresh before you are seeing him, Miss Rose."

"I don't care about what the Lord Guthanderkaz thinks. Where is Viktor?"

The sunken-eyed man focuses on Mom, and I see his lip twitch very slightly in the shadow of a sneer. "As I say. The Lord Guthanderkaz think you will like to refresh. The Lord *Viktor* Guthanderkaz." His expression doesn't change again, but he sounds smug.

I peek at Mom. Her face is ashen, her hair almost silver in the castle's white mist and deep shadow. "Viktor?" She repeats, voice barely a breath, and then more loudly. "*Viktor* is the Lord Guthanderkaz."

"For many years."

Mom is silent, shocked.

"This way, please. To your rooms."

Still, Mom doesn't move, her hand loose in mine now. More men peer from behind him to see what the fuss is about before averting their eyes and hurrying to the car.

"Mom," I murmur gently. "It's getting dark."

Mom blinks and refocuses, glancing at me, then to what parts of the grounds are visible in the rapidly disappearing twilight.

"You're right. We should probably head inside." She says reluctantly. She releases my hand and attempts to smile. I see no sign of her dimples but don't say anything. Together, we retreat into the castle's dark mouth.

I've never set foot in a more opulent interior. Gilded gold filigree frames the dark wood-paneled walls and marble floors, and lavish paintings adorn the walls. Potpourri doesn't quite mask the acrid scent of old wood. The lighting is modern, but there are also partially melted candles and gas lamps with blackened glass.

"Where is everyone?" Mom asks, eyes darting between the shadows near the heavy draperies. "There must have been a hundred people here.. ....last time."

I stumble, only Mom's hand stopping me from spilling onto the well-waxed floor. Is she actually talking about when we lived at the castle?

"Evening draws close. It is important time. I trust you remember this much." Our guide says.

Mom becomes rigid for a moment, then nods. I open my mouth, bubbling with questions, but Mom glances sharply at me and shakes her head, and that's the end of it. I sigh and glare at the man leading us.

The castle is a maze of stairs, hallways, and windows. It's a reversal of the Embassy. Instead of maddening repetition, I'm lost in the vast differences, overwhelming in their tiny perfect details, unique carvings, paintings, and decorations. Even the doors are subtly different. The man stops and turns his sunken eyes to me. "This room is yours." He says, holding an antique key primly in front of him.

"Mine?" I echo, staring between the key and him.

"You live here now." The man's tone implies that this should be evident, but his eyes shift to Mom as he speaks. I can sense judgment, even contempt, directed at her. What the hell?

Mom pays him no heed. She leans close to me, whispering, "Do you want to stay here?"

We are in the middle of nowhere. My phone lost reception an hour ago. We're in a completely foreign country. We can't leave even if I *did* desire it. Which I don't. "Yeah."

Mom looks resigned, but she nods.

I accept the key and heft it, surprised by the weight. It's a gold skeleton key with a hydra snarling at the bow. It's heavy enough to be solid gold. That can't be right. It must be gold plated; pure gold would be too soft to use as a key, especially one so large.

The door unlocks with a satisfying click and I shove it open to peer inside. The room could swallow any of the apartments I've ever lived in whole.

Behind me, the man urges Mom to her own room. I glance back, uncertain. To my surprise, Mom waves me inside and lets herself be herded away.

I plunge inside, closing the door behind me, abruptly muting voice and footsteps alike.

My feet echo against the stone as I cross the room, taking it in. The single rug does little to muffle the sound. The furniture is dark mahogany with gilded trim and carvings as elaborate as a dragonfly's wings. It looks more pretty than comfortable. Despite the furniture, the room feels vacant. I flop back onto the bed, sinking into the comforter with a poof of clean laundry smell.

"I'm home," I say, tasting the words. I swallow and close my eyes. "I'm going to see Dad and Basil, and everything will be as good as I remember. Better."

I speak with more hope than conviction.

I don't remember falling asleep, but that's what I do instead of "refreshing." Mom wakes me up, and long story short, when we go to see Dad, Mom is wearing a shiny new dress, and I have wrinkled several-day-old clothes and bedhead.

Not that I care. I'm seeing Dad, not going in for a job interview. Still, I desperately long for a shower.

Our guide doesn't waste time with pleasantries, simply knocking at the door, probably wishing to be rid of us as soon as possible.

"Show them in." The voice from the other side tickles at my mind like lost car keys. It's deep and rich, with the slightest trace of an accent. The man with the sunken eyes obliges, and I glance at Mom. She's inhaling slowly through her nose, hands flexed. I step inside. Best give her that extra minute to compose herself.

Dad stands before a large window, pure shadow against the falling twilight. He's tall, elongated further by too-perfect posture, his hands clasped behind his back, standing still as stone.

My skin prickles with… anticipation? Dread? Both? I feel the whisper of Mom's dress against my leg. The door thuds closed behind us. My father turns to face us.

I know his face. But photos don't compare to standing in front of him, solid and three-dimensional, and breathing. His assortment of straight, angular features makes him appear chiseled out of stone. His cat-shaped eyes glance between us, irises so dark I can't find the pupil. I don't wait to study more. I run to him, throwing my arms around him and squeezing. His cologne washes over me, spiced with memories. I'm suddenly a child again, unbalanced, clutching his chest instead of his legs. "You shrunk."

"You've grown." He counters, his voice noticeably gruffer. He ruffles my hair. "Your hair too quickly for the rest of you."

"My hair's fine," I say, rubbing at my face with a sleeve and tilting my head down to hide my tears. Seconds later, Dad's hand enters my field of vision, presenting me with a handkerchief. I guess I'm not hiding them that well.

"Thanks," I croak. I dry my face, hands trembling.

Mom approaches and I tense. What if they fight…? Curiosity pulls my gaze towards them despite my anxiety.

Tears shine in Mom's eyes, too stubborn to be shed. Her brows are drawn together as she stares intently at Dad, searching for something. She reaches out, touching his cheek. He stares back at her, expression neutral but his eyes shining almost as much. Then she smiles. It's a smile that eclipses every one I've ever seen outside of photographs, altering the constellation of her freckles, dimples burning deep into her cheeks.

"It's really you." She says, voice light with wonder.

"It's really me," Dad replies softly, placing his hand over Mom's, then gently bringing it to his lips to kiss it softly.

I avert my eyes, rubbing my leg with a foot. This is way too intimate. I desperately study every inch of the room that isn't where they are. I think it's an office. A throne of a chair towers before a desk far too big for the laptop that rests on it. There are more bookshelves than wall, filled as much with decoration as actual books. Unlike the Embassy study, these have that friendly worn quality they gain with repeat readings. I inadvertently glance at my parents. They're completely lost in each other, and I really need to leave. Besides, there's someone I'm desperate to see. "Where's Basil?"

My parents both glance down at me, broken from their reverie. Mom blushes and moves to step back, but Dad holds her there as he addresses me.

"I'm surprised you remember him. Perhaps I shouldn't be; you were always getting him into trouble..." He turns to Mom again, staring at her as he continues almost absently. "He's in his room. Metod will show you."

I hurry out without waiting for further prompting. I am glad they are getting along instead of fighting, but that doesn't mean I'm prepared for it. Halfway down the hall, I realize I forgot to ask who and where Metod was. I'm not about to go back, though. Besides, how hard can it be to find one room?

Half an hour of wandering empty halls later, I spot a timid-looking man. His attire is similar to that of the man who greeted us, except with a little less embellishment.

"Um, hello?" I call.

The man starts and spins to look at me. His eyes widen, and he goes very pale, stammering something in Fyrnekh. A puzzling reaction. I'm a lot of things, but I've never been called intimidating before by anyone. He looks around and then gestures for me to follow.

"I'm looking for Basil," I say hopefully.

The man hesitates, wringing his hands together. "Basil?" He repeats, eyeing me. He looks as if I requested he please take a stroll out the window. I nod, baffled by his terror, and offer a smile, hoping to calm him.

"Basil," I repeat since he doesn't seem to speak English, and I still don't understand Fyrnekh.

The man scans the room one more time, perhaps hoping to spot someone who might rescue him, before he arrives at a decision. "Basil," he says, followed by a stream of words I don't know. He gestures for me to follow.

The door he leads me to seems perfectly identical to mine, though perhaps there's a subtle difference between them that just takes studying to see. The man gives a mouse-worthy knock, but I still hear an unfamiliar voice respond in Fyrnekh.

Of course it's unfamiliar. Basil's my age; he isn't going to sound like he's still seven.

The man bows and gestures for me to enter. I step through the door.

Basil sits with perfect posture and an immaculate suit. He taps a pencil against a desk and stares at a computer screen, eyes glazed with boredom. I stare, brain struggling to stretch memories of my childhood best friend to fit his teenage counterpart. I have no idea what to say.

"Your room is bigger than mine." I finally blurt.

The tapping stops, and he turns towards me with an expression of bafflement that freezes into one of shock. For a disorienting moment, I'm staring at a color-inverted mirror. He has black hair and eyes, but otherwise, his features match up strikingly well. Straight nose, sharp chin, cat eyes. His face is a little longer, cheekbones a bit sharper, but that's about it.

This time, he's the one to break the silence.

"David?" He whispers.

I can't resist grinning, stepping closer. "Hey."

Basil jerks up, sending his computer chair flying. "When, how..." He trails off, then mutters something in Fyrnekh.

"Er, what?"

Basil blinks at me.

"I... um, don't remember much, Fyrnekh." I clarify.

"Forgive me," Basil says, shaking his head, expression dazed. "I'm just..." his hand brushes through his hair, so short it's practically a crew cut, even at the top. I hope that isn't what Dad has in mind with the comment about my hair. He smiles hesitantly as if he's asking permission.

"Same," I say, relieving him of the need to explain. "Dad didn't tell you we were coming?"

"No," Basil said. He clenches a hand, then relaxes it, gesturing for me to follow him deeper into the room. "I suspect he wished to keep you hidden from the rest of the family."

This piques my curiosity. Maybe I can finally get some answers. "Why would he want to do that?"

Basil reaches out a hand towards me as if to affirm my solidity but catches himself and draws it back at the last moment. "It really *is* you... Father said nothing?"

I fidget. "Mom never wanted to talk about any of it. Dad--well, we *just* got here. And, um, they're a little distracted."

Basil clears his throat and straightens, the red coloring his face matching my own embarrassment. "I see."

Crap. I made it sound like I was only here because I couldn't be with them. "I wanted to see you, though," I add quickly. "I mean, I wanted to before they got all..." I wave off the thought with one hand, eyes intent on my brother. "You're my brother, and..." I trailed off. *My best friend*, my mind finishes, but I don't speak out loud. The idea that I don't have a best friend besides my brother after ten years seems so damn pathetic, even to me. "I missed you."

Basil smiles more quickly this time. "I did as well. You always had a way of making things interesting."

"One hopes you missed me for more than being your personal jester."

"What? No! I mean, yes, I mean, that isn't at all-," Basil protests with utter sincerity.

I laugh and ruffle his hair. "You really *are* as serious as I remember, still! I have a lot of work ahead of me, but as your big brother, it is my humble duty to knock all that sense out of you."

"There's nothing humble about you," Basil retorts, but his smile is immediate and utterly relaxed.

The last bit of doubt dissolves. I have my brother back and a lot of time to make up. I wonder if it's too dark to play about the grounds. I'm about to voice the thought, but Basil speaks first.

"Father announced a late dinner today; I had wondered why.

Nonetheless, it shall be starting soon, and you seem… ill-prepared. It's probably best we all speak to Father first. Do you know where he is?"

"Dad's office," I say immediately. Then add, "I think. It *looked* like an office. I didn't exactly ask. Like I said. *Distracted*."

Basil regards me with disbelief before bursting into a laugh. "I suppose I should never expect certainty from you. Very well, it is a start."

He pauses in the hall, withdrawing a key identical to mine and locking his door. I raise an eyebrow. Just how universal are the keys? Do they work on more than just my room? Even the key wards look the same. Nevermind. Not exactly a priority at the moment.

Basil opens the door to Dad's office. He doesn't become emotional or embarrassed like I would expect based on the scene I left. Instead, Basil adopts the stiff-legged countenance of a sheepdog who spotted a bear. I peer past him, curious.

The atmosphere has transformed. The air crackles like the prelude to a storm, and a third person has joined my parents.

She's pretty, I guess; she has the dark eyes angled like a cat's and straight nose that I'm beginning to recognize as family features. Her black hair spirals around her head in a braid. Her dress clings to a body that is either wearing a very tight corset or missing a few ribs. Both clothing and hair are accented by ridiculous amounts of diamonds. Seriously, she looks like she just walked out of a Tiffany's commercial. She stands like one of those living statues, one hand folded over the other, so a diamond ring is in the forefront. She's smiling at Mom and Dad.

Mom's smiling back at her without a hint of dimples. Dad's face is impassive.

"David," Mom turns to me. Is that a tremor in her voice? The dark-haired woman looks at me and smiles the way I imagine a spider would. To my surprise, she speaks with a perfect London accent.

"Ah, Basil, David! It's truly a pleasure to see you two getting on so well. You shall have to introduce him to his sister, Basil. Not now, of course, after dinner."

"Sister?" I echo at the same time Basil responds, "Yes, mother."

The woman doesn't seem to hear me, floating over to Mom. "Oh, but it is good to see you again, Emily dear. I *did* miss you. Walk with me; we have so much to talk about, and we simply must prepare you for tonight. I do want you to make a good impression. I have a lovely necklace that would be stunning with your eyes..."

As she speaks, she takes both of Mom's hands. Her smile is as warm as her jewelry.

"Thank you, Margaret, you're very kind," Mom answers. I'm even more baffled. Mom isn't usually the type to flatter falsely for politeness.

"I have matters to attend to," Dad says suddenly, rising. He bends down, kissing Mom deeply, before sweeping past both women without another glance. He nods at Basil, pats my head, and then disappears down the hall.

I look back to see Margaret staring after him, lips pressed thinly together. Then her gaze meets mine, and that smile returns with a flourish. She turns to Mom. "Let's be off, we've much to do, and it's best to settle in early before everyone gets there." She glances back and holds my brother's gaze. "Remember, Basil, be sure David is presentable."

"Yes, mother," Basil repeats, in precisely the same tone as before. The women sweep through the door and are gone.

I stare after them, speechless for several long moments. "What the hell was that?"

"That," Basil replies, straightening his suit and not looking at me, "was my mother. Lady Margaret."

"But... we're brothers," I say stupidly.

"Half-brothers." Basil corrects slowly, pausing between the words as if trying to avoid stepping in something unpleasant. He's not meeting my eye.

I feel vines twisted in my guts. I struggle for coherency. "But, I... Mom..."

"...David, your mother... never married into this family."

"I know that," I snap hotly, blinking furiously, voice thick. It was a lie. It shouldn't have been; Mom doesn't have a ring, Basil is impossibly close to my age… Mom literally *told* me we were half brothers; I just… don't think I really processed what that meant. I feel so *stupid*. I don't even know why I'm upset. I have no reason to be upset, right?

"David…" Basil trails off. I see an echo of his earlier motion, reaching furtively toward me.

"Dammit!" I scrub at the tears that are forming.

Basil remains motionless, biting his lip in impotent empathy.

"C'mon, let's get out of here," I say. I feel embarrassed and upset, and I'm not about to let anyone besides Basil see me like this.

I march out and down the halls blindly. My skin is prickling, and there's a pulsing ache in my chest that constricts with each breath. I don't know what's worse; knowing that this woman who isn't Mom is married to Dad, or knowing that Basil, my brother, is hers. It feels wrong. I don't want to share either of them. I don't even want to share Basil with that sister Margaret mentioned. I just need one sibling, one brother. My brother. The one I played with when we were small. My best friend. And I hate myself for thinking it, for being so childish and petty.

"Where precisely are we going?" Basil's voice startles me, and I stop, glancing behind me. I can't hold his gaze, embarrassed at what he might be thinking of me. I survey my surroundings instead, but my eyes are drawn back to him. I muffle a sniff and shrug, trying to look nonchalant, before wiping my eyes and nose with a sleeve.

"Come on," Basil says, finally, carefully placing a hand on my shoulder. "Let's get you ready for dinner. I don't suppose you remember where your room is?"

I shrug, still not trusting my voice, then dig around in my pockets. I find the heavy key and hold it out to him.

Basil stares, then smiles radiantly. "You'll be near me."

"Good. I need some happy news," I reply. Crap, does that count as insulting Basil's mom? I push the thoughts away and attempt a smile. My left side has always been more eager to do so, and this time, it seems the only side able to at all. Basil blushes and clears his throat again.

"We don't have time to give you a bath," Basil notes after we find my room, glancing at a glinting pocket watch.

"What about a shower?" I ask. "I kind of need it; it's been over three days now."

Basil stares at me in abject horror. "Why on earth haven't you showered in three days? In more than three days!"

"I haven't had a chance!" I say defensively, a blush heating my face. "I've been traveling nonstop. I guess we were given a little time here but I kind of passed out immediately since I haven't exactly had much sleep either."

Basil's expression softens. "I… see. That sounds tremendously difficult. I'm sorry to hear you were treated so ill."

I rub the back of my hair but immediately stop, appalled at the greasy, gritty desperately-needs-cleaning feeling. I shrug. "It's kind of my fault. I-"

"As much as I'd love to hear the story, you're correct. We really must bathe you, and there's no time to waste," Basil interrupts. "Your hair will be wet… Well, we'll just have to make do."

"By bathe, you mean shower, right?" I question. "And don't you have blow-dryers?"

"I'm afraid there aren't any in the men's rooms, and we haven't the time to dig any up," Basil says, shaking his head and herding me towards a door I hadn't explored. "And we only have a bathtub to work with in here."

"How much time do we have, exactly?"

Basil practically shoves me towards the door to what I assume is the bathroom. "That depends on how long it takes you to put on a suit. Ah, but a bath hasn't even been drawn…"

"Suit? Just what sort of dinner are we going to?" I ask, glancing behind me but opening the door.

"Just a regular dinner," Basil says offhandedly, already turning away from me to open a wardrobe taller than him. I see him rustling through what looks like the exact same outfit in subtly different shades. "Go clean up; I'll pick out your outfit."

I obediently step into the bathroom, hearing Basil muttering just before I close the door, "I doubt they've had a chance to measure you, but it'll have to do…"

I focus on the bathroom. It's at least as big as the one in the Embassy, but much more opulently decorated. I turn my attention to a clawfoot tub and hop out of my clothes as quickly as possible.

I don't bother trying to fill it; I just use the faucet as half shower, half sponge bath. I even block the faucet with my hand to intensify and direct the spray.

I can't read the toiletries labels, so I just do my best to guess based on consistency. Even if I'm wrong, it'll be better than nothing after all my traveling.

I scrub quickly, wrinkling my nose at the color of the water. Gross. I can't believe Dad ruffled my hair without commenting.

"How are you doing?" Basil calls through the door. "Do you need help?"

"No, I do not need help bathing."

As soon as the water looks consistently clean, I turn the bath off and hop out, grabbing a towel and drying as I race to the main room. Basil stops pacing and looks at me anxiously.

"Good. I'll help you into the suit."

He dashes around me at a dizzying speed, half directing, half dressing me. He steps back after securing my tie so I can observe myself in the mirror. I'm bedecked in a night-black three-piece ensemble and polished shoes. A golden hydra is embroidered over the heart.

"The fit really isn't perfect, is it?" Basil asks anxiously.

I wave my arms. The material is luxuriously soft, but the structure limits my movements. "It is pretty restrictive, but it's probably fine," I say. "I think it is my size."

"It hasn't been tailored yet," Basil protests.

"I doubt anyone will notice," I say, smiling at Basil. He doesn't return it.

"Oh, they will, I assure you."

Well. That's... ominous. "Well, we can't really do anything about it. This is what I have, so it's what I'm wearing."

"I... suppose. But it isn't the best with first impressions. Especially with your hair."

I touch my hair, which is still very much wet. "We could try to find a blow dryer still?"

Basil rechecks his pocket watch. "We don't have the time. I'm sorry, David. I should have thought about this sooner-"

"Hey, it's okay," I say, squeezing his shoulder. I have no idea why he's so panicked. "Honestly, everything has been a rush so far. I don't think any of us has had a chance to process, which is kinda my fault."

I drop my hand, twisting my fingers together. "I just... I didn't want to risk... not ever seeing you again."

Basil gapes, taken aback. I bump his shoulder with mine and smile playfully. "Aren't we in a hurry?"

"Oh! Yes." He says quickly, then grabs my hand and leads me off as swiftly as he can without being accused of running.

The corridor expands into a vast atrium. It's crowned with a star-shaped vaulted ceiling, from which elegant arches fall like dead rainbows into the hands of stone angels. Gilded chains dangle in an intricate web, upon which hang massive chandeliers. Innumerable crystals shimmer from the flames of the actual candles that line them. The effect is stunning.

I peer down curiously. The central floor drops for three stories, each level caged by balconies. On the ground floor, a single line of tables spans the length of half a dozen swimming pools. The complexity of the table settings suggests a very fancy meal.

The dining hall is colossal. Even the giant line of tables seems lost in the ocean of dark carpeting. Schools of men in dark suits and women in colorful gowns drift around it like strange fish. The hushed roar of all of them murmuring at once drifts up to us.

I whistle. "What's with all the people?"

"They are our family," Basil replies. I glance back at him.

"Is there some sort of reunion going on?" What crap timing.

"No," Basil shakes his head. "This is normal, selective even. Only those of high rank may live and dine at the main house. Special events and reunions bring far more."

"More?" I stare down, trying to imagine it.

Basil waves a hand dramatically. "These are the most powerful people in all of Fyrnlendh."

"Sounds like you might have a nepotism problem," I mutter.

"This isn't the time to joke, David!" Basil hisses, eyebrows drawn together in a worried attempt at a glare. "You're in a very precarious position. People still aren't sure what to make of you or where you fit in. You are Father's son, but..." he trailed off.

He looks so sincere and concerned I don't have the heart to tell him I wasn't joking. Instead, I stare at all the people in their fancy clothes and finish for him. "...a bastard." Based on the bits I've seen and what Basil's said, they seem to be the type to care about things like that. Which I guess I kinda do too, but for a completely different reason. I shrug and smile. "So what? Don't get me wrong, I'm grateful for your help, but I couldn't care less whether they like me or not. I didn't come here for them."

Basil's accent thickens as he grows more distressed. "They know a great deal about making a person miserable, and you're already a target. Potestas, Stirpes, Dignatio. Power, Family, Reputation. These are what we have been taught to value. Everything you do will be judged, and they will find ways to make you unhappy if you fall short."

He reaches out, touching a damp lock of hair, then drops his hand in a gesture of helpless distress.

I recline against the railing and stare down at the sea of people. I shake my head, more at them than my brother. "Thanks, really. But I mean it too, Basil. I didn't come here to impress them. I came to be with you and Dad. I'm not a pushover. And if they're going to be assholes because I have wet hair after traveling for days, that says more about them than me."

We face each other again. Basil's lips are pinched tightly together. With a wink and a grin, I add, "C'mon. If they're as uptight as you're letting on, this could be hilarious. I wonder how much I could press people's buttons while maintaining a facade of innocence..."

"David," his voice is a mixture of exasperation and pleading, but I can see a spark of amusement now behind the horror in his eyes.

My grin widens. "If they're going to judge me either way, I might as well have fun with it." I push away from the banister, walking backwards towards the nearest stairway to look at Basil. "Coming?"

Basil lingers a beat longer. He surveys the crowd one more time before hurrying to catch up. I face forward again, smiling, and we descend together.

Two men flank the base of the stairs. They're both wearing suits, but I'm starting to realize which ensemble is meant to denote staff; white gloves are the biggest giveaways. They dip in perfect unison the moment my foot touches the ground floor. Another identically dressed man emerges, bowing before us. "Young Master David, Master Basil, good evening. I am to placing the sitting of the Young Master."

"Why am I 'Young Master?'" I mutter. "I'm older than you."

Basil chuckles, smirking and glancing at me from his corner eye. "You don't act older, little brother."

I strongly consider being as childish as he implies and sticking my tongue out, but I don't want to send him into another panic. Instead, I turn my attention to the room in front of us.

The hairs on the back of my neck stand up. The fish have transformed into sharks, and all their gazes are fixated on the two of us.

"You were not kidding," I mutter softly. Basil doesn't say anything in reply, but his smile has vanished again. That alone makes me dislike everyone in the room.

I pretend to be unaware of their scrutiny and follow the man to my place at the table. It's three down from the head of the table, assuming the imperious gold chair denotes the head. Every eye is on me as the man pulls out a chair for me.

I flop into it with comfortable ease, leaning back and making myself relaxed instead of presentable. Sound returns suddenly, whispers rushing over me like wind. I bite back a smirk, feigning obliviousness. Ignoring the unfamiliar faces, I try to catch Basil's eye. He doesn't acknowledge me, but I see his lip twitching against the urge to smile.

I scan the crowd as I wait. The suits are three piece, like mine, and like mine the style is a little different than I've seen in the states, but the style difference is much more obvious with the women. Their dresses remind me of costumes of victorian movies, maybe ones made by fashion designers who can't quite give up modern aesthetics and create a mismatch. I don't see a woman without a corset, all the gowns are floor length and most are as elaborate as wedding gowns, with bustles and trains and beading. I look back to Basil. Is this really supposed to be just an average night?

Basil moves to talk to someone instead of sitting, so I pull out my phone. As I told Basil, if they're going to think I'm rude for things I can't control anyway, I might as well indulge in the things I can. Unsurprisingly, there's still no reception, but I have plenty of books to read.

I'm lost in rereading one of my favorites when sudden pain wrenches me unwillingly back to the table. I blink and look around. There are only a few empty chairs left now. The pinch came from my right, and there, straight-backed and too skinny to have the right amount of ribs, sits Margaret.

Great. This isn't going to be awkward at all.

She gives me a thin-lipped smile and raises a pointed eyebrow. I glare and am about to return to the phone when I see Basil watching us over her shoulder, brows crinkled.

Dammit. I sigh and turn off the phone, slipping it into my pocket.

"Good, that cannot return for the remainder of the dinner," Margaret says in a single whispering breath, all while smiling like she's complimenting me.

I stare. Is she trying to act like my mother?

She gives me a disapproving once-over. "I must have words with Basil, you are not fit to be dining here, but it's far too late for that; the damage has been done. Sit up straight, and don't you dare use that phone again. You realize, of course, that every bad thing you do will be a reflection of your mother?" Her eyes move past me, eyebrows lifting, and I follow her gaze.

Mom is so far down I can't see her face, but her hair glows like the candles, serving as a gleaming beacon. She stands out starkly against the sea of black hair. I bristle in anger.

"Have a little more consideration," hisses Margaret in my ear. "Things will be hard enough on her as it is without you making things worse."

"Why the hell is she over there?" I demand. Why would Dad let her sit so far away from us if he's in charge? Isn't that what being the Lord Guthanderkaz means?!

"For heaven's sake, do not swear, especially here! Didn't you hear a word I said?" Margaret's voice rakes against my ears like splitting metal. I meet her eyes.

"If you think I give a single-" I begin.

Margaret beams and pinches me again, making me interrupt myself with an exclamation of pain. How are her nails so sharp?! I'm about to snap before I become aware that an eerie silence has descended over the table. I glance around nervously, but the eyes aren't on me this time. I follow the polite gazes and see Dad standing at the head of the table. Everyone stares at him with anticipation, like the play they're waiting for is finally starting.

"Good evening." Dad doesn't yell, but his resonant voice flows through the silent room without issue, not too loud but clearly heard by the entire room. This place must have superb acoustics. "Tonight is a time for celebration. It has seen the return of two of the people dearest to me, as I'm sure you've heard. Please welcome Miss Emily Rose and my son, David."

Around us, people applaud obediently, looking towards whichever of us is closer to them. Delighted smiles replace once-affronted expressions. The sudden change is unsettling.

Dad waits for the applause to die down before continuing. "They are both part of the family, and I trust you will do all you can to make their stay welcome."

More applause, more smiles. Dad sits, and I'm startled by a cheery trill of strings from behind me. I glance over my shoulder to see several well-dressed violinists energetically playing Mozart's string quartet.

Laughter and conversations erupt around me again. I turn back and find the first course waiting. There's a long flute of bubbling gold juice. A silver saucer has been placed upon the service plate, upon which wisps of cream are sandwiched between crisp pastries and heaping pearls of dark green...gunk. I stare, prodding it suspiciously with a fork. Round blobs roll off in a heap. Not exactly appetizing.

I peek at my neighbors through the curtains of my hair. To my left, a small girl with a crown of braids is devouring one with relish. To my right, Margaret is nibbling daintily at another.

I spear a green blob with a tiny gold fork and sniff it. Smells like fish.

"Don't you like caviar?" Pipes a soft voice. I glance at the little girl, who now is staring at me with wide eyes.

"I dunno. I've never had caviar." I admit.

The girl giggles furiously, and I glance at her again. "You sound so strange! I thought they spoke *English* in America, as Mother does."

"Adela!" Margaret's scandalized hiss interrupts our conversation. Adela flinches, ducking her head, her smile vanishing.

"I'm sorry," she says meekly.

"'S'okay, I just speak slang. I'll teach you 'case you decide to go to the U.S.," I say, as lazy in my enunciation as I can manage. Adela's large eyes flick between the no-doubt glowering Margaret and me.

"You most certainly will not," Margaret growls.

I ignore her, smiling at the little girl brightly. "So you're Adela? I'm David. Nice to meet you."

Adela smiles shyly, tugging at her skirt and bobbing her head in a seated curtsy. "It's a pleasure to meet you, big brother. Why are you sitting with the girls?"

"Like I know anything about the stupid seats," I mutter, rolling my eyes. I have a few questions about the seating arrangements myself, like why the hell is there a separate girls section at all? Why put me in it? Does Dad think my not-even-that-long hair means I'm trans or something? At least that could be well-meaning, though it wouldn't excuse the sexist setup. And why is Mom so far away?

I don't know how to phrase this without potentially upsetting Adela, so I moodily stab at more caviar instead.

"Seats can't be stupid. They're inanimate," Adela enunciates the last word with such conscientious pride I can't help but smile. Okay, maybe I can share Basil with one sister.

"Guess so."

"You should eat. The second course will be here soon." Adela adds. "It's tasty, really. Everyone *adores* caviar."

"Okay, okay," I say, smiling at her enthusiasm. I take a deep breath and bite down with exaggerated slowness. It tastes buttery and almost overwhelmingly fishy, but the cream and pastry help temper it. Adela's watching me breathlessly, so I hum in exaggerated pleasure.

Adela beams. I finish and grab the flute, taking a deep sip. Then cough, slamming it down and gasping. "That isn't Martinelli's!"

Adela tilts her head, puzzled. "It's Champagne. What's Martinelli's?"

"Sparkling apple juice. They gave me Champagne?"

"Of course! What else would you drink with caviar?" She asks with such candid perplexion I almost laugh. I don't want to risk offense, so I turn it into a cough instead. A white-gloved man bends over and plucks my plate from the table. "Hey!"

"I did tell you," Adela sniffs.

"It's wasteful," I grumble.

Margaret interjects coldly. "The chefs and servants are allowed to eat the meal's leftovers. None of it is wasted."

Kitchen workers often get to eat the food they make. But usually, that doesn't mean eating it off the *used* plates of those they make it for. I push aside my fork.

"What's wrong?" Whispers Adela.

I shake my head. "Not hungry." I lie.

"After two pieces of caviar?" Adela asks dubiously.

I poke the salad irritably. No wonder Mom hates this place. Sexism, classism, nepotism… what other fun surprises await? I steal a glance to my right. Well, beyond the fact that Dad is apparently married. I should try to tolerate her for Basil's sake, but does she have to act like such a complete harpy?

I lean over the table and peer past Margaret. Basil is eating slowly, watching Dad, who is leaning across the table and saying something to the grim-faced man on his right. Said grim-faced man is staring straight at me. His eyes narrow when I catch his gaze. I sigh, disregarding him and leaning back to inspect the chandeliers above me. I regard Dad again.

"Hey, Adela?"

Adela swallows quickly. "Yes?"

"That side," I point towards Dad, "is the, um, higher ranked side, or whatever, right?"

"Yes."

"And Dad's at the top?"

It's Margaret who answers. "Your father is the Head of the House."

I turn towards her despite myself. "So he's in charge?"

"Of course, dear."

"Then shouldn't where we sit be up to him?"

Margaret looks past me towards Emily. I expect some sort of triumphant smirk, but either Margaret's an excellent actress, or she's unhappy about it too.

"Yes," she murmurs. To my surprise, she touches my shoulder.

Her touch does nothing to quell the sick feeling in my stomach, and I shrug away. I stare at Dad, heart pounding. He's eating and conversing as carelessly as the rest. I glare, gripping the tablecloth tightly. Like everything is fine. This is being done with his approval; it has to be. This messed up table arrangement full of sexism and classism, where neither myself nor Mom is next to anyone we know.

"David?" I barely hear Adela's quivering voice. I clench my trembling fists. I'm not going to sit and pretend that I'm okay with any of this.

I stand abruptly, knocking the heavy chair aside. It screams against the stone, drawing the attention of those around me, but I don't care.

I turn from the table and storm toward the stairs.

"David!" Dad's voice resonates with force and halts me midstride. The echoes of his words eat away all other noise. Silence amplifies the sound of my heartbeat and ragged breathing until I'm sure everyone can hear it.

His tone shreds my assurance, leaving me small and vulnerable. What am I doing? This is a bad idea. I'm just making everything worse. I should just go, sit down, and accept this...

Accept this!? I shake my head to clear it. Like hell I'm accepting anything!

I will myself forward, ignoring the embarrassment, the vulnerability, the shame of disobeying my father, and the weight of the silence and the stares. He should never have allowed any of this to happen to begin with.

He calls my name again, but I ignore it, and with gaining confidence, leave the dining hall. I have no idea where I'm going, and I don't care. Just so long as I leave that nightmare behind.

Rage propels me down the endless hallways, so easy to get lost in. Doors and passages blur together, and my feet ache in the unbroken leather shoes. I don't want to be in the main halls and steer the darkest route possible at every chance.

At some point, pain overcomes anger, and I halt and lean against a wall. I look around. It's a dead end, save a set of french doors that lead to the garden. Two flickering candles glint like feral eyes from another corridor. Their stare is reflected in night black windows. The candles and their reflection are the only light around. The only sound is the rain flailing against the windows.

I'm just about to turn around when I hear footsteps approaching behind me.

My heart skips a beat, and I fumble with the door in the dark—unlocked. I push it open, battling against the wind, and let it spill the storm inside. Its howls drown out the quickening steps.

If you've ever been camping somewhere miles and miles from any city, you've seen something like the blackness I plunge into. With the storm, there aren't even any stars or moon to soften it, only sharp flashes of lightning that taunt me with glimpses of my surroundings.

I'm angry and ignore the darkness, the storm, the cold. The suit does surprisingly well against it, but soon enough, it's soaked, and then it's as much ice as the air around me, freezing each breath I take. I hear shouting behind me and run faster. The house is surrounded by a maze of gardens, which are surrounded by forest. There are plenty of places to duck and hide to avoid people.

Eventually, I curl under the wing of a neglected stone angel, shivering. The mossy stone barely breaks the storm, and I hug myself.

What am I doing?

Movement catches my eye, and I lift my head to look at the source. Distantly, I see a flickering; those twin candles again. I sigh and curl back against the storm again.

There's another flash of thunder. For a brief moment, it paints an image of the garden: statues, roses, trees... and a black mass where the candles are. I stare.

That isn't the house... I scan my surroundings swiftly. Behind me are the glowing windows and looming silhouette of the castle. I turned back towards the black bulk before me. The candles aren't gone.

And probably aren't candles.

The wind dies down, and everything grows still. My heart pounds against my chest as if trying to break out of my ribs to flee. I slowly uncurl, facing the dark mass. A flash of lightning. I count my breaths before the rumble of thunder, slowly backing up. Another flare of lightning illuminates the garden. Where the bulk and not-candles had been stands only trees.

Just a trick of the light, I lie to myself.

I hear a branch crack next to me. I bolt.

I feel something behind me. Like a dream, where you know something's there but don't know what it is, something terrible, closing in, closer, closer...

Light flickers ahead, and I see it: the open door, safe haven. There's a black figure there, but I don't care: it has to be better than whatever's behind me.

I careen into the room, lose my balance, and almost face plant, but a surprisingly strong arm grips my own. I jerk back, but it's only one of the white-gloved staff, his face hidden in the low lantern light. "Young master," he begins.

"Door," I interrupt. There's no time to be polite.

He blinks, looks at the door, and nods. He shuts it. I hear the sound of the lock and let out a long shuddering breath. I sink against the wall. I'm shivering violently; the room is just warm enough to remind me how frigid it is.

The servant speaks again. "Young master, I am come to return you."

"No!" I snap. He freezes, and I cover my face. "Sorry, I just. I can't. Just... leave me alone. Please. I'm *not* going back there."

For a breath, there's nothing. Then I hear his footsteps retreating. I shudder and curl against the cold stone and let myself cry.

Chapter Three

I wake on a couch, my shoes discarded, and a fire crackles in the corner of the room. Dad sits next to me. I flush and glare at the wall..

"David, why did you storm off like that?" Dad murmurs.

"Why did you make sure none of us were next to each other?!" I demand, turning on him.

Dad closes his eyes and rubs his head. "I did the best I could do, David. There are ways of doing things—"

"Ways of doing things?! Wha-no, you know what? There is! Like maybe actually spending time like any father would do if they actually gave a rat's rear end about their son!"

"David, I do care, very much. But I have responsibilities I can't ignore. I can't put my own desires first. No matter how much I wish to. If I had had a choice, those ten years-" he makes a strange choking sound and stops, taking another deep breath. "I will not coddle you, David. It's long past time for you to learn responsibility yourself. You will attend your lessons tomorrow, and I will see you at lunch. Goodnight."

"I-"

"*Goodnight*, David." He snaps. His tone softens just a bit. "I love you."

I swallow, looking away. There's so much more I want to say, to protest, but suddenly I can't voice any of it. The door shuts with a soft click. I kick a pillow and hug my knees. This was my choice, I remind myself.

But this isn't how any of it was supposed to go. I feel empty. At least before, even if I was lonely, I could hope that somewhere there was a Dad who loved me. But if he cares, why is he acting like this? I close my eyes and hug myself, mentally replaying our initial reunion. He felt something then, didn't he? So why?

The only light in the room belongs to an old-fashioned lantern. It casts shadows that dwarf me, and I shiver.

I stand up, trying to push away the unpleasant thoughts. I'm too restless to even attempt to sleep. I strip off the soaked jacket and toss it on the floor. The waistcoat follows, but just as I start to unbutton the undershirt, I realize I have no idea where my clothes might be if they're here at all. I really don't want to wear a suit to bed, too.

There's a soft knock at the door. I consider ignoring it, but Basil's voice calls from the other side. "David? It's me. Are you awake?"

I open the door immediately, stepping aside to allow him in.

He accepts the silent invitation and surveys my room as he enters. He holds a lantern and sets it down next to mine. "I... I um..." He stops, clears his throat, and straightens, clasping his hands behind his back. "Are you alright, David?"

"Yeah, fine," I trail off, the lie obvious even to me. "...no."

A trick of the light or a smile flickers across Basil's face. "I wouldn't expect it of you, honestly." He takes a seat where Dad did not long ago. "I can scarcely believe you did that."

I look away, and my eyes rest on the pillow I had kicked on the floor. "Did what?"

"Ran out at dinner," Basil says, leaning back against the couch, letting himself slouch for once. "If you wished to cause a stir, you succeeded."

"I wasn't trying to do anything," I reply, flopping down beside him. "I was pissed off. Why the hell would he assign seats like that?"

"You ran out because of the seats? I did warn you," Basil begins, but I interrupt him.

"You warned me about the rest of them; you didn't say anything about *Dad*."

Basil gives me a measuring look. "You still don't understand. Listen," he adds quickly as I suck in a breath to protest, "He placed you as high as he could get away with. Higher than most expected, I think. Uncle Leonid complained nonstop about it-"

"I don't care about being placed high on the table!" I snap. "I don't care about rank; I'd rather be with Mom!"

"He couldn't do that and also acknowledge you as his son."

"His son? Then why wasn't I next to you? Why was I with his daughters? Which, by the way, is a whole other can of misogynistic, bullshit-filled worms!"

Basil winces, blushing. "He… first, you must be proven. Uncle insisted on that much. In some ways, tonight…" He trails off, shaking his head, then smiles. "I look forward to sitting beside you. I'm sure we will soon."

I snort, unconvinced, and fold my arms. "Even if we did, what about Mom? She's still stuck away from everyone else."

Basil's smile slips away. He stares down, tapping a finger against his lip. "… I'm not sure. Perhaps…" He hesitates and stares at me again.

I raise my eyebrows at him, nodding in a silent entreaty for him to continue.

"I… it's hard to say for sure, but… as your mother, even if she was a mistress, I… believe he might be able to seat her higher after that. Possibly even next to my own."

I make a face. "Ugh, wouldn't-" I catch my words too late and flush. "Uh…" Right. Margaret is Basil's mother. "Crap, I'm sorry."

Instead of getting angry, Basil just smiles ruefully. "I have no illusions about your feelings towards Mother, David. I don't think anyone that saw you tonight does."

I rub my arm nervously. "Basil, I…." What can I say? 'I hate your mom but I still think you're awesome; please don't hate me' just doesn't feel right.

Basil laughs, but it's genuine, not a disturbing false laugh like Margaret's. "I'm not mad at you, David. I know how Mother is, and I know how you are. You two are fire and water, and you both can be difficult to deal with at the best of times."

"I am not!" I protest. Basil laughs, and I tilt my head, studying him. "You seem more relaxed all of a sudden."

"Yes, brandy is good for that. I was hoping to invite you, but after what happened…"

"Brandy? Just what is the drinking age in Fyrnlendh, anyway?"

"Sixteen, not that I'd let it stop me if it were older," Basil replies. "Sometimes you need a good drink."

"So you haven't forgotten how to break the rules." I tease. I manage a more genuine smile.

"No, just learned a bit of subtlety. I'd suggest you do the same, but I fear it's a lost cause at this point."

"I can be subtle."

"As an earthquake."

I lean back, folding my hands behind my head, and listen to the sound of the rain. "Hey. We should go explore again tomorrow, for old time's sake."

"Mm. Sounds nice," replies Basil.

"It's a deal, then." I sit up, looking towards him. "After lunch?"

"Barring the weather," Basil agrees, lifting his glass towards me.

I wave him off. "Oh, come on. It's just a bit of rain."

"It would make exploring more difficult, but we'll see." Basil concedes, smiling.

Not everything here is dismal. I still have my brother. I flop backward on the couch, hands still folded behind my head, legs dangling up and over the side. "Hey, Basil? Do you know where Mom's room is?"

"I've a good idea; why?"

I shrug. "I wanna talk to her."

"Mm… understandable, but perhaps it would be best to wait until tomorrow. She's likely…occupied."

"What makes you say that?"

Basil clears his throat and blushes. "Well… she and Father are… close. And she hasn't changed that much despite the ten-year–"

"Oh god!" I cover my face and groan. "I did not need to think about that."

"You did ask."

I throw a pillow at his face, but he catches it one-handed. I scowl. "You're supposed to be drunk." I accuse.

"I'm not drunk," Basil responds, raising an eyebrow. He smirks. "Not that being hammered would matter with a throw like that."

"Screw you," I say, starting to smile, but a yawn comes out instead.

"I've read about jet lag. Our time zones are quite different as well… somewhere near ten hours, I believe? You must be tired. I'll leave you to sleep." Basil says, standing.

"Hey, do you know where my stuff is?" I ask, stretching and straightening.

"They should have unpacked it by now," Basil said. "The clothes will be in the wardrobes. I'm not sure about anything else."

I wince at the reminder of how limited my pool of clothing is. And they aren't exactly fresh… But I don't have the energy to explain the whole story to Basil.

"Ah, I'll take a look. Thanks, and g'night, sleep well."

Basil lifts his lantern again. "Goodnight."

I carry my own to the wardrobe, and sure enough, hidden between rows of far fancier attire, I find my familiar clothes. To my relief, they're clean and worn out and inviting. I throw on a t-shirt and head to the bed. On it lies embroidered pajamas. Oh.

Well, I'll still be more comfortable in my own clothes. I push the pajamas aside and sink into the bed. It's fluffy and comfortable, half swallowing me. I struggle to figure out how to turn the lantern off for a moment. I'm left alone with the sound of the rain. My thoughts and the pains of my neglected stomach keep sleep at bay long after Basil leaves, despite my exhaustion.

Knocking yanks me from the dream I finally managed to slip into. I groan, rolling over. Something pokes at me from the comforter. I grasp at it, tugging it away and opening one eye to squint accusingly at the culprit, a downy feather. I'm too tired to even glare properly.

The knock sounds again, and I moan, heavy-headed. "What?!"

"Young Master David, it is time for your lessons." Says a voice.

I squint at the door, then the window, blinking into the pre-morning haze. The sun isn't even up yet. Is Basil the only person in the damn castle who knows what jet lag is?

"Young Master David, I must insist you rise." Says the voice, accompanied by the damnable persistent knocking.

With another groan, I will myself up, rolling off the bed and yawning.

"Young ma-"

"Yeah, I heard. I'm coming," I interrupt, wincing at the cold stone on my bare feet and retreating to the safety of the carpet. Upon opening the door, I see a white-gloved man holding a tray of several steaming mugs, some pastries, fruit, pickles, and grilled fish. My mouth waters.

"I don't have to go down to that stupid feasting table to eat?" I ask, relieved.

"Goodness no," replies the man, emerging from the bathroom. He's younger than most of the staff I'd seen, but his hair is startlingly white, contrasting his youthful face. His features are all slightly elongated; slender fingers, long nose, long face... and the combination brings to mind the beautiful elves I read about. His accent is also different, like a mix between Fyrnekh and English. Not to mention his mastery of the language. "Only dinner, young master. The rest of the meals you may eat where you please."

"Awesome," I plop down and set to work on the breakfast. I have not slept much the past few days, but I'm too hungry to care about sleep right now.

"I'm glad you approve, sir. I've taken the liberty of drawing a bath; it should be done by the time you've finished your breakfast."

I've just finished a pear when he speaks again. "Your bath is done. I shall leave you your privacy and return when it's time for your lessons."

I strip down and, noticing a clear spot near the bath, grab the food tray. I eat and bathe at once. After my day yesterday and the lack of decent sleep, I feel like I've earned indulgence.

I emerge to an empty room, save a suit that's been laid over the bed. I toss it onto the couch and sink back into bed without another thought.

When I wake, the sun is up, its light bleached by mist. I'm clean, no longer famished, and looking forward to rediscovering my old haunts with Basil.

The family has other plans.

Lessons, I'm told, are to take place in the library. I'd forgotten about the classes (seriously, not even a single day to deal with the jet lag?). Still, the thought of them taking place in a library is uplifting.

I've always loved libraries, almost as much as forests. They're quiet refuges. Most importantly, they're where books live. Shelves full of thousands of places to go and people to meet. People that will never ghost you, places you can always return to. Books are more dependable than reality. And they always have better endings.

The castle library is enchanting. Bookshelves span three stories tall, with sliding ladders to reach the highest volumes. Spiral staircases connect the ground floor to the slender balcony that wreathes the room. The walls are dominated by stained glass windows. Paired with the towering vaulted ceilings, I feel like I'm in a cathedral dedicated to the god of books.

Across the floor, tucked between bookshelves, are desks. Each has a child or teenager sitting in it and an adult looming above them, most speaking in hushed whispers. I dart around looking for Basil when a woman steps in front of me.

"David Rose, I presume," she says, with a smile as straight as the ruler she holds. She has neat hair the color of deep soil, a round face, and dark eye shadow, giving her a friendly, panda-like softness.

"Yeah," I respond, gazing wistfully at the bookshelves. I want to find Basil. There seem to be so many cozy areas to cuddle up to read, too...

"You're late."

I shrug. I'm tired, distracted, and jet lagged, and I honestly have never cared about being late at the best of times.

Her eyes narrow. "I am Miss Rigo. I have the misfortune of being selected as your tutor."

I raise my eyebrows. "The *misfortune?* I hope you're not supposed to be teaching me manners."

Miss Rigo gives a prim smile. "I'm certainly not looking forward to it. Your tardiness aside, I understand you come from America. Saints know I've witnessed the atrocities that pass as a school system there. I clearly have my work cut out for me."

"I mean, my schooling has been a mess," I admit, tilting my head, smiling slowly. "But we *do* cover how wrong bigotry is. Y'know, like what assuming someone's going to be a bad student because where they came from falls under. So I think you'd find you have plenty to learn in American schools. But don't worry!" I give her an elaborate bow and a cheshire grin. "I'll do my utmost to live up to your expectations."

"You certainly have a smart mouth." Miss Rigo growls, smile gone. She looks like she's going to say more, but I'm faster.

"Smart ass, too."

"Enough!" She snaps the ruler to a bookshelf less than an inch from me, and I jerk back. She then points the ruler at me. "This is the only warning I'm giving you. You will be a focused and obedient student, I do have permission from your father to discipline you, and you will not be coddled. Now come take your seat."

I glare at her but follow her to a desk in an alcove of books. If I have to study, it is an excellent place to do it.

I flop down into the chair, leaning back. My hand is immediately smacked with a ruler. "Ow!" I cry, cradling my hand, stunned. "That-that's illegal!"

Miss Rigo tuts with the barest hint of a smirk. "You seem to know painfully little of Fyrnlendh law. Didn't I tell you I have permission to discipline you as I see fit? You will be expected to maintain proper posture moving forward. Back straight."

I glare, rubbing my hand angrily. What the hell? There's no way Dad would approve of her actually hitting me... ..would he?

"We'll have to begin with an assessment, of course. I expect to find you years behind in every possible subject, but we won't know what's needed until we see, will we?" She slaps some papers onto the desk. "We'll begin with math. Your desk is well equipped with writing instruments, but you may not use the calculator for this test."

I gawk. It looks like more pages than an SAT test.

Miss Rigo taps the ruler against her palm impatiently. "Begin."

I glare at her, eyeing the ruler before I ruffle through the desk. I find the supplies she mentioned and retrieve a pencil and eraser.

The test is mind-numbing. I despise math. A headache forms almost immediately from staring at banal lists of numbers. The first few pages are insultingly basic. The next are slightly more complex addition, subtraction, multiplication, division, and the like.

I lean forward to write unconsciously, resting my head on a hand where I can rub at a temple. Miss Rigo smacks me with her ruler again. I hiss and glare.

"Back straight, David. If you are incapable of sitting properly, I will have to recommend your father dress you in a corset."

It sounds like a joke, but I don't think Miss Rigo is capable of humor. "Over my dead body."

"I don't imagine it will come to that. Continue, David. We have quite a lot of subjects to cover."

I flex and unflex my hand, gritting my teeth. Miss Rigo lifts the ruler warningly, and I return my attention to the page. I come across a problem that covers one of the many areas of math I never actually learned. I have quite a few, unsurprising considering my constantly fluctuating educational background, and trying to shore up the holes in my education has always felt pointless.

I skip the problem, moving to the next one, only to be slapped by the ruler again. "Ow! What the *hell?*" I demand, cradling my hand with my other. Which she smacks. I grit my teeth against tears.

"No swearing." Miss Rigo says dispassionately. "And do not skip questions."

"*I don't know it,*" I snap. "I have no idea how to do the problem. What exactly do you expect?"

"I expect you to make an effort." Miss Rigo says, lifting her eyebrows, intensifying the panda-like makeup.

"No amount of effort is going to magically make me know how to do something I don't know how to do! That's supposed to be your job; that's why you're the *teacher!*" I protest, frustrated.

She hits me again. I flinch. "No talking back. Now finish the test. *All of it.*"

I bristle, clenching my teeth. "Isn't this supposed to be an assessment? What's the point?"

Miss Rigo just taps the paper with the ruler. My hand is shaking from pain, and I don't know how much I can keep writing. My eyes sting, but I fight against it. I don't want her to see how much this is getting to me. I pick up the pencil with a trembling hand to start throwing random numbers at the page because, apparently, that's what she wants. This is torture. The fact that it's occurring in a library only makes it worse.

I have a hand full of bruises and am halfway through the so-called assessment when I start to notice the other library occupants walking past. I glance between them and Miss Rigo.

She gives a contemptuous sniff. "You're far too slow. I'd planned to be on the third subject by now."

I almost point out that I'd be done by now if she didn't insist on having me 'try' to solve impossible problems I don't know anything about, but she's keeping a firm grip on her ruler. She watches me for a long moment and looks pleased when I hold my tongue. Her expression makes me sick to my stomach. I want to say something just to wipe the smug look off her face, but she apparently decides I'm obedient enough before I think of the right words.

"Very well. We'll break for lunch." She says in the tone of voice I'd expect her to use to offer me a cookie. She collects the papers and slips them into a folder.

I stand, trembling. I'm mentally exhausted and in too much pain to think, so I just follow the crowd.

We pass through some double doors into a large, brightly lit hall. I halt, my stomach at once souring. The radiance of light illuminating the grand length of tables from the star-shaped skylight is truly a sight to behold. I absolutely despise it and everything it represents.

I'm not doing this again. Especially not with the morning I just have. I spin and face the way I came.

Directly in front of me stand Dad and Basil.

"David," Dad greets. "Not hungry?"

"I'm not eating here," I growl, glaring. Pain still radiates in my hands, pain that if Miss Rigo is telling the truth, he approved of.

"Very well. The servants will fix you something and serve it wherever you like. I will speak with you after lunch." Dad continues past me. I clench my fist. Bitterness burns in my chest. I turn to Basil.

"What was that?" I attempt to keep my voice lighthearted.

"I believe father just told you to eat in your room," Basil replies. I bite down on my anger with a grin.

"Screw that! Let's eat outside."

"I was thinking the patio."

"Too boring." And I didn't want to be found by anyone else.

"Do you just plan on raiding the kitchens?"

"Sure, why not?"

Basil groans, then grabs my arm and points at me. "Watch." He turns to one of the men standing like statues around the hall. "My little brother and I are having a picnic. Prepare us a basket."

"I'm not your *little* brother." I protest.

"You're the shorter brother," Basil smirks, staring down at me from all of an inch, *maybe* two.

"Barely," I say, nudging him with my elbow, but the ribbing is strangely soothing. It's not like I actually care about who's older or who's taller or any of it. It's refreshing to have someone to bicker with.

The man returns with a large basket. I grab it before Basil has a chance. "Thank you!" I chirp. Then I dash off to find us a spot to eat.

I walk through and past the gardens straight into the twisting forest. I follow a path half dream half memory, deep into the tangled branches. We've walked maybe half an hour when I suddenly stumble onto a meticulously manicured walkway, contrasting sharply with the thick undergrowth around us. I look forward and see walls of crumbling stone.

"Huh," I say, "I actually found it."

"Found what?"

I point.

"Why didn't you say that's where you wanted to go?"

"I guess I wanted to know if I could do it. Anyway, you know this place. If you lead the way, it'd hardly be an adventure."

"We could have arrived faster, at least. I am hungry."

"Hunger makes food taste better."

We pass through the hedges and into the clearing of trees. There, I stop to take in the ruins of my childhood.

For the first time since I arrived, I'm disappointed by something being smaller than I remember. They're just tiny walls green with moss, the highest parts barely as tall as my waist. Their original form can only be guessed at now. Then again... hadn't that been the fun of it? Dreaming up my own castle, my own history that could fit inside.

I close my eyes and almost feel the stones dwarfing me. Memories flitter at my mind like fragments of a tune with words long forgotten.

I smile and lean against one of the walls. It's cold, but the moss is springy, and I pretend I'm breathing air from a lost civilization. I pull out the now cold lunch. Basil settles across from me. He eats as if still at a table, unfolding a napkin and taking small bites. I pause to stare, bits of bread crumbling from my mouth.

"What are you doing?" I ask, then swallow.

He looks at me. "Eating." He raises a challenging eyebrow. "While still having a sense of etiquette."

I press my lips together, trying to wrestle my grin into the charade of solemnity. "You know, the only people who will care are the birds, and I think they'll like my way better."

He shakes his head and returns his attention to his meal.

"You can lighten up, you know. No one's here." I say, spreading my hands expansively and sending a few more crumbs flying.

"I am light," Basil replies.

"No. You're heavy. Because you're so tall."

"At least I'm the tall one."

"And the heavy one."

Basil eats with care and eats more than I do, but I talk through the whole meal and finish after him. I'm desperate to break the suffocating atmosphere of the castle. As lighthearted as I'm trying to be, everything has been pretty sucky except him, and I don't want any reminders. Even his manners threaten to drown me.

I lay on my back next to the blanket, staring at the bright white sky through the trees. The sun is peering defiantly through the upper layers of fog. According to Basil, this is considered sunny in Fyrnlendh.

"Well, we've had time to digest," I say. "Let's go have some fun."

Basil bites his lip. "I should be working."

"Work can wait. We have grounds to explore, adventures to have, princesses to steal!"

"We aren't kids anymore," he says, but he's smiling.

"Race you!" I laugh and dash away without waiting for a response. I hear the thud of his feet coming up behind me, and I grin, leaning forward and charging into the fog, allowing myself to laugh. I glance behind me and see him catching up, a look of determination on his face.

I smirk and face forward again. I suddenly dart deeper into the forest, bounding over a log.

"Hey!" I hear him call, voice filled with surprise and indignation.

"You're too sloooow!" I call behind me teasingly.

"I'm not!" He exhales in one breath, sounding focused, "You're cheating!"

"Can't cheat when you're making up the rules as you go!"

We race through the woods. My heart pounds in my chest like clattering hooves. I feel more alive with each breath, darting about, changing directions randomly, staying ahead through my own capricious nature.

A root comes out of nowhere, and I fly forward, throwing out my hands, carried over a foot by my own momentum. I barely turn the fall into a roll, sticks and rocks stabbing vengefully across my body before a treetrunk forces me to a bruising halt.

"David!? Are you alright?" Basil cries, skidding to a halt near me, sending a few more sticks and a cloud of leaves over me.

"Just my pride," I croak, then wince. "And my ribs. And hands. And legs..."

"Well, thank goodness no one knows where we are, klutz."

I help myself up gingerly and brush off the suit. Generally, I'm not the type to revel in needless destruction, but I find the layers of dirt coating the abominable suit gratifying. "I'm not a klutz, just practicing flying."

"Going well for you, is it?"

"Gotta start..." Something just past him catches my eye, and I trail off, wandering towards it. It's a stone cave with a line of large iron bars and a door across it, barred with a heavy padlock bigger than my hand. The low, swirling fog trails down into the darkness. Yet, it almost seems to be the other way around, the cave expelling it like the breath of some enormous animal.

I touch one of the bars and peer through them into the depths. The iron is cold as icicles and popped and chiseled with age, poking my flesh. I can see a whisper of stone stairs. I press my forehead against the bars, ignoring a shiver, trying to figure out how far they go.

"David?"

I look behind me as Basil emerges from the fog. He looks at me, then over my shoulder into the cave.

"What is this place?" I ask. "Part of the old castle?"

"No, not quite. I don't think it was ever part of the castle. But it's old, not safe anymore. Not used very much for anything." Basil walks next to me, still staring down a moment, before looking at me and nodding over his shoulder. "Let's go."

I stare at the padlock, shiny and new against the old bars. "Didn't I say adventure?"

Basil's footsteps stop, but my attention remains fixed on the cave. I hear a low sound from the cavern's mouth. I tilt my head, so my ear is at a better angle. "Do you hear that?"

It's the type of deep rumble you feel in your bones. A distant throb, like a heartbeat. Something about it draws my attention.

"Sounds like wind. Happens with old caves."

"No, it's not like wind," I mutter, sinking to one knee as I inspect the padlock.

".... let's go, David." Basil insists, but I ignore him. I turn the padlock over in my hand, but there's no sign of a keyhole or any way to open it at all.

Suddenly, there's a loud caw and furious wing beats. I pull back just as a black blur whizzes by where I'd been. The raven twists and settles on top of the cave. It unfurls its impressive wingspan and shifts foot to foot like a tiny gorilla, cawing angrily.

"Its nest must be nearby," Basil whispers, taking my arm in his hand. "Let's go."

Why does he sound relieved?

We're barely back in view of the castle when one of the white-gloved staff members rushes to meet us. He speaks rapidly in Fyrnek, and I stare blankly.

"You started lessons already?" Basil asks me, glancing back.

"Right? It's like you're the only one in the castle who knows what jet lag is," I say, running a hand through my hair to collect some larger pieces of debris.

Basil winces. "Perhaps this was a bad idea."

"What are you talking about?" I ask, pausing in my motions. "I thought it was fun. I was hoping we could hang out again tomorrow."

Basil glances at where the messenger stands and watches us nervously. "I… don't think that's a good idea," Basil says.

We head inside together, but Basil stops. "I have work to do. Father wants to talk to you. He'll lead the way," he gestures to the staff member as he says 'he.'

I absolutely don't want to talk to Dad. But I nod so Basil doesn't worry more, and obediently follow him to Dad's office, trying to decide what to say.

Dad is sitting at his desk when I step inside. The door closes behind me, but Dad doesn't even look; he just continues writing with a fountain pen. I give him a few moments to speak first, listening to the oddly soothing scratching of metal nib on paper. He says nothing.

Being ignored hurts more than I expect. I should be used to

it after ten years, right? But those ten years were full of hopes and might-have-beens. Not a reality where he doesn't care.

Either way, I have no intention of standing here and taking it. I turn back to the door. Just as I clasp the nob, there's a gentle clink of the pen being returned to its spot and he speaks.

"How was your day?"

"Crappy start. Lunch was nice."

"You skipped your lessons."

"No, I didn't; that was the crappy part I mentioned."

"There were more lessons after lunch."

"I don't know if you can qualify them as lessons." I glare over my shoulder at him. He's standing now, and halfway across the room. I didn't even hear him. "Was having me start them the day after I arrived your idea too?"

He pauses and watches me for a moment. "Yes. There is a good deal for you to learn. Things are already going to be hard with you not speaking the language. But…" He closes the distance. "…perhaps you need more time to settle in."

"Oh wow, you think that might have been helpful?" I ask, eyes widening in a sarcastic mimicry of innocence. I turn to face him all the way, hands clenching. "Too bad you couldn't find an actual teacher instead of throwing me at that abusive lemur that couldn't teach a frog to jump."

His eyes narrow, and his mouth presses into a thin line.

"Your teacher is highly accomplished and well respected. Miss Rigo taught your brother and several of your cousins." He closes his eyes and takes a deep breath. Touching the tips of the fingers of one hand to the bridge of his nose while tilting his head.

"Oh, trust me. I've had a lot of teachers in my life, but Miss Rigo takes the award for being the worst, hands down. She may know a variety of subjects, but teaching is absolutely not among them." I snap.

"She comes with the highest credentials." He retorts, an edge beginning to creep into his voice though it has not changed in volume.

"Credentials for what?" I snort. "She doesn't even know what a goddamn *assessment* is. Are you really okay with her hitting me with her fucking ruler?"

"History, language, communications, education, social science, mathematics, chemistry, biology, language. Shall I go on? And yes, we do discipline children here. This is not the United States." He sighs and places his hands on my shoulders. I immediately jerk back, bumping into the door, hands clenching. His hands hover in the air where I was for a moment before slowly lowering. I determinedly blink back tears. I didn't want to believe it. I hate how easily he admits it.

"I called it then. She's a scholar, not a teacher, and you don't know the damned difference. I've been here less than a day, and I already can see why Mom wanted nothing to do with this place!"

"I did not want things to be this way. I wanted you to be here this whole time! But you're here now, and this time I am the head of the family. I don't want to drive you away, David. Please. Bear with me and our family. Some changes can be slow, but I have the power to make those changes."

"Let's ignore the utter bullshit from last night." I snap and hold up a hand to display the bruising. "*This* is your choice and your responsibility! Why are you talking about changing shit when you've both already told me that *you approve of this?!*"

"That's how your brother was taught. How I was taught. How your grandfather was taught. I fail to see the problem. I've had much worse horseback riding and fencing. Not to mention *boxing* and *wrestling*. Are you telling me you can't handle a few bruises?"

"Oh wow, it's not as bad as injuries you obtained during some of the sports most known for inflicting permanent brain and spinal damage, guess I should be fine then." I say, voice dripping with sarcasm. "Clearly that makes physical abuse okay." I narrow my eyes. "Mom doesn't know shit about this." It isn't a question, because nothing can convince me I'm wrong.

He watches me for several seconds, his breathing slow and controlled. He's clearly trying to maintain an impassive expression, but a million things give him away. His nostrils flair and the corners of his lips twitch slightly. His jaw muscles stand out on his chiseled face, tense and clenched. I can hear his teeth grinding. Despite all this, he speaks with an even, steady voice.

"Your mother and I fought like this on our first date..." he turns his back to me and clasps his hands behind his back and he paces towards the window and stares out. "She always was very good at pointing out that I can in fact be wrong. That the old ways may not always be the best." He draws the curtain aside and looks out the window and lets out a heavy sigh. "You're so very much like her. I shouldn't be surprised."

"Are you saying that before you met Mom, you didn't even consider the fact that you could potentially be wrong about something?"

"I'm saying that I led a very sheltered existence in a tiny, foggy, damp, isolated corner of the world. One whose xenophobia is only overshadowed by its arrogance. Trust me, I'm leagues more understanding and progressive than my grandfather. I'd suggest you ask your mother for confirmation, but I'd rather not remind her of any of that." His arm drops and he turns to face me once more.

"I don't give a shit about how bigoted he was, this isn't about him, this is about you." I snap.

He gestures to the chair across from his.

"Sit," he says. He sits in his throne-like office chair, which looks more ostentatious than comfortable. "...and I'm admitting that I may be wrong. That our methods however traditional may be outdated. You're right. She doesn't know anything about this." He steeples his fingers. "I want you both here. I want you both happy. I'd rather explain how I made a mistake to her, but then listened to you and fixed it, than have the same fight with her."

I fold my arms, staring at him, but I lean against the wall instead of sitting down. There's dozens of things I could say, but none of them will do anything but make things worse. I'm still furious. He lets out another heavy sigh.

"No more physical discipline. I'll speak with Miss Rigo personally. But you need to attend all of your lessons. It is important that you learn quickly and make a good impression." He snaps the quill from its stand and dips it in an inkwell before writing himself a quick note. I glance between the ink and the computer, and then back at his face.

"That's it?" I ask.

He looks up, "Is there something else you wish to address? I will need to have Miss Rigo notified and a space in my schedule made to meet with her. I'll make sure it happens before your next lesson. My other duties today are all time sensitive."

Is he just… dismissing me? Like this meeting wasn't his idea to begin with? "How about a fucking apology."

He lifts his head to stare at me a moment, expression blank. "What exactly am I apologizing for now?" He sighs again, irritation evident. He looks at the grandfather clock looming over one wall of the room. "We can finish this discussion another time. I'm very busy."

So that's it, then. I grit my teeth together, and swallow my anger and disappointment. I clench my hands and storm out, not trusting myself to try to say another word.

Chapter Four

I lock the door to my room and huddle at the window. I don't have the focus to read, so I escape the only way I know how, into music. I choose songs echoing my own anger and grief, letting them scream where I must bite my tongue. I watch a nearby raven, its feathers lit by gold, then rose and purple as the light dances its swansong before draining from the sky.

I stretch and pull my earbuds out, letting myself return to the world. Even now, in the twilight, the eternal fog hides the roots of the trees. I blink, rubbing my eyes, and only then notice my tears. I flush, even though no one's there to see it. Why is everything such a mess?

I rub my face. I don't know what to do. This isn't the relationship I want with my father.

There's a soft knock at the door. I bite my lip, debating. "Come in," I say at last.

It rattles. Crap. I forgot to unlock it.

"It's-" Basil's voice calls.

"I know," I interrupt, hurrying over. I unlatch it and pull the door open for him. "Sorry."

He enters and glances around my room, adjusting his suit. "I... I wondered if you intended to come to dinner." He says softly. He glances at my red eyes and then quickly averts his gaze.

I sigh and flop onto one of the couches. Basil sits across from me.

His eyes flick up at me, then down to his clasped hands.

"I hadn't decided," I answer honestly.

"I'm sorry," Basil says suddenly, startling me.

I stare at him, perplexed. "For what?"

"You... father was angry with you," Basil replies quietly, looking unhappy. "I shouldn't have... I should have waited until your lessons were done. I should have known you had started. Especially..." He glances at my hand, still covered in bruises, then away.

"Basil, that's not your fault. It was my choice, not yours. And Dad and I are very much angry at *each other*. I wouldn't have gone back even if we hadn't had lunch together. And I don't regret it," I add fiercely. Seeing Basil's obvious discomfort, I force myself to focus on something other than my anger. "I didn't see you there. At lessons, I mean."

Basil blushes, squirming in his seat. Apparently, I've made a poor choice of subject change. "I've already... graduated, so to speak. Mastered the subjects to an acceptable level. I work now."

I raise an eyebrow. "You're younger than me, and you've graduated and are working?"

"It's not your fault," Basil says quickly, "Everyone knows how miserable American schooling is-"

I let out a bark of laughter. "Firstly, American schools aren't the only ones I've attended. Secondly, I can assure you that this morning was literally *the worst* 'educational' experience I've had." I use finger quotes when I say educational and shake my head. "Graduating and working at seventeen isn't the norm anywhere else, you realize?"

"Well, yes, but we are encouraged to learn quickly, to excel-"

"To have no sense of self, want, or time to play?" I interrupt, irritated. "You realize that's actually necessary for development, right?"

Basil goes quiet. He has a strange expression. Like a sneer, but his eyes are sad, not angry or disgusted.

"Basil?" I ask, straightening. I curse myself inwardly. Why am I taking this out on him? None of this is his choice any more than it is mine. I swallow, groping for the right words to apologize.

His head snaps up towards me, and he blushes. "I... sorry David, I was... ...you really need to wash that suit, it's filthy. You'll be giving the servants a good deal more work, rubbing it everywhere like that." I glance at the couch guiltily. I hadn't considered that someone else might have to clean up my messes for me; I'm used to them being mine to deal with. But a quick scan around the room confirms it's as immaculate as when I first arrived. Even the bed is still made. Great. Now I'm being a jerk to random people who probably couldn't even ask me to stop. "Fuck."

"I wish you wouldn't do that," Basil murmurs quietly.

"What?" I ask.

"Swear so much. It's unbecoming and dangerous."

I have no idea how swearing could be dangerous, but I don't feel like arguing the point. "I'm upset. People swear when they're upset, and cry, and do other things. Not pretend to be statues."

Basil stiffens. Dammit, I'm doing it again.

"Sorry Basil, I… I'm just…" I hug my knees, searching for words. "This has been a lot. And a lot of bull-…shoot. I don't give a single crap about propriety or whatever. I have no interest in family legacy or pretending to be better than everyone else, and I sure as he-…ck don't support the clear misogyny I've been seen." I say, having to consciously stop myself from swearing several times. "The reason I reached out wasn't so I could be some sort of pampered lost prince. I just wanted my family back. And by family, I mean you and Dad."

Basil relaxes again, his eyes softening. "David," the door to my room swings open, interrupting him. I turn, expecting Mom or Dad. Instead, striding in as if she owns the place, is Margaret. I bristle.

"Leave us." She says to Basil without looking at him.

I look at Basil. His eyes dart from her back to me, conflict contorting his features. This time he doesn't answer with an immediate, "yes, mother."

"Now, Basil," Margaret snaps, with those few degrees louder moms do when they want you to know how serious they are.

"I'll wait for you outside," Basil says quietly.

A tiny, childish part of me wants to call him a traitor, but I know how illogical and unfair that is. She's his mom, after all. I wonder if that's always going to stand between us. The idea leaves me with an unpleasant taste in my mouth. He leaves, and I turn my attention to Margaret. I'm not in the mood to put up with her crap. I'm polite enough to wait for the door to close, so Basil doesn't have to hear any of it. "Get out of-"

Margaret slaps me.

I'm not prepared. This is the second time anyone, adult or child, has ever hit me, the first being Miss Rigo. I'd wrestled and play-fought, but that's completely different. This is aggressive, hard, and painful. The sting shoots all the way down my spine and spins me to face the wall, and some detached part of me wonders how someone that skinny can have such a strong arm.

I touch my cheek, half numb with shock. The skin pulses hot against my fingers.

"You disobedient child!" Margaret hisses. "Do you enjoy causing other people suffering? Is that what this is about?"

I just stare. I want to say something. I want to say a lot of things. I open my mouth, trying to sort through my thoughts and feelings, to find the words that convey half of what I feel.

"Don't try it. I'm not one of those sheep, David. I can resist your little tricks. Open your mouth again, and I'll shut it for you."

I close my mouth. I don't like the idea of being cowed by anyone, especially not someone like Margaret. But I still have no idea what I'd even say. I'm shaking from pain, shock, anger; I don't even know myself. Maybe all of it.

"Your parents fought today because of you," Margaret hisses. In the still room, her hushed voice is booming. "Your mother's crying now. Does that make you happy?"

How fucking dare she? I remember Mom's face as I passed her, and I feel cold.

"Despite it all, I would have thought better of Emily's child. Perhaps it isn't your parentage. Perhaps it's simply the nature of being a bastard, but whatever it is, it stops. Now. You are dancing on fog, David Rose. With every step, you threaten to fall through and take both your parents plummeting with you, and I will not allow that. I have put far too much effort into getting where I am. You will act as you should. You will attend your lessons, eat dinner with grace, and earn enough of a place that you do not shame your parents further than you already do with each undeserved breath. Am I understood?"

I stand slowly, meeting her gaze. I gather my courage, my anger, and my pain and lace it into each word. "I'm not your pet," I say quietly. "This is *my* room. Get the hell out, and never come in without my permission again."

I want to say so much worse. I want to tear Margaret apart with words like she's trying to do with me, to make her suffer like all of today has. But I just don't have the energy, and I don't want a fight. I just want her gone.

She stares at me, lip twitching and eyes widening in anger. She lifts her hand for another slap. I tilt my face forward, presenting a better target, daring her. But her hand drops, and she turns, leaving just like that, not saying another word.

I watch her go. The moment the door closes, I collapse. I miss the couch, falling onto the hard marble, because apparently I don't have enough bruises. I blush. God, I hope that slap doesn't bruise. I really don't want a constant reminder. Why can't the day be over already?

I take in measured breaths. I won't cry again. Not because of her. I try not to think about Mom crying, but I can't shove it out of my head. I've only seen her cry a few times, and it's always a chilling, unpleasant experience. Margaret's words were barbed. She seems to know exactly what to say to hurt me most.

I remember Basil's words again, what he said about everyone here being experts at making someone's life miserable. I hadn't taken him seriously enough. I really should have. I shiver, cold creeping into my very heart.

I can't leave now. If I go, I'll be leaving my father, my brother, and the only chance at a real home I've ever had. And that's assuming leaving is even possible.

The door creaks open, and Basil peers into the room. He gapes when he spots me. After a moment, he closes his mouth, then the door, not speaking a single word. He steps forward and pauses, wary as a wild deer.

I imagine facing dinner. Mom, who's been crying and fighting with Dad, and Dad, who's been fighting with us both. And Margaret, the ice-hearted terror, and every other person in the room who is just like her, smiling while they try to cut me down. I know I have to do something, face it sometime. But I have no plan and no strength. "...I think I'm going to go to bed early," I say quietly. Seeing his face, I add, "I didn't get much sleep."

Basil stares miserably at me, clearly unconvinced by my excuse. "I'll bring you something after dinner." He promises quietly.

My stomach growls, and I lick my lips. "Will you get in trouble if you do?"

Basil shrugs, though he pales. He's clearly far from unconcerned. "I've nothing to worry over. It isn't as if Father explicitly said anything against it."

I doubt things are that simple. But it also would pain me to discourage rule-breaking. More than that, I don't want to turn down Basil's help. "Thanks. Um, if I pass out before you get back, can you wake me up, so I actually eat?"

Basil's concern becomes even more apparent. Dammit. "Of course."

I stare at the delicately embroidered fabric on the top of the four-poster bed, listening to the groaning and creaking of the castle settling. The sounds are annoyingly reminiscent of footsteps, so I keep thinking I hear Basil returning. Or maybe they are footsteps, staff members darting back and forth to attend to whatever duties are involved in making an ancient castle look spotless. My stomach growls again. Just how long do these dinners usually take? I should probably sit through one at some point, if only to know the answer.

I roll over, facing the window. I can see the wind by the shadows it casts, black ivy dancing against a deep ocean of sky.

"David?"

I ignore the voice, groaning, not wanting to return to the waking world. A hand touches my shoulder, shaking gently, and I jerk up, wincing. "Ow."

"Sorry, I didn't… I was trying to be gentle," Basil stumbles over his words apologizing, sounding guilty.

I pull my shirt aside to reveal an ugly bruise where he'd touched me. "…I think this is one of the ones that's actually my fault. Or the tree's fault, depending on your perspective."

I sit up and look at him expectantly. Basil's gaze drops down, then he turns away, flushing beet red. "You're naked!"

I blink slowly, confused, staring down to confirm I am, in fact, wearing clothing.

"You're in your undergarments!" Basil clarifies before I can point this out. "Which is nearly the same!"

"So… you're saying I might as well take my clothes off?" I ask, quirking an eyebrow.

"That isn't what I'm saying at all!" Basil almost squeaks, and I burst into laughter. He tries to glare, but he's so flustered it's closer to a pout. He truly has a talent for making me feel better, even when he's not trying.

"Guess it's pretty different after all, with that reaction," I say, smirking.

Basil huffs. "Aren't you going to get up and eat?"

It's my turn to pout. "I thought you were going to bring it here."

"Absolutely not. You can walk to the table to eat it properly." Basil snaps firmly.

"You're only saying that because I'm right, and you're pissy about it," I smirk. No one else is around, so I stick my tongue out. It's apparently very effective; all Basil seems to be able to do is glare as I slip from the bed.

"You didn't bother with pants, yet you're wearing socks?" Basil grumbles.

I shrug. "Floor's cold."

On my table is a tray covered in a silver cloche. Not exactly what comes to mind when I think of sneaking someone dinner. My stomach rumbles its approval as I lift the lid. My eyes brighten at the wide assortment of food before me, and I laugh. "This really isn't what I was expecting."

"Sorry," Basil says immediately, and I look up, lifting my eyebrows.

"Basil, unexpected doesn't mean bad. It's a nice surprise."

"Oh." Basil pauses and then sits down next to me.

"You still feeling snackish? I remember you eating more than me at lunch," I say.

"Well, I'm much taller. There's more of me to feed."

I snort, relieved that he seems to have relaxed. "Have some, then. I'm more used to eating with company," I say, then grab a plate that drew my eyes as soon as I'd lifted the cloche. "Except these, these are mine."

"The Caprese bites? I was expecting the lemon crème brulee." Basil says, smiling.

"Dessert too," I say, "but I love fresh tomatoes, and everything has been fresh as fuck so far."

"I've known intercourse to be described as many things, but I do believe this is the first time I've heard 'fresh.'"

I choke on my tomato. Basil looks pleased with himself, proud even, and honestly, I am too. I tilt my head and tap my lip thoughtfully. "Oh, I can think of reasons to describe it as 'fresh,'" I muse.

Basil is instantly disarmed "what, how- I mean-"

I laugh. "Words can have multiple meanings," I say with a wicked grin, reaching for the fish.

"I think this conversation is becoming rather inappropriate," Basil says with a cough, red as my tomato.

"You're the one who brought it up," I tease. Basil opens his mouth to protest, and I add, "but sure, what would you like to discuss instead?"

Basil huffs. "Perhaps that you're eating the food out of order."

"I can eat my food in whatever order I want," I say petulantly.

"It's culinary art, David. Each course is designed to flow naturally into the next and flavor it based on the one that comes before." Basil explains. Then, in a moment of inspiration, he adds, "it's adventuring for your taste buds."

"Hm." I look thoughtfully at the dishes. "That *does* make it sound interesting," I admit, putting down the fish. "So what's first?"

Basil brightens and pushes a plate towards me, explaining as I eat.

"You actually started correctly; the caprese bites were the amuse-bouche, the first course. Excluding, of course, the Hors D'Oeuvres, which I didn't bring. Next up is the soup," he passes me a bowl. "It isn't going to compare to when it's fresh and warm, but it's lovely. Our kitchen staff are led by a weekly rotation of chefs, so they may fully focus each day on a unique menu with a mixture of local seasonal-"

"Basil?" I interrupt, studying him.

"Yes?" Basil asks, more nervous than miffed at the interruption.

"You sound like a commercial. Are you trying to get me to attend dinners again?"

Basil blushes. "Were my intentions so transparent?"

"Maybe a little." I rest my head on a hand. "This is really important to you, isn't it?"

Basil's expression turns solemn. "It's important for *you*. Avoiding it will just make everyone think less of you, think you're weak and don't belong-"

"Maybe I don't," I mutter. I go to take another bite.

"You can't mean that," Basil implores, voice cracking, and I pause to look at him.

"I don't think I *want* to, Basil," I say seriously, frowning. "Why the hell would I? Literally, the only things I care about here are you and Dad." Even Adela isn't enough. I liked her, she's cute, but I don't have the same bond I do with Dad or Basil, and I've left more people I care about than I can count. "And at this point, I don't even know *what* I feel for Dad."

Swallowing is suddenly difficult, and the soup just lost its taste anyway, so I put my spoon down, blinking. My face is hot, and admitting it out loud solidifies my feelings in a way that aches.

"David-" Basil starts, then stops. There's a long silence. He begins again, voice softer. "I don't know what's happening between you and Dad. I know he's frustrated-"

"*He's* frustrated?!" I snap, glaring at Basil, but then flinch, regretting my anger when I see his face. "Sorry." I look away.

"...he is. There's a lot you still don't know or understand. He is not as free as you believe he is."

"He's still responsible for his own choices," I say, glaring at the bruises on my fist.

"Then, at least do it for me?" Basil asks softly, sounding helpless. "David, I don't want you to leave."

I swallow. I don't even recognize what I feel anymore; I have no idea how to sort through it. But I look at the food that Basil risked his own punishment to bring me, then at his eyes, which echo the same loneliness I felt for so long. I might not be the only one without a best friend for a decade. "I'll try," I promise. "I'll eat dinner tomorrow, at least."

Basil sighs, slumping in intense relief. I resume eating. I can't shake the feeling that there's something more he's not saying. Why is he so invested, so *concerned?*

I'm woken by the same white-haired man as yesterday. I'm more than half alive this time and actually able to ask questions.

"How did you learn English? Your fluency is really impressive."

The man blushes and brushes some invisible dust from his chest. "I trained in England for several years. I'm sure the details are of no interest to you."

"Why not?" I ask.

He adjusts his gloves and clears his throat. "Well, because... you are... I am..." He trails off, then straightens, holding his hands behind his back. "It wouldn't be proper."

"Sounds like you had a lot of fun in England," I say, grinning.

The man blinks and goes beet red. "That wasn't what I meant by improper-" he falls silent and clears his throat. "I... I shall leave you to prepare, but it's my responsibility to ensure you arrive on time today, so I shan't give you as much time to bathe."

I scowl at the mention of lessons, then notice the man's expression. He's staring at me like a puppy expecting to be kicked. Dammit. He probably thinks I'm pissed at him, which is dumb because it's obviously not his fault. But this also means I can't even ditch, not if it's his responsibility to get me there on time. I sigh.

"Sure. Just knock first."

"Of course, young master," He looks only slightly relieved.

"Um, can you just call me David?" I asked, wincing. "Also, can I get your name?"

The man stares with slowly widening eyes. "I… it wouldn't… I…"

I sigh. "Nevermind," I mutter and poke at my fish.

I enter the library with a scattering of others, the youngest dragging their feet and yawning.

The room is warm. Morning light filters through the stained glass windows, dyeing the motes of dust drifting through rainbow. I want to curl up on those pillows by the window and read in this magical, multi-colored warmth.

"The prodigal son returns," Miss Rigo greets cooly. She's wearing the same dark eye shadow, only today, her soil-brown hair is pulled back in a bun. It emphasizes the roundness of her face.

"I am probably the *least* extravagant person in this entire castle. I'm lazy, not prodigal. There's a difference." I say, annoyed. Miss Rigo's eyebrows shoot up in surprise. I smirk and drawl, "you didn't expect me to know what that word meant, did you? I thought teachers were meant to impart *correct* vocabulary. And here you would have happily enforced an inaccurate-"

"That is quite enough," Miss Rigo tightens her hands around her ruler. And then chooses what I assume is her go-to when she's wrong and ignores rather than refutes it. "You will be staying extra to make up for yesterday."

My eyes narrow. "You're the one that insisted on wasting *both* our time for no god damn r-"

The ruler slaps at the bookshelf millimeters from my eyes. Shock freezes me. I guess it's not physical discipline if she doesn't actually touch me.

"You really are a slow learner." Miss Rigo sniffs. "To your desk. I'm not having you waste any more time."

I glower at her back but follow. However, she must agree with me because instead of dumping the remainder of the math test in front of me, her selection is history.

Which is probably my second-worst subject. Do you know just how much variance there is on what things are covered when in different schools? Or at all? A fishing net has fewer holes than my knowledge of history. I sigh. Today is going to be a long day.

Ironically enough, I get through history quickly *because* I don't know most of the answers, so I can just put a random date, place, or name. Judging by her indignant little huffs and grunts of disbelief, Miss Rigo finds my selection less suitable.

"Well, we certainly will have a lot of ground to cover," Miss Rigo says, voice a little high. One of her eyes is twitching. It's immensely satisfying.

She takes the test and places another stack in front of me.

I stare at it. None of it, not a word, is in English. I don't even recognize some of the letters. I lift my eyebrows and meet her merciless gaze. "Get started, David."

"We're really doing this, are we?" I ask.

She smiles coldly. "It's a very standard assessment test for Fyrnekh."

"Standard for a native speaker," I say, glancing back down.

"This is your home now." Miss Rigo says. "Fluency is essential. I'll need to review these, but I expect to see pages filled out by the time I'm done."

It's like she's just looking for an excuse to assault me again. She's definitely some sort of sadist. She leaves.

I listen to her footsteps until I can't hear them anymore. The library is stunningly quiet; I can barely hear anything from the other students, even though I know they're working here. Cautiously, quietly, I stand.

I *did* say I'm lazy. Why should I attempt an impossible task for that miserable excuse of a teacher? I take a step and then remember Basil's face the night before.

I freeze. *I didn't promise Basil anything beyond dinner*, I tell myself. And it's not like I'll do any better if I stare at it longer. I sigh heavily and sink back down, staring at the first page.

I knew this once, didn't I? Long ago, maybe. But I've always had a talent for languages. I close my eyes and focus on just being in the library for a moment. The tranquility, the stillness, the warmth. I take a slow, deep breath, letting all of that fill me. I feel warm and focused, and open my eyes.

The letters almost shimmer before my eyes. Maybe it's nostalgia that tugs at the back of my mind, whispering long-forgotten meaning, pattern recognition, or both, or perhaps something else entirely.

But I start getting a sense of meaning. Not enough to write in Fyrnekh, at least not yet. But enough that I think the answers I write are answers and are relevant.

It's meditative, and while there's some effort, something about it, and the library itself, is exceptionally invigorating.

"Well," Miss Rigo purrs, her soft voice jolting me out of my trance. I blink up at her and see her smirking haughtily. She *wants* me to fail, I realize suddenly. But *why...?* "I wasn't sure you'd make an attempt."

She snatches the page up. She lets out an amused little snort at the first line. "I think there's an American saying about this, something regarding monkeys and.." her eyes dart to the next one, then the next, and she trails off, scowling. Then she snaps, "I see you enjoy feigning ignorance. But I expect you to write your responses in the *correct* language. Do it again."

Behind her, I see the other students and teachers trailing out to lunch. Finally.

I start standing when a ruler slams down on the unfinished pages. "Not you," says Miss Rigo. "You are to stay here during lunch."

I look at Miss Rigo, then at the paper. Then I walk out of the room. Miss Rigo calls after me, "You are the most disrespectful child I have ever encountered! You can expect your father to hear of this! This is disgraceful!"

I'd hoped to have lunch with Basil again, but I delayed too much, and he's already in the dining room, sitting between father and the harpy. I can't manage dinner *and* lunch, especially after dealing with the lessons. I turn away and, remembering yesterday, stride up to one of the suited men standing around the room. "I'd like to have a picnic. Would you mind getting me a basket?"

The man stares blankly. He answers in Fyrnek, and I'm pretty sure it can be summed up as, 'Sorry, I don't speak English.' Crap. I sigh and, noticing his expression becoming worried, smile disarmingly. I don't want him to think I'm mad or anything. I really do need to study it more. The bits I remember are unreliable, and understanding seems easier than speaking. Too bad I have a terrible teacher.

I set off again. I still haven't found the kitchens, but I can probably grab some food myself...

I spot the white-haired man who brings me breakfast. "Oh!" I cry, then grope for his name. "Right, you... didn't want to tell me your name. Sorry about earlier. I wasn't trying to make you uncomfortable."

"Uh, no, of course not, Young Master! It's not that. There's just no reason for you to learn my name." Says the man.

I silently pray that his reasoning for not wanting to talk wasn't something like that. "I'd like to know. I mean, I don't want to just call you 'you.' It's rude."

"If it means so much to you, my name is Alfrèd," Alfrèd responds, straightening his back and dipping his head in a small bow.

"Um, nice to meet you, Alfrèd." I hope I'm pronouncing his name well. "I was wondering if you could maybe grab me some food? I wanted to eat out again. Doesn't have to be a whole basket or anything fancy; just some bread would be fine."

"Of course," says Alfrèd with an enigmatic smile. He leaves, and I wonder if I made him uncomfortable again. What did I say this time?

He returns with almost as big a basket as before. Far more than I could eat, and something else I'd need to carry around. Nonetheless, I smile and thank him before setting out.

I'm determined to get so far away from the grounds that no one will find me until I'm good and ready. I put on music to listen to as I walk. The combination of music and forest soothes me, but something still feels off, a little pang in my chest. I'm always on my own when I walk like this; it's how I escape. So why do I feel so lonely?

Everything has the vague familiarity that made missing Basil and Dad all the more poignant. With nothing but time, there's nothing to distract me.

I try to remedy it by going further from the castle and deeper into the forest. I walk towards the sun, so I'm consistent with direction when it's time to leave. But it becomes more difficult to tell where the sun is as I go deeper into the forest. The curling branches ahead of me choke out what little light isn't already scattered by fog. Eventually, I'm simply looking for the spot where the leaves look a little more emerald than turquoise grey.

I don't recognize most tree species here; I wonder if they're exclusive to Fyrnlendh. They're beautiful. Their bark is so dark it almost looks black, with branches and roots that twirl in elaborate patterns. The end of each branch is overflowing with teardrop-shaped leaves. Several trees are dressed in twisting gowns of ivy, which drape from tree to tree like decorative ribbons.

The ground is scattered with broad, pale mushrooms and curling ferns. I have to keep an eye ahead as frequently as I glance upward to avoid mossy logs and stones. The smell of the forest is familiar and welcoming: naturally decaying wood and growing things, a perfect balance that seems to say, all is well, all is pure.

If only home could be so stable.

...is it really home? A small, doubtful voice asks in the back of my head. I do my best to ignore it. I don't want to give up. I walk faster, trying to outpace the thought. My passage is abruptly halted by a looming gate. Ivy nibbles at its cobblestone base and grips at the spears of intricate cold iron which rise from the cobblestone to threaten the sky.

I stare up at it, indignant. I don't like feeling caged, least of all in a situation like this. I look over the gate carefully. The top may be pointed, but the intricate latticework looks easy to climb. It'd be far more difficult holding a picnic basket, and anyway I'm hungry, so I break to eat.

I leave the basket and what I don't finish sitting on the wall. The ravens can enjoy the rest.

I hop the fence and continue on my way.

The trees gradually loosen their grip on the sky, and the forest opens up to an old road. It's stone, not paved, but free enough of weeds that it's clearly been tended to. Strange, isn't this the middle of nowhere? Am I trespassing? What if the gate doesn't belong to the Guthanderkaz estate?

Either way, I'm curious. And even if things go wrong, I'm sure I'll be able to talk my way out of it. It's the one thing I'm good at. Usually. Less so here, I guess.

I shake my head and kneel next to the road, making an arrow with stones that points at the castle. Then I step onto the street. One side curves back into the forest, the other extends into the mist.

I set out towards the latter. The tiny droplets of water raise a pleasant chill against my skin. I've always loved the fog. I pass rocky outcroppings, and I even spot the entrance of some caves, but I stay on the path. I'm not going to go spelunking on my own, and I doubt these ones have stairs. Still, it does make me wonder about the structure of the island. Unfortunately, Miss Rigo is absolutely useless. Maybe I could ask Basil about it.

The fog thickens and thins on a whim. Sometimes I can see the ghosts of trees, and other times I can't see my own feet.

I hear something echo through the mist, a wordless, deep hum that makes the stone at my feet tremble, not like an earthquake but like someone's playing some intense bass underground. The sound and sensation fade out and are replaced by the distant roar of surf and the cawing of birds.

I walk more slowly, not wanting the fog to trick me into walking off a cliff. Then the mist withdraws with the sudden embellishment of a magician flicking back a curtain to demonstrate a successful trick. There, back against the sea, is a small stone church. It has only the simplest stained glass, forming a single star, and the stone cross at the top is also crowned with a star. The church appears ancient and hand-built but is well taken care of. I see no weeds outside it or ivy growing along the walls, and there are patches of new stone where the weather had no doubt worn the old away. A soft light subtly illuminates the stained glass window, and two cars are parked outside, so I approach the church. A thrill of excitement races down my spine. Finally, something to explore.

As I approach, I hear voices in Fyrnekh. Angry, loud voices. Dread freezes my footsteps. It's not just that the raised voices seem out of place for a church. There's a slithering quality to the voices that's indescribably disquieting. Like they're not so much speaking words as gulping at them with mouths full of too many tongues.

Curiosity propels me past my hesitation, and I slowly make my way inside. On the inside, the church is pretty close to what I'd expect. I see wooden latticework at the entrance with images of angels pointing at a star. Past it sit rows of pews and an alarming number of candles. At the front of the church, where the pastor would speak, I see two figures adorned with what looks like old-school monk robes, their bodies braced in anger.

I step forward, trying to get a better look.

"Ah, stranger! English? American? Русский?" A heavily accented voice asks from my left, making me jump.

I face the source. A pale man with very round eyes and greasy hair stands before me, wearing his own set of black monk robes, a necklace of the same cross and star shape that caps the church, and an anxious smile. His thick fingers are clasped together, twitching nervously. Nervous or not, he's friendly and eager to communicate, so I smile back.

"American," I reply. "I… don't speak Fyrnekh well."

"Is ok. I know some. Many come to… old church of Fyrnlendh." He shifts so that he stands between me and the lattice. The angry voices have stopped, and I hear a shuffling, retreating step, and…something being dragged? I lean to peer behind the man and see one of the robed figures disappear behind one of the pews. The priest bends with me, so his face is in front of mine, smiling still. "You want to be making the old church… eh… sight.. eh… tour?"

"Um, sure," I say and follow the priest. He sighs in relief. Then, smiling, begins showing me around, pointing out a glass case lined with gold. It holds a leather-bound book with no label that looks ready to crumble with a whisper. "Old bible," he says proudly, if not very helpfully.

"Does everyone in Fyrnlendh just… really like candles?" I ask.

Every corner of the room is full of candles. There are even some melting on pews and all across the back of the church. There are even candles around the book, which makes me inwardly nervous despite the case. Fire and books don't mix. Triply so if the books are also important relics.

The man looks puzzled, perhaps reviewing the question in his head, then he smiles. "Candle is… holy. To… to make pray. You want to buy Holy Candle? To make pray?"

I hold a hand up. "Ah, that's ok. Sorry, I don't have any cash or anything."

The priest smiles. "No, no. Is good. You be welcome. Church is welcome, is holy. Church is good."

I smile back. Some churches certainly aren't any of those things. But this one certainly seems to be trying. The peace of it is welcome, and I thank him. He concludes his brief tour, which does not lead me to the doors the cloaked figures had disappeared into, and even I'm not rude or oblivious enough to just shove my way inside. Instead, I wander the small church for maybe ten minutes and wave when I leave.

I glance toward where the cars had been parked as I leave. Still there, both of them. Apparently, whoever was arguing never left. Curiosity gnaws at me, but I let it go for now. I don't want to try hopping that fence in the dark.

I make my way down the road until I spot my stone arrow. From there, I follow my shadow back to the castle.

CHAPTER FIVE

I return to halls busier than I'm used to. Everyone who sees me smiles politely, but their eyes linger far longer than is polite, curious, assessing. Apparently, no one I run into is comfortable enough with English to try talking to me, for which I'm thankful. I ascend the first staircase I find, and things are quieter.

I don't return to my room right away. Instead, I go to my Dad's. We have a lot to talk about. I knock, but there's no answer. I try the door. Locked.

"Dad?" I call, hopefully.

Silence.

I glare at the door, then sigh. So much for facing things.

I glance out the nearest window. It's too late for lunch and too early for dinner. Maybe Dad's with Mom…? But even so, what then? What if my conversation turns into a fight? Adding Mom into the mix will only make things worse, and I'm angry, but… I don't like fighting with him, either.

…and I don't want to see Mom cry. Margaret might be lying, but I don't want to risk it. Besides, things are weird there too.

Mom was so protective the entire trip to the castle, staying close to me, and now I've seen less of her than Dad. And things aren't exactly unresolved there, either. I really need to talk to both of them. Separately.

Maybe I can ask Basil where they are. Would he be offended? Going to see him just to ask how to see someone else? *Now you're just being paranoid*, I tell myself, shaking my head.

I weave my way back to Basil's room. I don't run into anyone else on the way. In fact, the fifth story seems far less populated than the lower four. Is this another rank thing? Basil did seem excited that I was near him… I finger my key. If my theory is correct, I finally found something I like about the Guthanderkaz obsession with hierarchy.

Basil's room is empty as well.

I stare at the door, fingering my key. I check my own room, scanning every polished surface for some sort of note, and find none. The lack of reception for my phone is becoming maddening. If I could just text them, I wouldn't have this problem.

I drum my fingers against my arms and think. Where else could they be? I still have no idea where Mom's room is, so I can't even look for her.

I stride out and look for a staff member to ask. I'm hoping to find Alfrèd. He seems to frequent the upper rooms, and unlike most of the staff, he's fluent in English. And even if he doesn't know where anyone is, he can still show me where Mom is staying.

"You missed lessons." Says a cold voice I vaguely recognize but can't place.

I blink and turn. The man with the sunken eyes who guided Mom and me the first day is sneering at me. I glare. My lessons are none of his business, not for any stupid reason like him being a member of the staff or propriety or some bullshit like that, but for the much more relevant reason of him not being my parent. I'm about to tell him as much when I realize that, while he isn't as friendly as Alfrèd, he can, at least, communicate with me. He also is top of the list for most likely to know where everyone is.

I straighten and give him a smile more friendly than I feel. "I'm looking for my Father." I somehow doubt he knows the word 'Dad.'

The man's sneer softens to a slight frown. "He is taking a Brandy."

"Can you take me to him?" I ask brightly.

"He is busy."

"I thought you said he was drinking brandy," I tilt my head, "how does that make him busy?"

The man makes a noise somewhere between his throat and his nose. "Lord Guthanderkaz is meeting with all important family Lord." He finally states. "Important matters to be discussed over brandy. Is very private."

I perk up, intrigued. "Can you tell him I want to talk?" Could I get away with following him to eavesdrop?

The man bows stiffly. "Yes, of course, Young Master." I hear the slightest emphasis on the word 'young.' "I am to tell."

"Now?"

"I am not to interrupt without inviting." The man says, shaking his head. "I speak when…. appropriate."

I bounce on my heels, biting my lip, thinking. As tempting as it would be to follow him to the meeting, it would be rather obvious. Especially since I have no idea when he'll leave, and hanging around would be suspicious. I want to disarm him. Basil had mentioned brandy the night before. It could be a coincidence, but I have a feeling it isn't, especially with Basil's seat next to the head of the table, since he already 'graduated.'

But it might help me learn why he's so worried.

The man returns much faster than I expect. Maybe I could have followed after all.

"Lord Guthanderkaz awaits." He says, bowing and gesturing for me to follow. The route between my room and Dad's office is familiar by now, but I follow him there.

"The Young Master," announces the sunken-eyed man outside Dad's office.

"Thank you, Metod." My father answers. So *that's* Metod. Should have guessed. I step inside the room. The moment I meet Dad's eyes, staring dark from thick brows, I know he's in a bad mood.

Dad waits for the door to close. He leans back in his chair and holds my gaze with a long, measuring look, tapping one hand on his desk. I hold his gaze. He isn't the only one who's angry. At last, he speaks. "You missed your class. Again."

"She wanted me to skip lunch," I say, controlling my emotions as much as I can manage. "And it takes up too much time as it is, especially with such pointless, monotonous supposed lessons from the worst excuse for a teacher I've ever had the displeasure of encountering.

He folds his hands in front of him. The tension at his shoulders eases. "You are already behind, David. You have a lot of time to make up for."

I press my lips together to hold back all the angry retorts I want to make and take several measured breaths through my nose. "Dad, do you want me to be happy?"

Dad's eyebrows lift. "Of course I do. But I am much older than you, David, and I have a better idea of what you need to be happy in the long run."

I grit my teeth and clench my hands tightly, closing my eyes. "I really don't think you do."

"David," Dad begins, but I plunge forward without waiting for him to continue.

"Dad, you don't know anything about me. You don't know my hobbies, interests, favorite classes, or books. You have no idea what I like doing in my spare time, much less what I want to do with my *life*. How could you possibly know what will make me happy?"

Dad becomes absolutely still. He stares at me, pain is etched across his features. A moment later, his careful poker face obscures it, but the memory of it throbs at my heart like a hornet sting.

"Do you want to be part of this family?"

"I accept most people here as family about as much as they accept me," I snap. "You and Basil are my family. But you barely. You're too busy being head of the house to be a father." My voice cracks at the last words.

Once again, his mask cracks for just a moment, but my eyes are blurry with the tears I refuse to cry, and by the time I blink them back, his face is stony again. He's still and silent for another moment. While I can't read his emotions, I can tell by the intensity of his gaze that he's thinking hard about his following words.

"Then make me proud." He says.

I stare, wait. But he says no more. Bitterness and dissatisfaction gnaw at my stomach. *A father's love shouldn't be conditional*, protests a small, desperate voice inside me. At the same time, another part wants to bite back, *You first*. I don't voice either thought.

I just turn away, pausing briefly before stepping out. "Where's Mom's room?"

Dad speaks so softly I can barely hear him over the clock's ticking. "I will have Metod show you."

I nod, then retreat to the window to wait. I will not cry. I refuse. I refuse to let any of them know how much they're breaking me. I put in my earbuds and retreat into music.

I don't take them out when Metod comes to show me the way. Metod stops, gestures at a door, bows stiffly, and walks away.

I remove the earbuds and knock on the door. Then before waiting for a reply, I push the door open, peering in. To my horror, the first thing I see is Margaret. Panic lances through me. Did Metod bring me to the wrong room?

Margaret turns to me with an iron smile. My cheek burns in memory, and my traitorous hands sweat unbidden.

"Who is it?" Mom calls from behind the door, and I push it further open to stare at my mother's face with utter relief.

"Mom," I say, and hurry inside, hugging her. The strength of her frame makes me realize that I'm shaking.

"David! What's wrong?" Mom asks, returning the hug.

Margaret's laugh freezes the air in my lungs. "It's so hard to remember how close he and Basil are in age when he does things like that. I think the last time Basil hugged me was, oh, I don't know... seven? Eight?"

My ears burn, not so much at the clear attempt to insult me but at being spoken about as if I wasn't there. It might have been easier to handle if I had been calm coming here, but somehow, Margaret always manages to rile me. If Mom weren't there, I'd point out how her words say more about *her* than *me*.

Mom smiles. It's a small smile, but its tugs at her dimples. What the hell? For *Margaret?* "I'm sorry to hear it. I have heard that Americans are more open with our displays of physical affection. Perhaps that's why I'm biased, but I find the idea of ever outgrowing it to be sad."

Margaret is silenced, thankfully. I pull back from the hug and look up at Mom. "Can we talk alone?" No matter who was there, I would have asked, but triply so with Margaret.

"Of course… I hope you don't mind, Margaret?" Mom asks for some strange reason. Why is she being nice to Margaret at all, considering the whole thing with Dad? Or visa versa. Shouldn't they be clawing at each other's throats? Besides, how can she *trust* Margaret? It's pretty obvious she has it in for both of us. Maybe she hides her true nature better around Mom? Maybe Mom is being too trusting or oblivious or something… though that would be pretty out of character. Whatever's going on, it's unsettling, and I feel even more paranoid.

"I think that's a wonderful idea. David's been so busy for the past few days and having such trouble adjusting. I'm quite sure he needs his mother right now." Margaret's voice is pure honey, but there's no way Mom can miss the barbs there. When I turn back to Mom, however, she's clearly oblivious. What the *hell*.

Mom cups my face in her hands, brushing some hair from my face, then licking a finger to rub at some dirt.

"Mom, gross!" I cry, pushing the hand away.

"If you don't like it, you should clean yourself next time." Mom rebuffs mercilessly.

I grumble but push it aside, turning serious. "Did you and Dad really fight?"

Mom freezes mid-motion. She's still a moment, then folds her hands on her lap. Her eyes are dark, and she's no longer looking at me but out the window. "Everyone fights, David."

"Over me."

Mom turns her gaze sharply back to me. "Your father and I have… several disagreements, David. It is in no way your fault."

I look away. That's the clichè, right? The parents get divorced, and the kid thinks it's their fault. It's not even like things were going well before. Which… brings me to the primary reason I need to talk to her, which has nothing to do with Margaret's poisoned words. "But you hate it here, and we're back here because of me."

"No," Mom says firmly, and I look at her, thrown by the reply. "I'm not going to blame you for wanting to see them, David. God knows I missed them too. I... I know how hard moving has been for you. I didn't realize how much you remembered them, how much you mourned. I'd hoped- no, that doesn't matter. But I made a mistake in not telling you, not preparing you, and not listening to your needs." She gives a sad smile, stroking my cheek. "I'm very proud of you. You have my tenacity." Her expression grows serious. "You're going to need it here."

I hunch over. "...yeah. I can see why you didn't want to come back here." I swallow, head full of questions, but decide to ask the most pressing. "Why haven't I seen you much?"

Mom rubs her temple. "I've been trying to make arrangements after our... abrupt departure. And your father, Margaret and I, well, all have a lot to discuss with each other. And... I thought you might want some time to settle in and recover after all that traveling. You know you're welcome to come by, don't you?"

I flush. "I... didn't know where your room was," I admit. But everything she said makes sense. With everything that happened, it's easy to forget this is barely the third day. I frown. I'm about to ask about Miss Rigo and the lessons... ...but what if she doesn't know? What if I say something that causes a fight between her and Dad? They already have so much between them, I don't want to be the cause of more fighting. Besides, this is something I should handle on my own. "...are you ever going to tell me details about when we left? The first time, I mean." I ask instead.

Mom stiffens immediately. This topic has been dangerous for a long time, but it seems pointless now that we're here. "David, you know how I feel about bringing this up."

Bitterness returns to squeeze at my chest, and I stare away. "Yeah," I say without bothering to hide it.

"Please understand. I have my reasons." Mom says more softly this time.

"That's what you always say," I say, trying to keep my voice steady.

"You've seen a few of my reasons now." Mom reminds me.

I flinch, then glare at her. "I'd rather go through this bullshit and have Basil and Dad in my life."

This time Mom's the one who looks away. "...I know. That's part of why we're still here, though I don't like it. There's a lot I still don't trust, either. This place is dangerous, David, in ways that-" she stops, then shakes her head.

"Ways that what?" I press. She remains silent, and I grow frustrated. "Didn't you just say you should have told me more last time?" I demand.

Mom winces and seems torn for a moment, then stares outside. "...yes. Maybe I'm making a mistake again. I'm not perfect, David; I'm not always going to get it right. But I'm going to do my best to keep you safe. However I can. And sometimes that involves not doing things I'd prefer to do."

I glare at her. She just *admitted* not ten minutes ago that she was wrong to hide information from me, and she's doing it again! I fold my arms tightly, hunching over.

Even here, even after everything, I'm still alone.

"David?" I ignore her. She sighs. "I'm sorry, there's... ... there's a lot of factors."

"Sure."

We sit in awkward silence. Mom speaks again. "I'm trying to get our things back here. I'll make sure yours get to your room."

Not that there's much. I wish my life had been more stable, not for the first time. I wish I had posters and sculptures and decorations to transform the sterile room I'm staying in from a vibe that's less museum slash luxury hotel and more me. I just nod.

Another briefer silence, and she tries again. "I heard about your picnic with Basil. Did you have fun?"

"...yeah." While it lasted.

"Next time you go on one of your picnics, why don't we all go? Your father and I, Basil, Adela, and Margaret?"

It's a peace offering. I could ignore it, but things are shitty enough here as it is without us turning on each other. I sigh softly, reluctantly straightening. I don't want Margaret there, but I guess I can't have Basil without her. "Sure," I say, Mom smiles, relieved, and I can't quite match it. "I... I'll see you at dinner."

And there goes the smile. "You don't have to go, David."

Neither do you, but you do, I think. *Probably for the same reason, at least in part.* I shrug and give her a lopsided smile. "Yeah, well. Food's best fresh, right?"

Mom searches my expression with worried eyes. I don't blame her. It's a pathetic excuse to my ears, too. But I don't like feeling like I'm hiding, and I don't feel like talking to her about Basil.

"I should go get ready for dinner and find Basil," I say, standing.

"Of course. And David?"

"Yeah?" I glance back at her, too late to prepare for the sudden tight hug she gives me.

"I love you."

I squirm. Why is this worse than when Margaret was there? Probably because I'm still kind of ticked off at Mom now too. "I love you too. But I really should get ready."

Mom kisses my forehead before releasing me. I hurry out before I can change my mind.

I ask Basil to help me prepare, more for his peace of mind than mine. He's delighted at the opportunity, though he's utterly baffled about what to do with my hair. He attempts to tame it with a comb, but my hair refuses to bend to his will, and I refuse oil.

"It'll just look wet again," I protest. "Which I'd like to avoid, thanks."

Basil sighs. "I doubt we're going to get much better then. We should be off."

I nod and follow him to the dining room. This time I'm determined to sit through the whole thing. Margaret and Adela are like the metaphorical angel and demon sitting at my shoulders, one trying to make me happy and the other trying to make me miserable. Adela has lots of natural talent. Unfortunately, Margaret's years of practice win out.

Dinner extends for what has to be hours. I lose track of how much food is brought out and left, some of it untouched. How can anyone eat like this *every night?* Especially when the rest of the day is already so structured. Why would they want to waste precious leisure hours on *this?* More than that, how can anyone live with so much of their schedule dictated to them? It's baffling, no, *terrifying.*

Finally, Dad stands up. I watch him, but this time, he doesn't make any sort of speech; he just walks out of the room. Apparently, it's some form of signal because everyone follows suit. I start after him and Basil, but Margaret takes my arm. "No, David. They're off to take a brandy. You're not mature enough for such things."

I know the drinking age by now, but I don't bring it up. After all, I already know what's really going on. They're attending a secret meeting.

I yank my arm back and stomp off, pretending to be angry. I'm careful to keep an eye on the path the Brandy Drinkers take. I leave the hall, meandering around. I give them time so no one, especially not Margaret, knows of my intentions. Unfortunately, this also makes it challenging to figure out exactly where they went. I wander, trying to act casual. I wear my earbuds for effect, though I don't actually listen to music.

It seems to work; no one pays me much notice.

I'm almost ready to give up when I notice a particularly fancy door. The family Hydra is stamped in gold on the front. It's the first Hydra I've seen on one of the lower-floor doors.

I can definitely get to the dining room from here following the path they were taking, and no one else is around. Seems worth a shot.

I pull out my earbuds and press my ear against the door, but I can't hear anything. I hear footsteps approaching from my side of the door. Quickly, I try opening it. I don't care about getting in trouble, but I might not get another chance to learn more.

Luckily the door is unlocked, and I slip inside, closing it softly behind me. I'm in a large room, lit primarily by a fireplace, but I've seen enough of the castle by now to know this is considered foyer-sized. I cross the room, and as I approach the door on the far side, I can hear voices.

I grin, press my ear against the door, hold my breath, and listen.

The words are Fyrnekh, which I suppose shouldn't surprise me, and I have to strain, only catching bits and pieces. I take steadying breaths and concentrate. The warmth of the candles, the heartbeat I can feel through the stone my hands are pressed against, the voices of the people within... All seem to aid in my meditation. I'm half dreaming, half awake. The air is staticky and tastes of ozone. Through the haze, I hear their words as plainly as if they spoke English.

"...know I am not alone in this sentiment." Growls one voice.

"It's a disgrace," agrees another, "he's a bastard!"

"You speak out of turn" I immediately recognize Dad's voice, though it sounds cold and alien.

There's a poisonous silence, and the first voice speaks again, this time with a slight quiver. "You seem to be placing personal affections above what is right-"

"What is right is for him to be placed near me. He is my son!"

"Come now," says what must be an old man. "Surely this can be resolved to the pleasure of all. Now, Lord Guthanderkaz, there are proper ways to go about things. To Nurture the Blood, and then no one would complain of th-"

"Oh, I'm certain you have one of your daughters in mind."

Arguments break out, but the cold seeping into my bones interrupts my trance, and the words become muddled again. As I pull back, ready to leave, I hear one more word.

"Silence!" It's Dad's voice again, commanding in Fyrnekh.

I hold my breath, afraid I might be detected in the utter silence that follows. Dad speaks again, nothing I can understand.

I take the opportunity to slip away, returning to my room. The elaborate gilded carvings along the walls and ceiling make the large space feel claustrophobic. There, I play the events over in my head. How do I keep doing that? It's like I'm slipping into my childhood memories of fluency. Or just have some sort of savant-like epiphany of understanding at random. But that makes less sense with the way it comes and goes. I have to talk to Basil about getting some sort of internet connection. Not being able to look things like this up on the phone leaves me feeling helpless.

More importantly, what exactly did I hear? I can think of few phrases full of more foreboding than 'nurture the blood.' I shake my head. It must be some sort of Fyrnekh colloquialism. I want to ask what it means, but I can hardly do so without explaining why I'm asking since this is the first time I've heard it.

Either way, one thing is inarguable: Dad has been supporting me under the attack of everyone else, just as he claimed. Still, there's so much I'm missing.

I visit Basil directly after breakfast. I'm not really a morning person, and he doesn't have school, so I expect him to be as groggy as I usually am (especially because he attended the secret meeting, and that meant he was both drinking and enduring a bunch of assholes,) but he's already dressed and presentable enough for a Guthanderkaz dinner when he opens the door. He looks startled to see me. "David?"

"Hey," I say, rubbing the back of my neck. "I... was wondering if I could ask a favor."

His eyes narrow in suspicion, and he arches an accusing eyebrow. Oh, come on, what have I done to deserve *that* kind of reaction? "What did you do?" Basil asks, sighing.

"Wha-? Nothing! I mean, not yet."

Now Basil really looks worried. "What are you planning, David?"

I bounce on my feet, rolling from heel to toe. "Plenty of things I'm not going to tell you about yet, but. I.." I stop, fidgeting with my shirt. How do I even ask this?

"Wait," says Basil, as my fidgeting draws his attention away from my face, "are you standing in the hall wearing nothing but a... ..what even is that?"

"It's a t-shirt," I say, releasing the shirt so it covers my boxers. "An oversized t-shirt."

Basil looks horrified and yanks me into his room. "Thank God we're on the top floor," he mutters, closing the door. "David, you can't just walk around the house naked!"

"I thought we already established that it doesn't count as naked," I say. "I can't believe you don't even know what a *t-shirt* is."

"Other than shapeless fabric with a gaudy painting on it? I can't believe you prefer that over a suit…"

"It isn't gaudy," I protest. "A Perfect Circle is an amazing band. I mean, Leonard Byrnstein is a musical genius in general, but-" I trail off.

Basil is staring blankly at me. I grimace. "Please tell me you know a genre of music besides classical?"

"Well, I know *of*…pop," Basil mutters.

"Ah yes, the two genres: classical and pop," I tease. "You really need to expand your musical range. Luckily, I have a magical device full of fantastic music of every genre-"

"Shouldn't you be preparing for class?" Basil interrupts testily. I blink, surprised at the short temper. Why is he angry? Maybe he actually is hungover.

"Um…" I search for an appropriate response

"You aren't planning to skip it entirely, are you?" Basil asks wearily.

"I still think it's a waste of time, and Miss Rigo is a terrible teacher," I grouse. "But maybe I should go."

"Yes, you should."

"Probably not like this though" I hold my hands out dramatically.

"Absolutely not like that!" Basil sputters, blushing to the tips of his ears.

"Then I'll need your help," I admit, blushing.

Basil stares, puzzled. "My help?"

"That's… why I came here." I let out my breath in a huff. "I know there's more going on than anyone's telling me," I note Basil's sudden nervous straightening. "I don't want to play the game. And I still don't give a shit about most people here. But I do give a shit about you. And the way you're acting… this is about more than just showing up to lessons, isn't it?"

Basil hesitates, then nods silently.

"So I'm going to play the game. Or, try, anyway." I say. "No matter how much I think most of this is utter bullshit." If only to find out what's really going on. "Especially because you implied that if I do things right, I'll sit next to you at dinner, not your mom."

"And my mom," Basil corrects, crushing my dreams. "But your mother would also likely be allowed to sit further up and away from… well, everyone she's near at the moment. Which likely would be preferred."

I sigh but nod. "It's about playing the part. And part of that is the costume." I gesture towards his wardrobe. "All those suits look exactly the same to me, but you keep choosing some of them over others for some reason. And different ones. I have no idea why."

Basil opens his mouth, and I hold my hand up. "I'm not asking you to teach me. I've got enough information I need to stuff my head with, thanks. I'm asking you to help me pick out the right outfits."

"Oh." Basil looks surprised, then smiles. "Very well, but I have one condition."

I fight the urge to pout. Condition? I'm doing this for him as much as my curiosity! Unfair. "What's that?"

Basil's smile turns wicked.

Chapter Six

"You're trying to humiliate me, aren't you?" I mutter, glaring into the mirror.

"It's… not exactly how I intended things to turn out," Basil says. I can tell he's resisting the urge to laugh. "Your hair really is as willful as the rest of you."

His condition turns out to be using oil to slick back my hair, which looks ridiculous. My hair looks incredible if I just let it do its thing. It's light, and the wind-tousled look suits me. I've never concerned myself with looking sexy, but I've had many guys and girls compliment my hair. With the suit on and hair wet and slicked back, I look like a disgruntled cat stuffed into one of those terrible Halloween costumes.

Basil eyes the results. He's definitely losing that battle to hold in his laughter. "Well. You do look more… professional." He reaches forward to smooth back a lock of hair that managed to escape. Another springs out to take its place.

I try not to glare at him. I *did* ask for his help. "That isn't exactly a compliment," I mutter. "It's like what you say when you can't think of a real compliment. And I'm not sure it's even honest."

The corners of his lip are twitching. "You look fine, David. Other than your hair-"

"I swear if you suggest cutting it, I will melt every pair of scissors in the damn house," I say seriously.

Basil bursts into laughter. "Actually, I think I like your long hair." He says, trying to keep a straight face. "It's very… you."

"And that is the number one thing said when you don't have anything nice to say," I say.

"It's different," Basil says, shaking his head. "Which means something here. Most of the others my age were allowed to go to boarding schools, but Father says, as his heir, there's too much I must learn first." He laughs. "I never realized how tiring it could be looking at nothing but black hair."

I don't laugh with him, staring. "Wait, you mean… you haven't left the house?!"

"Oh, I have," Basil says quickly. "We do family trips, sometimes, across the island and such… but it isn't really the same as truly living somewhere else. Everyone in Fyrnlendh knows who we are…" He sighs and lets some of his wariness show for the first time. "I am glad you came, David."

I swallow, disturbed. What's worse, never having a real home, or having a home you can never leave? I'd feel so trapped in his place. "I'm sorry, Basil," I say softly.

"For what?" Basil looks genuinely surprised. "Skipping class?"

For your childhood, I think, but I don't want to hurt him by saying it. Instead, I smile, "well, then, I guess I'll have to introduce you to it all. We'll vacation together, I'll show you the U.S., and then we can see the world! Isn't that what rich, traditional Europeans do?"

Basil smiles. "I would enjoy that, I think. You certainly have a way of making things interesting, and you'll need me to bail you out of the jails of all those countries."

"You only end up in jail if you get caught," I counter, winking.

Basil moves his hand as if to ruffle my hair, remembers his careful handiwork, and lets his hand drop. "You should get to class, or you're going to be late and spoil your effort."

"Ok," I say. I make it to the door before remembering the other thing I need to tell him. "Oh yeah, we're having a picnic for lunch."

"Are we?" Basil asks, smirking a little.

"Yeah, with Mom and Dad," I'm not going to bring up Margaret if I can help it. Basil gapes at me. I wave, then dart off without waiting for an answer. He deserves to stew with any questions he might have after what he did with my hair.

Miss Rigo is waiting for me. She lifts an eyebrow at my hair but doesn't comment. "I will not tolerate another outburst like yesterday. Do not think things will be easier for you because you sniveled at your father for special treatment. I can be very creative with my punishments."

It takes everything I have to bite back my instinctive reply. I desperately want to challenge her. But I'm supposed to be playing the part and doing things right. I hate that she may think she cowed me with her words, but I smile brightly. "I understand. Let's get started with the lessons, shall we?"

Her eyes narrow, but she nods. She looks neither pleased nor displeased, only a little suspicious. I sit at my desk, and she dumps the next stack of tests, and for once, luck is with me. English has always been my best subject.

I may not always use it, but I have a pretty good vocabulary and am well-read enough to intuit grammar when necessary. Alliteration also amuses me, appropriate or not, and I have a decent ear for rhyme. Which I wouldn't expect to matter with the type of assessments she does. I expect essays and the like, but there's a poetry assignment too.

I finish the entire thing before lunch and give her my most charming smile as I finish. "I hope this is to your satisfaction?"

"It seems you have at least one point where education hasn't failed you," Miss Rigo says, not quite as begrudging as before, as she skims the pages. I consider reassuring her that my skill isn't from school; I just like to read, but decide against it. I just smile at her. She frowns at me, thoughtful.

"I had planned on having you stay for lunch to make up for lost time. We should have finished your assessment days ago." She says absently.

I press my teeth together harder, biting down on the words that desperately long to be said. It's her own damn fault this has taken so long; most of that was pointless busy work. Instead, I say, "I have an appointment with Dad at lunch."

She presses her lips together. "Hm. I'll be confirming that with your father later. I do not appreciate being lied to."

Is the idea that Dad wants to spend time with me that hard for her to believe? I force cheer into my voice as I reply, "good thing I'm not lying to you, then. I'll see you after lunch!"

"I expect you to." Miss Rigo says.

The lunch hall is buzzing. Apparently, once it became evident that the great Head of the Family planned a picnic, it became in vogue. Instead of lining the room like statues as they usually do, the poor servers are running around frantically passing picnic baskets like a fantastical fire brigade.

I observe the chaos I've wrought with mixed feelings as I join my family and Margaret. Basil looks ridiculously excited, though he's obviously trying to hide it. He keeps biting at his lips, trying to prevent his smile with his teeth.

"We're going to have to walk a while to get away from all of them, aren't we?" I ask Basil.

Dad is the one who answers. "No. This picnic is meant to be a private affair, and I've assured it will be, whatever the others may intend."

"You certainly do know how to make things interesting." Margaret muses. Mom laughs softly.

"Well, where are we going?" She asks.

"There's a cool chained-up cave in the middle of the forest I found," I say, not because I want to picnic there but to study their reactions. Dad looks sharply at me and then Basil, who looks panicked. There absolutely is something there.

"I see why you always return so late from lunch. We won't be traveling far from the castle; you still have classes to get to." Dad says firmly. "I've already ordered an area of the garden kept clear for us."

I huff, but Mom smiles. "That sounds lovely."

There's tension in her voice, and I glance at her, then between Dad and her. Whatever's going on between them isn't resolved. I feel Margaret's eyes bore into mine but disregard it.

"Are we eating on the patio?" Adela asks curiously.

"It doesn't count as a picnic if you use tables and chairs," I say.

"We're eating on the *ground?*" She asks, disbelieving.

"On a special blanket, dear." Margaret corrects. Adela is still looking between us like she's uncertain if she's being pranked.

"Let's get our basket and go then?" I suggest, bouncing on my feet and looking around. No one is holding any, even though this was clearly Dad's idea, which seems a little unfair.

"Our picnic has already been set up. We were just waiting for you." Dad answers and begins walking off.

I pout. "Dad, I don't think you fully get the point of picnics."

Dad glances at me, lifting a single eyebrow. "Are you planning to enlighten me then?"

"Let's not dip into anything that might turn into a debate," Mom says firmly. "I'd like to enjoy this. No debates, no discussions of lessons, or anything like that. We're going to have a pleasant picnic together."

I can't argue with that. I haven't had a pleasant interaction with Dad since the first night, and never with all of us together.

The location Dad chose is a cluster of grass and sorrel, surrounded by high flowering hedges, perhaps some sort of rose.

I flop onto my belly to eat while lying down, kicking my legs absently. Adela looks between our parents and me with wide eyes, but after they fail to reprimand me, she follows my lead. Her delighted smile at being allowed to do something so different is infectious.

Dad pours everyone some drinks, then passes out the first course because we obviously can't have a simple meal when he's involved.

The start is a charcuterie of meat, cheeses, fruits, and even a cut of fresh honeycomb. I eagerly compare favorites with Basil and Adela and try mixing things to see how they taste with each other. Mom and then even Dad and Margeret join in, and soon everyone is laughing and enjoying themselves. It's a little surreal. Some small part of me doesn't trust it; this happiness surely can't last, can it?

The main course is the most colorful salad I've ever seen, full of nuts and seeds and flowers and cheese. Mom's face brightens when she sees it.

"Is it still your favorite?" Dad asks, leaning in close to her and murmuring right near her ear.

Mom laughs like I've never heard her do, almost a *giggle*, and answers playfully, "A girl can have more than one favorite."

I avert my eyes, blushing. It's still weird to see them flirting, even if it *is* better than fighting. I look to my siblings instead. Adela is watching them with wonder, and Basil… He's watching them too, but his emotions are more complicated, harder for me to read. Regret? I wonder what he's thinking, but I don't want to ask in front of everyone.

I decide to take advantage of our parents' distraction to make him squirm in a different way instead. I lean in, resting my head on my hand. "So, will you tell me what the deal is with that cave?"

Basil tenses, eyes widening and darting between our flirting parents and me. Luckily, even Margaret seems to be occupied. He hushes me.

"Not here," Basil says softly. Then, quietly. "Maybe."

I lift my eyebrows. Maybe is promising. Maybe *also* confirms that there are secrets there worth telling. "Maybe depending on what?"

"On father," Basil whispers.

"Why do you need his permission?" I ask, trying to match his volume.

"He'll know," Basil responds, shaking his head. "Trust me." He looks at me, licking his lips, and then adds, "but I think I can convince him. Especially with today."

He flashes me a genuine smile. "Moreso if you don't mind me sharing this morning?"

"This morning? Why?" I ask, eyebrows pressing together.

"Because he needs to know how much effort you're putting in," Basil whispers sincerely. "It *does* matter."

I chew the inside of my lip but shrug. "Sure. You don't have to give Dad details, right?" I don't like the idea of conversations between Basil and me being privy to other people. Especially not Dad, after how he's been.

"I don't imagine so, though I'm not sure what you're worried about,"

Basil replies quietly.

I shrug. "Nothing in particular, just..." I trail off and look at Basil as a thought occurs to me. "You're acting like the cave is a huge deal in a way that I don't understand."

Basil doesn't respond, just nods.

Whatever else we might say is interrupted by the next course. Mom conscientiously pulls Basil and I back into the conversation. It's pleasant, even with Margaret there. Hell, even Margaret acts nicer than I've ever seen her. None of her words are barbs, and she's smiling, not even the cold way I'm used to. She's not being strict with Adela or Basil at all. She's even laughing, nudging at Mom, and offering her bites of food.

This is it, what I wanted when I reached out. Maybe with fancier food, but the essential part. The family.

"So," I say to Basil. "You're going to talk to him?"

"After lunch," Basil promises and gives me a pleading look. "You'll return to your lessons, won't you?"

I nod. Even if I hadn't already made up my mind, now I *have* to know. Basil looks relieved and smiles again.

Unfortunately, the picnic can't last forever. Dad checks a pocket watch and looks at me. "You should really be getting back to your lessons."

"Already? We're having such a nice time." Mom protests, frowning. "It's only been a few days-"

"-And he has a lot to make up for. It's already been an extended lunch. The food has already been eaten-" Dad argues, and I sense tension building between them. I interject quickly.

"It's fine, Mom. I really do need to finish the assessments anyway." I say.

Mom frowns, then looks to Dad. "Why can't you just use his school records?"

Dad pinches the bridge of his nose. "Even if he had only attended a single academy, it wouldn't work. The school records don't have enough important information about what knowledge he actually has and doesn't."

"Mom, it's *fine*," I say more firmly. I really don't want them to fight. Mom looks back at me and finally seems to drop it, looking troubled. "You guys have fun!" I say, forcing cheerfulness into my voice.

It helps that I really do have something to look forward to.

I turn a corner near the library and see Miss Rigo talking to an elderly man, his back to me. I hesitate. Should I wait for them to finish?

"-hardly a surprise he hasn't returned." It's the man. Are they talking about me? I slip back around the corner, hiding and listening from the hallway. The man continues. "This is precisely why discipline is so important."

"The Lord Guthanderkaz expressed a desire for a balanced and well-rounded education. He has shown quite an aptitude for-" Miss Rigo is interrupted.

"I do not care about his aptitude. His *attitude* is what is in most need of adjustment. He doesn't know obedience, he doesn't know how to bow, and he doesn't know his place! Some lessons can only be taught by pain. Everything else comes after that, and that is where you will focus. Do you understand me?" There's a tone in his voice that grates on me. Instinctively my fingers curl. I suddenly want to punch or scratch him, and I'm not a violent person. It isn't just the words; something about his tone just pisses me off.

"Yes, Lord Kolya. But the Lord Guthanderkaz was specific about avoiding physical discipline."

"The Lord Guthanderkaz has a weakness and coddles him. He hardly needs more people joining in! Do not coddle him, do not be gentle! If you can no longer beat his lessons into him as you should, find another means! Am I understood?" Kolya growls. The desire to punch increases dramatically.

"Yes, Lord Kolya."

"Good. I have matters to attend to. Keep me abreast of his progress."

"Yes, Lord Kolya."

I hear Kolya stomp off in the opposite direction. After a moment, I hear softer footsteps approach me. I force a cheerful smile and relax my hands before walking around the corner.

Miss Rigo almost bumps into me and jumps a little, looking

startled. I smile brightly at her. "Good afternoon! We just wrapped up lunch… Did you not eat yet?"

"No, I did." Miss Rigo replies, recovering, smoothing out her dress. She tries to scowl at me, but her expression seems conflicted. "I was just getting some more supplies."

"Do you have the next assessment for me to start while you get things?" I ask.

She seems taken aback by my volunteering for work. After a moment's hesitation, she pulls some papers out of her folder and holds them out. "Here are your things. Do you remember where your desk is?"

"Yes, Miss Rigo," I say politely. Hilariously, the more polite I am, the more thrown she seems to be. It's the best encouragement to be polite I've ever had.

"Good, you're excused. Go get started." Miss Rigo says, sniffing and lifting her chin.

I start off, but she calls back, "And David?"

I stop, looking back. "Yes?"

"Formality. I am your teacher; you are to wait for me to address you first. Am I understood?"

I smile wide while swearing at her internally. I almost say, 'got it,' but catch myself. "My apologies. No offense intended."

Miss Rigo gives a little sniff. "Well, lunch with your father certainly has done wonders for your manners." She mutters, then gives me a little wave.

I dart off again. I hate the whole bowing and scraping thing, but if I look at it as a game I'm playing, putting on the act of the polite, obedient child, I can enjoy it.

Well, other than the work. Science is next. Wonderful. I sigh and try my best to answer the problems. I try to channel that meditative state again, hoping for another epiphany like with the Fyrnekh. No such luck.

But I continue playing my role for the rest of the day, despite the headache and how much I want to do anything else, and Miss Rigo doesn't hit me again. She does seem heavily torn the whole time. She almost compliments me several times but stops herself each time and snaps instead. I pretend not to notice.

Isn't Dad head of the family? Why is she listening to this Kolya guy, anyway? I guess she's technically obeying both at this point, but it's a dangerous and foolish game.

I intercept Basil on the way to dinner. "Did you talk to Dad?" I whisper.

"Hush." Basil glances around. "I'll find you tomorrow."

I struggle not to pout. "Tomorrow? Why not tonight?"

"I'm busy after dinner, and you should head to bed early. You'll do better in your studies with proper rest."

I sigh dramatically, but he's not wrong. "Well, can't we at least hang out before dinner? I mean," I lower my voice, going on tiptoes to speak closer to his ear, lips curling in a conspiratorial grin. "If this whole thing is about putting on a show, us being on good terms will look good, right? Or even better, plotting. Keep them all on their toes."

Basil smirks back at me. "I don't think it will hurt. When you first arrived, I was concerned about you doing things to draw attention to yourself and make things worse, but I'll never be able to prevent that, will I?"

"Absolutely not." I agree, grinning.

"Very well. Let's converse about things that aren't in the least bit suspect and see who braves entering our conversation," Basil responds, plucking a drink from a passing waiter's platter. He frowns at me. "David, stop bouncing."

"I'm not bouncing," I say, halting my movements. Which were more rocking than bouncing anyway. I hadn't even been aware I was doing it.

"You really do not sit still well, do you?"

"It's physically painful," I say plainly.

"Father will enter in a moment. We should both take our seats," Basil says, glancing toward the door.

"That was fast. Guess no one was up for braving my presence after all." I grin.

"Perhaps they're worried your willfulness will rub off." Basil teases.

"Or they just don't want to chance garnering anyone else's disfavor."

We head to our seats. It's much earlier than when dinner started yesterday, but Basil's correct; Dad appears a moment later, and everyone hurries to their seats.

I scan the head of the table, wondering which person is Kolya. I doubt I can hear them speak from here, and I didn't see his face. And 'old, gray-haired man in a suit' could describe half the people on this end of the table.

Margaret's good mood seems to be lasting. She's much less abrasive than usual. She still smiles politely as she corrects me, but she's less insulting, especially when I keep up my polite charade.

At least until one point at the dinner, where, for no discernable reason, she seems to get angry again. Oh well. It was nice while it lasted. I mostly talk to Adela, who's sweet, but… a kid. She's cute as a kitten, but it's not the most engaging conversation.

The food is rich and delicious, but I'm already tired of it. I long for a thick, juicy burger and some steak-cut fries. I'd even take fast food, which Mom forbids me from eating.

I consider trying to spy on the post-dinner meeting again, but Basil's right. Putting on a facade like this is exhausting, and I require sleep.

Basil does come in the morning, but the first thing he says is, "before you ask, the answer is later. Would you like to break our fast together?"

I huff, inwardly squirming. But I accept his offer, and we chat over the meal before he selects a suit for me. He debates longer than usual, and part of me wonders if there really is any difference or if he's just messing with me because they seem so damn similar.

In the library, Miss Rigo informs me that the last assessment is over, and it's time for the real lessons to begin. I'm not excited to know what she can teach me, but I'm relieved that I don't have to keep writing more pointless bullshit.

She has me take notes while she lectures, confiscates them, and tests me. Miss Rigo has found a way to implement the 'some lessons can only be taught by pain' directive. For each question I get wrong, I have to stop and fill an entire page with the same correct sentence, over and over. I feel like my mind is melting from the monotony of it, more than math usually inspires.

I am absolutely not learning math and definitely not learning obedience. It makes it more challenging to keep up the charade of compliance. I'm at my limit when lunchtime arrives, and I leave without waiting to be excused.

Basil waits for me just outside the library. I smile in relief. "It's good to see you," I say, and I'm not sure he comprehends just how sincere I am.

"You as well," Basil says, though his smile is pained, and his eyes linger on my hand. The bruises aren't new, but they'll take a while to heal, and they look pretty bad. He clears his throat. "Shall we?"

"Is it time?" I ask eagerly. His only answer is to hold a finger to his lips and wink. "After lunch. Let's eat in the garden; I don't want to drag around a picnic basket."

We stand before the cave I had discovered that first day. I watch Basil, eager to see how the key works, but he only extends his hand.

I hear a click, and the lock falls open.

"What the?" I pick it up, inspecting it. I still don't see any indication of a keyhole. Is it some sort of magnetic system? "How...?"

"Magic," Basil replies smugly.

"You aren't going to tell me?" I demand.

He only smirks. Then he takes my hand and leads us into the darkness.

"Uh, shouldn't we grab a light or something?"

"It's fine," he replies.

I shift closer to him, glancing nervously down. Carved stone stairs descend in a wide spiral, and the light from above disappears quickly.

Shadows deepen around us as we walk. Basil's footsteps are confident and rhythmic, but I feel vulnerable and clumsy in the pitch black. I tighten my grip on Basil's hand and find the cold stone wall with my other, trying to reassure myself with its solidity. I swallow, feeling each step with my toes before I take it.

My foot catches on the top of a stair, and I yelp, flailing. My heart all but leaps from my chest. There's a weightless moment, and I imagine myself plunging down endless stairs into an eternal black pit, lost forever, every bone broken. Then I feel Basil's other hand catch my shoulder, steadying me.

"You ok?" He asks.

"Y-yeah...." I swallow. My voice sounds squeaky and strange.

"There's some light just ahead, at the base of the stairs." He reassures me.

"The stairs need their own light!" I protest, but I follow. Belatedly, I add, "Um, thanks, by the way. I think you just saved my life."

He laughs, and his hand finds my head, ruffling my hair again.

At last, I see a warm flicker ahead. Soon enough, the stairs unwind onto a rocky path lined with sconces of actual flame. It sprawls before us, ten feet wide, maybe. One side is bordered by stone, the other...

I lean forward, peering down. "Holy shit," I whisper. The words echo down the jagged stone that slants down...and down... and down... "Helloooo!" I call, and the words reverberate off the stone walls back at me. There's another sound, too, though it's hard to hear. "It looks like you'd keep falling down to wonderland."

"Something like that," Basil replies enigmatically. I blink and give him a weird look.

"Come on." He turns, unperturbed by the expanse. I follow him carefully, wary but intrigued.

A few minutes pass, and a thought strikes me.

"Basil?"

"Mm?"

"...when were the sconces lit?"

I look at them more closely. They're all roaring strong, with no indication that they will go out any time soon. There's no way they've been lit for long.

"We'll get to that."

I glare at his back, making a sound half laugh, half grunt of frustrated accusation. "Jerk."

"It will be worth it," he promises, glancing over his shoulder and giving me a genuine smile. "Trust me."

I sigh but can't argue further.

We wind down into the earth, my mind occupied with stories of giants and dwarves and dragons. I stare in awe at stalactites many times my size, at the patterns dancing on the rocks from the flames. The passage continues far ahead at a slow downward slope, the sconces lighting the way.

At last, I see a door ahead. It's smooth and gold and etched with purposeful markings, standing out against the rough grey walls. I don't recognize the carvings, but some of the shapes bring to mind Fyrnek's written language. Rivulets of etchings curl around the edges, towards the center in mesmerizing swirls, catching one's gaze like a whirlpool and leading it across the door, stopping at each symbol.

"We're here," Basil announces, stopping before it. I let my gaze drift upward, staring at the strange pictures. Some of the depictions are recognizable. I think those are angels at the top. But some of the things... I have no idea what they're supposed to be. Some look less like intentional designs and more like amateur graffiti, nothing but arhythmic, jagged scribbling.

The doors opens, and my gaze drops down again to stare at Basil.

He steps inside, up a few steps, and I follow.

The room we enter is filled with books. Everywhere, huge, old looking, most leatherbound. Lines and symbols are carved into the stone walls, some that I recognize from the door and others new to me. The air smells strange; musky, spicy, and slightly acrid. Sconces, torches, and candles are the only light sources. Is no one concerned about the poor, flammable books?! The door clicks shut behind me, and the flames dance in the rush of air.

I look at Basil, and he smiles at me, striding to a table in the center of the room. He pushes a large book forward toward me. The cover looks to be written in some variation of Fyrnekh.

He opens it up, and the interior is written in the standard Fyrnekh I'm used to. I stare, pressing my lips and eyebrows together, trying to get focused enough to translate.

I don't think I translated correctly. That, or…

"This is a joke," I say, sounding strangely flat.

"No." He says. "I wasn't joking up there either."

I look up at him.

He smiles at me. And then he vanishes before my eyes.

Chapter Seven

I yelp, jumping back. Laughter echoes from behind me. I whip my head around, and Basil stands there, leaning against the wall, looking almost like me in the orange firelight.

"I... how...?!"

"I said it upstairs. The book said it too. Magic."

"Magic?"

"Yes." He says, eyes twinkling.

I gawk at him. "That's incredible! When.....how did you...!?"

Basil smiles and shoves off the wall, striding lazily towards me. Suddenly, he's inches from my face. "Do I have to say it a third time?"

"I know it's magic, but how... ...can you teleport? Can you teach me?"

He chuckles. "Teleportation is far more complicated and draining. That was something closer to hypnosis. I simply..."

He's sitting at a nearby table now. "...altered your perception for a little bit. I moved then."

I frown. Altered my perceptions...?

"But I can teach you. And will."

My anger vanishes. I smile brightly.

"But-" he quickly interrupts, holding up a finger. "On one condition. You must continue putting the work into your studies you've shown these past two days. It's father's condition, so there's no arguing against it," he adds as I open my mouth.

"Dad too?"

"Magic is in our blood, David. Powerful magic. We are wizards. You, me, and much of the family. Those in the inner circle all have magic. It's the most important requirement for having the highest rank."

I only half hear him, my mind abuzz with what he's saying. Magic, wizards... it's so unbelievable and yet so utterly fantastically awesome. Dad being so obsessed with standard schooling when we have *this* is laughable.

Basil lets out an exasperated sigh. "David, if you don't stop squirming, you're not going to be able to learn anything." He chides. "I used to think Miss Rigo was singling you out with how bruised you always are, but now I'm starting to get an idea of why you've gained your spotted coat."

I freeze, his words stinging more than I think he realizes. *I didn't earn any of this. That's not something you earn.*

My hands squeeze, and his smile falters. "David?"

"Can we get started?" I ask, trying to find the excitement I felt before, to dismiss the cold in my stomach.

Basil clears his throat, straightening and lifting his chin and eyebrows as one. "As I'll be your tutor from here forward, I expect some respect."

I smile at him. "Basil, I *do* respect you. *You* actually deserve it."

Basil turns bright red, jaw dropping open. Apparently, that was not the reply he was expecting. I can't help but laugh a bit. "I'm still going to tease you, though. You're still my brother, and my friend, teacher or not."

Basil looks away, clearing his throat again and covering his mouth with a fist, still red. "Well, I suppose that's acceptable. Now, let's begin with the basics."

I nod.

Basil lectures me about the structure of magic, doing a much better job than Miss Rigo ever could. It probably helps that he starts with demonstrations; summoning shadows into his hand and snuffing out and relighting the candles, as he explains basic concepts.

"Will alone, no matter how powerful, is not enough to cast a spell of real complexity. You need to refine it with a conduit. The most common are symbols, words, and sacrifices-"

"Wait, wait, wait, sacrifices? Like human or animal sacrifices?" I interrupt. I don't like the idea of either.

Basil chuckles, "usually something small, like a drop of blood. Some big spells need larger things, an entire animal, as you said, for example. Some exceptionally advanced spellwork involves more esoteric sacrifices, but I recommend against ever using them. They're complicated, hard to understand, unpredictable, and frankly, not worth it when you can simply do what you want more reliably merely through preparation and effort."

He continues, painting an overview of how magic, *real* magic, works and what it entails.

"The simpler the spell and smaller the scope, the fewer requirements for a conduit. Powerful sorcerers can even learn to do some spells without uttering a word at all, as I did earlier." Basil explains. "Of course, doing so requires more focus, and many still must *think* of associated words. For now, we'll focus on simple, basic spells. But you should know they can become quite complex and large. The larger the spell, the more potent it is. Additional casters working in unison also boost a spell's capabilities, though the need to stay perfectly synchronized also adds a layer of challenge."

"Do you use magic often?" I ask curiously.

Basil smiles. "Every day, but only small things. The larger spell-casting is much less frequent, partly because of the energy needed to cast them."

"What happens if you run out of energy?" I ask.

"You get very tired and must recharge," Basil says. "Ones own inner magical stores will refill on their own, but quite slowly. One can naturally absorb it more quickly from natural places, such as forests, oceans, and caves like this. And there are points around the world where energy naturally gathers from the entire planet, and those fill up even faster. The entire island is like that, but the castle was constructed on the absolute nexus of that power, so casting spells is quite easy here, even for those not attuned."

"Attuned?" I press eagerly, but he holds a hand out.

"Let's focus on less advanced topics for the time being. The important thing to know is that all those with natural proclivities towards magic are born with a well of power within them, though learning to utilize it as intended takes time, training, and knowledge of various conduits."

Basil's brief overview of magic continues. There's an overwhelming amount of information. Luckily for me, I drank up fantasy books growing up, and while none of the stories match up perfectly, there are enough overarching similarities that I'm able to grasp the concepts.

When he's done explaining, Basil gives me the tome and has me read a section. It's a bit of a struggle because it's written in Fyrnekh.

"I won't read it for you. Fyrnekh is a highly magical language, even as bastardized as it's become through time. It's important you learn it. I am impressed you've covered so much in your lessons already."

I snort. "I haven't had a single lesson on Fyrnekh. Mostly I've just remembered things from when I was a kid, I think."

Basil looks surprised. "You haven't studied Fyrnehk yet?"

"I told you she's useless," I mutter.

Basil bites his lip, looking thoughtful. "Very well, I'll help you through, but only this chapter. After this, you'll have to do it all on your own. I don't want to be your handicap, but what you haven't learned is hardly your fault."

"Thanks, Basil," I say, smiling in relief. It'll be nice to focus on what I'm actually meant to be learning.

He helps me with the first chapter, and then it's time to cast my first spell: putting out a candle. I'm both excited and disappointed, but Basil insists I begin with the most basic spell there is.

I review the notes and concepts, close my eyes, breathe in, and speak the word. I open my eyes.

The candle taunts me, bright as ever.

I blush, trying to ignore Basil's subtle frown. I figured 'most basic spell' would mean 'you can do this the first try easy.' I chew my lip, reviewing everything, and say it again. And again.

I can't do it. Basil directs me himself, giving me pointers. I do everything he tells me; I find what he's talking about, that sensation of power deep inside me, the strangely familiar, fuzzy-headed feeling.

But when I try to pull out that energy and snuff the candle, all I get for my efforts is a headache.

Basil frowns, watching me. I'm frustrated, exhausted, and confused.

"Let's break early; that's enough for today. Don't worry, David. You'll get it, I'm sure you will. Perhaps you're simply unused to it. You haven't been training since childhood, as I have. It's simply a muscle you must learn to use, I suspect. Besides, I'd only planned to cover the concepts today, and you absorbed them much faster than I expected. We're already ahead." Basil says with a smile, but I can tell he's disappointed. Worried, even.

Basil closes the book. "We'll come back tomorrow after your other lessons." He promises.

"Why can't you just teach me everything?" I ask. "You're much better at it anyway." I mean it, too. I don't think the candle thing is his fault. He's good at explaining things and actually cares about teaching me instead of torturing me.

Basil blushes but looks pleased. "I have my own duties… but if you like, I'll talk to father about it. Are you sure you wouldn't be embarrassed to have your younger big brother teach you?" He teases.

"I guess I can tolerate it, but only as long as I don't grow two inches and you remain my *big* brother," I tease back.

That night, I'm so busy dwelling on what I've learned that I barely even notice dinner go by.

Miss Rigo's following lessons are very focused on Fyrnekh. Dad hasn't spoken to me about it, but I assume he's pissed that she hasn't even started teaching me the language, which I'm almost positive is his biggest priority. Miss Rigo seems stressed.

I don't pity her. She shouldn't be listening to that other guy over Dad.

Once again, Basil is waiting for me outside the library at lunch, and he has good news.

I'm not excused from Miss Rigo's lessons entirely, but my time with her officially ends at lunch. After that, I get to study magic with Basil. Basil goes over more concepts before I practice again, perhaps hoping that something he explains might help make things make more sense. I truly appreciate his effort.

He watches me as I close my eyes, going over the spell in my mind again.

A distant noise nags at my senses, but I try to ignore it. A chill seeps in that's harder to ignore. It's so freezing in here, with only stone and candles. Is it colder than it was before?

The sound is louder, more distinct. There's a strange shuffling, a low hum, and other noises that I can't even describe. I open my eyes and look at the door. I know in my gut that whatever is making that sound is also responsible for the sudden cold.

The shuffling stops. A subdued banging against the door makes me jump.

I look at Basil. He lets out a long-suffering sigh.

"It's alright," He reassures me, standing, and strides to the door. He's confident, and I'm curious, so I follow him.

At least a dozen figures stand outside the door, hidden under dark robes. They bow at once and make a sound somewhere between drunken greeting and gregorian chant. The robes are identical to the ones worn by the two strangers arguing in the church.

One of the figures lifts their head and steps forward. The rest remain bowed, but even standing, he's slightly hunched.

Alien sounds rippled from beneath the hood, slippery sounding. It's similar to Fyrnekh but distorted. The hairs on the back of my neck prickle. I don't know if it's their strange words, slurping breaths, or something else impossible to describe, but I feel a deep, innate repulsion.

I frown, focusing, desperate to understand this exchange. I take a deep breath and close my eyes, listening.

"Praise be to the Pure Ones." The man's voice sounds slurred.

"Myrkr'on. What brings you here?" Basil asks, his posture more rigid next to the priest's bowed back.

"A gift," something indecipherable, "Pure Ones." Rumbles the hooded man and bows once more. His hands moved forward, trembling and holding a large golden chest out.

The motion pulls back the dark fabric, revealing his hand and arms. A spider web of veins the color of old oil are made milky by his semi-transparent skin. The skin is hairless, slimy, and peppered with strange lumps, ranging in size from Mardi gras beads to overripe grapes. One of the larger ones appears to have spilled open, long and tapering like another finger or oddly placed tail. His fingers are long and strangely uneven, a few thicker or thinner than others.

Basil waves a hand, and shadows creep from around the room, coalescing at the chest and lifting it away. The man's hands withdraw, but not before I realize that he has more than ten fingers.

I want them to leave. I know I sound awful, but it's not just how they look or sound. Their presence freezes the room and whispers a warning to something deep in my chest. Suddenly, the hoods turn towards me as one, and their chanting falters.

The heaviness of their unseen gaze weighs on me. Is it curiosity, accusation? Can they smell fear?

Before they can dare to ask about me, Basil speaks again, "You may go."

Shadows slam the door.

"What were those things?" I breathe, trembling. I swallow, feeling sick.

"We usually just call them the Corrupted," Basil replies, running a hand through his hair and returning to sit in one of the chairs. "They... ...most people, really... can't use magic like we can. Even some of the Family can't. If they try, well..."

He trails off, then nods towards the door. "You probably saw a little. It... warps them. Not just their bodies, either."

I stare at him, then double over as my lunch abruptly demands to revisit. Basil decides to end lessons early and walks me back to my room. I distract myself from what I've seen by playing him songs he's never heard and try not to think about how difficult the candle spell is for me and what that might mean.

That night, Basil spends most of dinner whispering to Dad. What he's saying is clearly troubling Dad, and they keep looking at me. It has to be about me not being able to do the spell.

I poke at the food. It's hard to find an appetite. Maybe I should spy on the after-dinner meeting again to confirm it. Except Dad and Basil head upstairs together, leaving the rest behind. The others near the head of the table exchange confused looks, and the one who sits at Dad's right looks pissed.

Then he glares at me and narrows his eyes. I pretend not to notice, retreating to my room. Though I do wonder if he's the one who was speaking to Miss Rigo.

I'm still tired when Alfrèd wakes me and informs me he is no longer required to escort me to class.

Basil doesn't stop by at the usual time, so I pick a suit at random. I don't think I'll ever get used to wearing them. I feel so stiff in them, and movement is so restricted.

I'm tempted to just skip lessons today and get more sleep. I can't break my word to Basil, though. Besides, if I miss a lesson the moment I'm not escorted, I'll probably never be able to go anywhere alone again.

I yawn as I step out of my room, rubbing my eyes groggily.

"Boy," says a stern, unfamiliar voice from behind me. I startle and spin to face the source. I recognized the man who usually sits to Dad's left, opposite Basil. The memory of his face is well-imprinted, thanks to his time spent glowering at me last night. He stares at me with the somber gaze of a funeral director. "I have need to speak with you." He continues.

I don't respond immediately, simultaneously trying to shake off the sleepiness and comparing his voice to those I heard during my eavesdropping session and, more importantly, the one who spoke to Miss Rigo about me. But his voice doesn't match either occasion. His hair isn't the right color, either, it's only starting to grey.

"Who are you?" I finally asked.

He narrows his eyes at me again. "For all the fuss over your education, they neglect to teach you that which is most important. You aren't even aware of the principal members of the household. I must speak with your father about this."

"You and I are in agreement over the inadequacies of my education, but that's not a name," I retort, annoyed that he didn't even attempt a reply during the long-winded ramble. I finger my earbuds with one hand, the other drumming impatiently against my thigh.

The man stares at me, grim countenance unchanging. "I am Lord Leonid Guthanderkaz, your Uncle." His hair may be graying but his eyes are deep and clear. He looks a bit old to be my uncle, but even as tired as I am, I have enough tact not to mention it. He continues. "And you are everything I have been led to expect. Lazy, disruptive, immature, ill-mannered. All of which will be remedied in time. But I digress. I came here to discuss the conditions of your departure ten years ago."

I freeze, suddenly very awake.

"A curious reaction," remarks Leonid, staring piercingly into my eyes as if he's reading my very soul. *Can* he do that? Basil hasn't exactly made a list of cans and can'ts, but considering he can alter my perception without any effort, it seems possible. If it's true, I have no way of defending myself. Hell, I still can't put out a damn candle.

Leonid watches me, unsmiling. "Quite defensive. I wonder, is it because of what you know or what you don't?"

"It's way too early in the morning to talk in riddles and expect anyone to understand." I snap, attempting to evoke confidence. My voice sounds shaky. Crap.

"I'll have to be blunt enough for your deaf American ears to process." Leonid sneers. People really have a thing for unnecessary, irrelevant insults here. "What do you remember of the day your mother fled?"

I hesitate. Part of me wants to send him off just for being an asshole, but this is the first time anyone has offered to speak about it. "Why are you asking?"

"Answer my question!" Leonid demands, eyes blazing. I see shadows in the corner of my eye that disappear when I turn my head to focus on them. I feel a heaviness in my mind, prodding me to answer.

Oh hell, he *is* using magic on me. He has to be. I glare. "Answer mine first." *Asshole*, I think fiercely and hope he has just enough telepathy to hear it.

Leonid's eyes widen. It's the first emotion I've seen on his face other than varying shades of anger and disdain. After a moment, Leonid speaks, voice soft. "Are you not aware? The night you and your mother left was the same night your grandfather and great-grandfather died. Both of a stroke, both simultaneously. An interesting coincidence, is it not?"

Cold bleeds into my bones. "What?" I ask. It's a ghost of my normal voice; I'm barely even aware of speaking. I can't hear his reply through my pounding heartbeat. He can't be implying what I think he is. I shake the shock off as if dislodging snow, forcing myself to focus. He's still rambling, and I interrupt him without bothering to listen. "My mother is not a murderer! She'd never hurt anyone! And why *would* she ever, anyway?!"

"Why indeed?" Asks Leonid, cooly.

I clench my fist, glaring at him, unable to frame a retort. Leonid simply watches me, letting me drown in his words. Finally, before I can think of anything to say, he speaks. "You should be off. We wouldn't want you missing class again when you so desperately need it."

"Go screw yourself," I growl.

"Don't be crude," Leonid replies without batting an eye. "It's unbecoming of our name."

I glare and storm off. Part of me wants to ditch, to go straight to Basil and ask a thousand questions. Based on his words, I can't decide if going or cutting would be more spiteful.

But I am not in the mood for another argument with Dad, and I want Basil to actually talk to me. Which means waiting.

Besides, if he didn't show up, he might not be in his room at all. I still don't know what he does most of the day.

I shake my head again. Even Margaret hasn't rattled me so thoroughly. But then, Margaret never implied that... I swallow, thinking of Mom and her evasiveness whenever I ask about us leaving or about our previous time at the castle. No. No matter what secrets Mom is hiding, there's no way she could ever kill anyone.

I stop, trying to collect myself and sort my thoughts. I lean against a wall, half hiding behind a heavy velvet curtain and rubbing my arms. I fumble with my earbuds, planting them and playing music.

Mom *couldn't* have done it, anyway. He said stroke, and simultaneously. Which probably means magic, right? But my magic came from Dad's side, not her.

I sigh in relief. I'm late, through no fault of my own. Miss Rigo berates me for my tardiness, and I don't bother to defend myself.

My attention drifts as her angry barrage continues when a thought hits me.

Mom doesn't have magic. But Dad does. Could he have…? No. I tell myself firmly. Still, I long to discuss it with Basil, if only for reassurance. Lessons are always agonizing, but more than ever, they cannot go by fast enough.

When I finally see Basil again, I can't bring myself to actually speak. That I have to ask at all is horrible. Now that I know, I can't think of a way to phrase the question.

Basil frowns when he sees me. "You're still worrying about the candle, aren't you?"

I swallow. Right. And there's that.

"Don't worry. You'll get it soon." He says, placing a hand on my shoulder and smiling. "Let's go, shall we?"

I force a smile I don't feel and follow mutely. Basil casts troubled glances my way, but I have no idea if it's related to magic, spells, or my own behavior, and I'm not about to ask.

I stare at the book, uncomprehending. I can feel the weight of Basil's gaze. He'll talk to me. I'm sure. I just have to gather the strength to ask. "Basil?"

"Yes?" Basil responds, sounding like he's been waiting for me to speak.

"Do you… do you know anything about Mom and me… about… why we left?" I ask, staring at the page without seeing it. I steal a glance at him when he doesn't reply right away. He doesn't meet my eye.

"I was still very young. I didn't think about why for a long time… well, not objectively." Basil replies slowly, trying to find a path through his own memories. "Most of what I know is mere rumor. The one certain thing is the day you left, Grandfather and Great Grandfather died." His words chill me. It's bad enough coming from Leonid. To hear the same words from Basil…

"Great-Grandfather was still Head of the Family when you were here last. But after that day, Father became in charge. Father never speaks of it. I did ask once, but he made me promise to never ask him about it again. Some people think that… I think that…" He pauses, staring at nothing. "I think he killed them." He adds quietly. "And I think it had something to do with you and Miss Rose."

Numbness spreads through me. "You really think Dad could, *did* kill his own father?"

Basil looks at me. "The only one who was there was Father."

"Didn't they die of a stroke?" I ask defensively.

"Yes," Basil says. "At the same time." His eyebrows draw together. "How did you know that?"

I flush, caught, and rub the back of my head. "I… sorta got interrogated about it by Leonid."

"Ah."

"He was saying the same thing, that… .well, he didn't specify Dad, but…" I trail off.

"Well, Miss Rose couldn't have done it. And if it was someone else, Father doesn't know who because he didn't punish anyone else. From what I've heard, Great Grandfather never approved of her."

"If he did it, wouldn't we have stayed? Doesn't that kind of defy the point?" I ask. Dad's expression when he spoke of 'those ten long years' is still etched in my mind.

"I don't know," Basil replies, brows furrowing. "In truth, I don't even know if Father is good enough to do away with both of them, even now. Great Grandfather's magical aptitude was legendary, and being the head of the family only amplifies it. This place is… old."

"What's that have to do with anything?"

"It's a place of Power, and whomsoever is in charge may tap into it."

"You mentioned something about that the other day, too. But I still don't know much about it," I say, frowning.

"You know that well you're tapping into when you cast a spell?"

"Well, theoretically, considering I haven't actually ever successfully cast a spell yet," I mutter bitterly.

"Yet you can feel it, can you not?" Basil presses.

I shrug. "I guess…"

"Well, imagine it as a… a pond." Basil continues. "You may be able to build up power for a particular spell through ritual, like redirecting a stream. But the castle is connected to the energy of all of Fyrnlendh. It's akin to wielding an entire ocean, and you never need wait.

"Father's position as head of the family is" he searches for the right word, groping the air as if he could catch it with a hand. "Coveted for that reason. It's even said that the most powerful family secrets are only revealed to the head of the family."

We sit in silence, mulling this over.

I ask, "Do you really think Dad's capable of something like that?"

Basil looks puzzled and answers without hesitation, "yes."

I gape at him. Just how little do I know my own father?

"We are trained to kill, if necessary." Basil continues slowly, watching me.

"Wh-what?" I demand.

"I know a few spells that will kill you," Basil answers, baffled by my reaction.

"What?!"

"I know spells that kill," Basil repeats. "I also know how to use a gun, a sword, and a knife. They're tools."

"Why would you ever need to learn anything like that?!"

"In case there's an assassination attempt or some such," Basil replies with a shrug.

"Why would you expect an assassination attempt?" I say, my voice shrill with panic.

"We're wealthy and powerful and live in a dangerous world," Basil says as if it should be obvious.

I swallow. And here I thought I couldn't be more disturbed.

"We have dealings all over the world," Basil continues. "Despite our country's size, we are very wealthy, and Father is essentially the king."

"I thought Fyrnlendh's a democracy," I say, frowning. It was one of the first things I read. I assumed the royal title was basically meaningless.

Basil sighs heavily. "Technically."

"Meaning what?"

Basil gives a half sigh, half groan, looking embarrassed. "Fyrnlendh was founded by our ancestors. We're royalty, similar to England. Most things get handled by Parliament, but if Father wants something done, it's likely to happen." As he continues, he clears his throat, becoming more awkward with each word. "Also… there's a.. pseudo-religious aspect to it."

"Religious? Isn't most of Fyrnlendh Catholic? Do you mean like old school, the king is chosen by God?" I ask, frowning. I don't actually know much about religion, and my vague ideas are mostly coming from tales of King Arthur.

"Well, yes, it is, and there is that aspect," Basil replies. "But pre-catholicism, one of our ancestors was worshipped as a god. When Fyrnlendh was converted, they declared him a Saint. Outside of Fyrnlendh, he isn't well known. Saint Gersavius. It wasn't an uncommon practice at the time. It happened with Greek and Roman gods as well. Mars became Saint Martin, Nike became St. Nicolas…"

"Well," I say. "That's… awkward." I run a hand through my hair.

"I suppose it would be if you're not accustomed to it." Basil gives me a sympathetic look. As if he himself wasn't embarrassed when the topic came up.

I push the book back. "I can't do this right now. Not after that." Maybe not ever, but I don't add that. I stand. "Why don't I give you more music appreciation lessons instead?"

"I'm a little busy…" Basil says.

I fold my arms. "I thought this was supposed to be training me time?"

"Yes, it is. We should stay focused. And unless you intend to sing your incantations to some sort of… pop."

I shake my head. "I just learned that my Dad might be a murderer, and we're descended from saints."

"A Saint." Basil corrects. "…Slash God."

I gesture wildly as if, through enough emphasis, I might demonstrate exactly how that makes it even worse.

Basil sighs and chews his lip, and I press. "Basil, please."

"Alright, alright." Basil finally agrees. "Let's take a break. I suppose it is a lot to take in if you're not used to it."

"Thank you," I say, relieved. "Alright, Lady Gaga or Eminem…"

Basil stares blankly. "Uh… don't you have something more… …adult? I don't want to listen to musicians who name themselves after baby sounds or candy."

"Wow," I say brightly, "You know what M&Ms are?"

"Yes. I own stock in Mars Incorporated."

I groan. "And here I was beginning to have hope. Come on. I suppose I should ease into it more anyway." I smile playfully. "Okay then, Queen or The King?"

"Which Queen?" Basil asks, looking lost. "And which King is the King?"

"No spoilers. We'll get to both eventually, but you gotta pick one now."

He sighs. "Queen," he says, shaking his head, an uncertain look on his face.

"Why Queen?" I ask curiously. "Not that I don't love Queen, though technically that will put it out of chronological order…" I maybe should have just started with Elvis, but I couldn't resist presenting the choice as I did.

"You said it first, and I have no notion or preference about either. I presume that they are stage names?"

"Queen is the name of a band, and Elvis Presley is called 'the King of Rock and Roll," I reply.

He stares blankly. "…Oh," He frowns and looks thoughtful for a moment, "We will get to them both. If Elvis is the King, I presume then that he is acclaimed to be better. Therefore, we should save the best for last," he says his words gaining confidence as he speaks.

"It's a bit more complicated than that," I say, tilting my head as we head back to the rooms. "It's more based on their popularity when it was bestowed, which is way back in the 1950s. The band Queen didn't even form until the 70s and didn't become the industry powerhouse they did until the 80s, so both of them are generally considered classics by people who listen to music written after the 1800s. By the way, do you ever listen to modern classical music?"

"I listen to what the performers play. Honestly, music has never been my focus."

I look at him, frowning a little. "Do you not even know the names of the songs? Or have favorites?"

He narrows his eyes, his brows draw together, and his mouth puckers slightly. "Favorite, not really. Generally, they play to add ambiance. I can't say that any have actually stood out to me. And of course I know their names. Shall I write you an essay on Leonin or Perotin?"

"Why the hell would I want to read an essay?" I ask, wrinkling my nose. "I'm just interested in your preferences. What's the point if you don't actually care?"

"Just because I don't have a preference yet doesn't mean I can't form one in time with exposure. I don't have a particular affinity for automobiles either, but I've only ever driven one car."

I clap a hand on his back and give him a smile. "Well, exposing you to new and wonderful sounds will be my job. We'll teach each other."

The time we spend listening to music together gives me the strength to get through dinner and ignore Leonid completely. I can feel him trying to catch my eye, to read more through me. I don't even glance in that direction. I speak to Adela about music throughout dinner and am delighted by how much everything I say seems to fill Margaret with impotent disapproval.

After dinner, instead of leaving as quickly as I can, I press down the length of the table, past the politely filing extended family, and find

Mom. She smiles at me.

I consider asking her about her side of what happened but decide against it. I don't know if my information will lead to her offering up anymore, and I don't have the strength to fight.

Instead, we read quietly together, as we used to do every night before bed. I enjoy the brief moment of peace

Chapter Eight

Days pass with no progress.

Basil goes over every little enunciation of the spell. I spend hours just practicing pronunciation until even he declares it perfect.

I glare at the candle. The flame dances and flickers, mocking me. Gritting my teeth, I reach for that sensation inside me. I shiver, feeling light-headed and empowered, almost detached. Yet as I recite the words, there it is again; a pounding in my head and behind my eyes, and a twinge of pain running down my spine as I finish the incantation.

I curl, breath hissing. It feels like the wind's been stolen from my lungs. I hold my mouth open, tasting bile in my saliva, and wait for the nausea to pass.

I'm still sweating when the nausea at last recedes. My hands are almost entirely white where they grip the tome. I slowly lift my head to gaze at the candle.

Nothing.

No, worse than nothing.

I slam the book closed, frustrated. Some basic spell...

Doubt returns, gnawing at my insides like a rat. What if I'm not meant for it after all? Worse, what if, by trying, I end up Corrupted? The thought fills my bones with ice, and I hug myself, shuddering.

I'm vaguely aware of Basil comforting me, trying to reassure me.

And for the first time, I voice the fear that's left me sleepless and reluctant to touch magic. "Basil... I.... I don't want to be like one of those things." Basil's hand stills where it had been rubbing my back, then he squeezes my shoulder. "You won't."

"You said some people in the family...." I trail off and swallow. "How can you know?" I demand, voice cracking.

"I know," is all he says. "Come on, let's end it for tonight."

I sleep in the next day. When I finally wake, I ignore the rows of suits and pull on one of my favorite t-shirts, my hoodie, and an old pair of jeans.

My sneakers squeak loudly against the waxed marble of my room. The portraits on the wall seem to sneer at me, offended that any relative of theirs could ever wear such things. Instead of attending my lessons, I go to Mom's room, knock at the door, and pray Margaret isn't there. It's been over a week, anyway. I deserve some days off.

I deserved some days off when I first arrived, too, but I can't time travel to give them to myself.

Mom opens the door and smiles, dimples winking at me. "David. I was just thinking of going for a walk. Care to join me?"

"Um, just us?" I ask nervously, remembering Margaret's intrusion last time.

"Would you prefer bringing someone else as well?" Mom asks.

I shake my head quickly. "We haven't really had much one-on-one time since we got here," I respond, fidgeting.

Mom's smile fades. "No, we haven't. It isn't your fault." She brushes some hair from my face. "You've been working hard, David, and you should be commended. But I don't want you to feel as if you have to... have to change yourself here. Have to become more like them."

I blink, startled at the words, and swallow. I'm not changing myself... am I? "I don't think I'll ever be anything like any of them," I say. But how many days had I endured the suits, the lessons, the judgment...? I shake my head. I don't want to think about it right now.

Mom's brows draw together, and she smiles without dimples. "Let's go." She says. "Before anyone comes to drag you to the library."

I smile. "Did you just encourage me to cut school?"

Mom snorts, but her eyes grow stormy. "That isn't school, and I still don't approve of it. I've told your father as much, but-" she stops, catching herself. She continues in a much lighter tone. "Besides, it's a Saturday."

I frown. How many of Mom and Dad's fights have been about that disapproval? I fight the urge to look at my hand. I doubt Mom knows about that. If she did, there's no way she'd allow me to keep going, even if the ruler has been banned.

Her words make me realize something else too. I have no sense of time anymore. I only realize it's Saturday when she says it.

We wander through the gardens. Past untamed rose bushes and stone statues and terraces half swallowed by ivy. The day is unusually bright, and it's easy to find a path without the curling roots and mossy logs tripping me. We speak like we used to, about every day, pointless things.

Mom's never really been my confidante. How could she, when she kept secret the one question I most longed to have answered?

But as we talk about books, what I've learned, and what I want, I keep thinking about Margaret. More specifically, about why the hell Mom trusts her and how she *can* trust her when Margaret is clearly waiting for a chance to stab both of us in the back. No matter how I turn it over in my head, I can't think of how to begin, much less phrase the entire sentence.

There's also the other question left unsaid, the one I'd asked countless times. I have new information, but... that didn't matter in the past, with finding out about Dad's letter, did it?

Speaking of Dad... well, Mom clearly doesn't know about that. She was shocked when she discovered Dad was the current head of the family, so she definitely had no idea they'd been killed. Anything she heard would come from Dad, and I doubt he'd confess fratricide to her, if it is a thing. Which... I hope Basil's wrong about.

The gardens aren't what I expect. I'm ready for precisely manicured conformity to match the rest of the castle, but there's only a hint of that in a small perimeter around the inner walls. The rest resembles unbridled nature.

We walk down old cobblestone paths edged by wild roses, past stone walls half eaten by ivy and various flowers and vines crawling up the marble pillars and statues. There are countless little nooks and alcoves to explore and hide behind, perfect for games of hide and seek.

Mom leads me across an overgrown stone bridge that arcs over a small stream. She halts at an ancient stone gazebo that overlooks a small green lake.

I wonder if the freedom the garden is allowed is based on what Basil said about magic and how it's easier to recover in wild places. Maybe taming flowers into perfect structures has an actual effect on magical recovery. I've always preferred forests over gardens, but I can't help but adore this garden.

Mom points at a dragonfly that skims over the water. Then she sighs softly.

"It's gorgeous here," Mom admits, staring across the lake.

"Yeah." I agree, looking around us. There's an abundant variety of plants, different textures of leaves, various soft flowers… "Feels out of place with the rest." *Feels like me.*

"More our style." She says. Guess we had the same thought.

I make a sound of agreement and hop onto the gazebo's stone railing, letting my legs dangle over the edge. The stone is smooth, unexpected considering the age, though its surface is softened by forest detritus and bits of moss.

I feel free, so much more myself. This is so much more me, enjoying nature, wearing my comfortable old clothes instead of those restrictive, fancy suits. "I'm surprised more people aren't out here."

"It's a good time to come," Mom says, leaning on the railing next to me. "Most those who walk this far out do so nearer to twilight, and the rest prefer the more maintained paths directly near the castle."

She nods to a set of iron tables and chairs in the middle of the gazebo decorated with filigree. "This is my favorite place to have tea. Maybe we could have some together sometime. Or tea and hot chocolate."

"Sounds nice," I say, kicking my legs.

We fall into silence. But nature plays its own orchestra, full of the buzzing insects and wind dancing through leaves, branches scraping against stone, and the pleasant babbling of the creek water rushing over rocks and lapping at banks.

Maybe this is an excellent place to try talking to her if I can figure out how. It's private, and peaceful, and she clearly prefers it over everywhere else. Why not take advantage of her positive mood?

Mom starts walking again, and I hop off to follow. I still haven't found the right words. I look at Mom, and am startled to see a reflection of my own expression. Maybe there's something she's finding difficult to tell me as well.

We wander back, and soon the castle looms in view again, blotting out a quarter of the sky.

I stop walking and look at Mom, silently pleading, trying to give her a chance. Maybe she'll speak about when we left. Maybe she'll shed light on things or prove irrefutably that there's no way that Dad ever hurt anyone.

Maybe there's something else she'll tell me, something earth-shattering, and everything will be okay again.

She stares at me in the green-tinted light under the canopy of trees. I wait, but in the end, she just pats my head and walks off, and that's it, the end of our walk.

I feel the familiar bile taste of disappointment, and I kick up a shower of tear-shaped leaves before trailing slowly after her.

I catch up with Mom, and Margaret is there again. Of course. My stomach sours as any hope of her telling me whatever was on her mind shrivels away. I watch as Margaret says something I can't hear. She plucks a flower pedal from Mom's hair and presents it to her, and they laugh carelessly.

I don't feel like dealing with Margaret, so instead of rejoining Mom, I head straight to the stairs. Better this way, I'll avoid the crowds that can form on the lower levels.

The fifth story is blessedly devoid of people.

I retreat to my room and close the door behind me. A heartbeat later, I realize I'm not alone. Goosebumps prickle my hair, and I jerk my head up. Metod stands statuelike before me, hands folded behind his back, studying me.

"The Lords Guthanderkaz wait for you." He says.

Dad's probably upset that I missed my lessons again. I wonder if he's going to cancel my magic lessons with Basil. I'm not sure how I'll feel if he does. I treasure the time spent with Basil and the chance to learn magic. But the implications of my inability to cast horrify me. The image of those twisted hands flashes through my mind, and only Metod's presence prevents me from comforting myself.

"They wait," Metod repeats pointedly.

I shake my head, trying to banish thoughts of the things below. "Lead the way." Might as well get this over with.

I listen to music and zone out as I follow. I don't pay much attention until we start going down unfamiliar flights of stairs. We enter the dining room, and I pull the earbuds out, confused.

Brilliant light made white by fog radiates through the star-shaped skylight and makes the room heavy with sharp shadows. It's the first time I've seen it empty, and it feels strange, like stepping backstage. Somehow, it shatters the magic of the place a little, making it feel less grand. It also makes the already massive room feel larger and emptier.

I stare up at the chandeliers, heavy with dead candles. The bleak reminder only heightens the feelings of dissonance, and I tear my gaze away. The hairs on the back of my neck stand up, but I don't know if it's the mood of the room or the terrible feeling that I know precisely where Metod's taking me.

My feeling is confirmed when he stops before the door with the hydra crest. I know what lies beyond it, though I'm not supposed to. It's the room where they drink brandy and have secret meetings.

This isn't just a meeting with my father.

Why did he bring me here? What's going on?

I swallow. Metod leads me through the foyer and knocks at the same door I had eavesdropped at several nights ago. The sound is painfully loud in the tense silence.

I hear no reply, but Metod holds the door open, gesturing for me to enter without following himself. He bows as I pass by and closes the door behind me.

The room is larger than I expect. It holds a liquor cabinet the size of a small library. There's a roaring fire in a large fireplace and smaller bookshelves. A large grandfather clock made of dark wood with a gold pendulum stands in one corner, its glass face unreadable in the firelight. There are no windows, and the walls are stone, not gold-lined wood paneling like most of the house.

Even the decor is comparatively minimalistic. There are a few tapestries and a massive portrait of a man I don't recognize. On the opposite end of the room from the picture is a heraldic crest of the same size, featuring that same Hydra and made entirely of gold. Emblazoned on a banner at the bottom is 'Potestas, Stirpes, Dignatio.' Underneath the crest is another door.

Filling the room are some of the most comfortable-looking pieces of furniture I've seen in the castle, half occupied. All the occupants are men of various ages, Basil being the youngest. Their sharp black eyes bore into me.

There's a clinking of ice falling into a glass. I glance back at the cabinet and see my father's back as he pours himself a brandy. He doesn't look at me. There's the rattle of more ice, and he pours another cup. He turns and carries both drinks to me. He sets one down on the table nearest to me, then takes a long sip of the other and sighs.

"David, let me introduce some of your relatives. This is Kolya, your Great Granduncle, and his son Nickoloz, your first cousin, twice removed. Your Grand Uncle Leonid, and his son Oleksiy, your first cousin, once removed. Your Uncle Stathis, and his son Levent, your first cousin..."

I stare blankly, the names and connections blurring together. The fact that they all are related and bear similarly antagonistic expressions doesn't help things. Basil's gaze is the only sympathetic one, but he doesn't meet my eye. I stand rigidly, tapping a hand compulsively against my thigh.

There's a suffocating silence, and they continue to stare, expectant. What am I supposed to say? "Um, hi." I see Basil wince. For his sake, I add, "nice to meet you." It's definitely a lie. They still don't look pleased.

How could such a big room feel so claustrophobic? I look at Dad. *Why are you doing this to me?* I think. *Why am I here?* However, I don't speak out loud, and his back remains to me.

Part of me wants to leave, but pride and stubbornness stop me. They'll just take it as me running and feel justified in their imagined superiority. Still, the silence is maddening. I squirm, ready to blurt out something, anything to end it, when Leonid speaks.

"How are your studies, David? I hear you have been inducted."

"Wha- inducted?" I repeat, distracted. I can smell the smoke from the candles, but I can barely hear the clock over the thunderous roar of my own heartbeat. There's something palpably oppressive in the air. Like the weight of their stares has something physical behind it. Hell, they're magic; it probably does. I shiver.

"Your Thaumaturgy. Magic David. We are a family of Sorcerers. Your father leads the family. You are of the Blood. We of the inner circle are the strongest, and as Lord Victor's son, we have high expectations of you. So, I will ask you again, how are your lessons?"

"Well, you could have been more specific," I fold my arms.

Leonid exchanges looks with those near him.

"Ignoring your insolence, we are again astonished by the American educational system. Shall we move along to the matter at hand?"

I narrow my eyes. "I know what the damn word means. It just didn't make any sense in context." I snap. "You accuse me of lazy speech, yet you didn't even bother using an object in your sentence. How is that my fault?"

I latch onto the debate as a distraction. I don't want to think about spellwork or the candles. The smoke from the fire makes the air strangely thick.

"You're stalling, boy. Answer the question before we rip it from your mind." The voice instantly grabs my attention, and I focus on the speaker. It's the first person Dad introduced, Kolya. It's also the voice that berated Miss Rigo, insisting that pain and discipline be the most crucial focus of my learning.

He sits across the room from Leonid. He has perfect posture that belies his age. Nor does he look old enough to be a generation above Leonid. His eyes are sharp, his hands steady, and while his hair is bone-white, there's no sign of balding.

The idea of thoughts being ripped out of my head is more than a little alarming, and I stiffen, back becoming almost as straight as theirs. "Bad, probably," I admit. I don't think my honesty is the result of any sort of compulsion. I never lied about things like that with Mom, and I don't see why I should with them either. They mean far less to me. "But I wouldn't really know."

I look at Basil. How well am I doing? And why isn't he saying anything? He sits tight-lipped, nostrils flaring with each breath. A candle next to him, with flame stretching as long as a hand, flickers slightly with each breath he takes. He stares straight ahead and doesn't look at me at all.

"Have you mastered the first lesson?" Leonid continues. "Do you truly have any talent, or was all your father's power washed away by your mother's blood?"

Rage tightens my fist, but I'm silenced by fear, haunted by the twisted grotesquery of the Corrupted. I don't want to end up like them. Is that what's in store if I continue practicing magic?

"Only a privileged few—those of great merit to the family—may live within these walls. You must demonstrate magical talent and resistance to its corruption, or you will be forced to leave. Should you become Corrupted, you will be sent below ground. If you cannot demonstrate the necessary talent, you must work to prove your worth in mundane means and will be expected to excel in a field that is beneficial to the family's interests if you wish to stay."

Anger burns away my fear. "I don't know what the hell is wrong with all of you. I don't care who you are or what you can do. I didn't come here to impress you, and frankly? I don't have a reason to give a shit about you. What I do will be my choice, not yours."

A heavy silence descends. I focus on the way the ambient sounds blend; the crackling flame, the rapid fluttering of my heartbeat, countered by the slower, more rhythmic ticking of the clock, backed further still by distant rumbling thunder. My own personal symphony. I call it, Percussive Tension.

Leonid breaks the silence with a snort. His face twists into something between a sneer and a smile. "He has some backbone, Viktor. How unfortunate he's a disappointment in all other regards. You have Basil, at least. It's a shame you do not have more."

"Insolence! How your mother managed to hide you all these years is beyond me," Kolya interjects. Kolya, the eldest, the instigator of my misery. "Should have been raised here from the beginning. You don't care what we think, David? Your priorities are severely misaligned."

"Demonstrate a talent in magic to us, and you'll be allowed to return to your room with some semblance of the leeway you have been allowed." Says Leonid. "If not, there will be... changes."

I focus on Dad. Why isn't he saying anything? Why is he just letting this happen? Like before, with the seats... I have to swallow another surge of anger. It feels like I've swallowed glass, tiny pinpricks stabbing my insides, and I plead silently. *Say something, Dad. Anything. Just show me you care as much as I do. That you care at all, please.*

"Don't look at him; look at us." Kolya snaps. "You cannot hide behind your father any longer. He used his influence to bring you here, into this great house. By rights, you and your mother should be in a cottage on the mainland. Instead, you are treated like his legitimate son, given everything entitled to a noble upbringing. No longer. Prove yourself, or you'll be treated like the Bastard you are." He turns to Dad. "This whole event is shameful. I propose he be sent away should he prove unable to demonstrate magical ability by the next ritual."

My belly drops to the floor. Out of my corner eye, I see Basil jerk as if slapped. No one else seems to notice. Dad doesn't react at all.

I don't care about most of the men in the room. The castle... the castle I have mixed feelings about. Nostalgia, yes. And I've always loved old buildings. Plus, it's cool. The grounds are endlessly fun, and yet... it feels dead here. So many strangers, so suffocating. As much cage as home.

But all of that is eclipsed by a simple fact. This is where Dad and

Basil are, and I don't want to leave them. Even if Dad's presence is an increasingly painful one.

Basil's first warning echoes in my head. They know how to make your life miserable... ...had I listened and done everything they wanted, would I be here? I feel the beginnings of doubt and force it back. It wouldn't have mattered. Especially considering what Kolya said to Miss Rigo.

All they want is an excuse, a reason to feel superior.

Besides, I'd rather be standing here, interrogated by my supposed family, than be turned into a living doll. Studying diligently, sitting straight, and ignoring my desires so I can become a cog in the Guthanderkaz machine.

That will never be me.

Dad finally turns away from the shadows he'd been hiding in and towards the group.

"Let it be so. I am confident that David will demonstrate his talent to the satisfaction of all. If he does not, the situation will be re-addressed. Is there anything else?" The assembly remains silent for several moments.

Leonid is the one to break it, "Business."

"Business, I trust in your capable hands. If you'll excuse me, gentlemen, I wish to confer with my sons." Dad says, finishing his drink and leaving the glass on the table. He gives Basil and me each a look before heading out.

His gaze inspires such mixed emotions I get a headache: relief, anger, bitterness. Part of me doesn't want to follow, to punish him for ignoring me, but I do. I can't leave things as they are, and I want to hear what he has to say. I want him to give me a reason for ignoring me, to reassure me, to show me he really does love me, he had good reason for turning his back like that...

I gulp in air once I step outside the room. It tastes fresher outside. I glance at Basil. He tries to smile at me, but the effort only makes his expression grimmer. Dad leads us to his office.

He sits on his couch, not his throne of a desk chair, and pats the cushion next to him. Like how one would gesture to a pet or a child.

I fold my arms and remain standing, staring back at him.

"I'm sorry they were so unpleasant, David, but let's focus on proving them wrong. We do not have much time, but I am confident in your ability."

"Why?" I ask stubbornly. I sound childish even to my own ears.

"I was under the impression that you wanted to learn magic. Basil expressed a great deal more excitement over the thought than you're showing now." He looks between the two of us.

I swallow, and look away, feeling miserable. "I can't," I say quietly, then more firmly. "And that's not what I meant. I mean, why do anything for them?"

He inhales slowly, holds it, and scowls. "If you meet with their satisfaction, then you and your mother will be redeemed, and I will be vindicated. They will stop fighting me regarding your presence here, and you and your mother will be free to pursue your own endeavors."

"I'm free to 'pursue my own endeavors' anyway," I snap. "Why would I let them stop me?"

"No, you are still a child. You have yet to graduate or master your Thaumaturgy. I'll not have you spend your life uneducated or squandering your potential. You must show progress, and soon."

I narrow my eyes, feeling that bitterness welling in me again. "This isn't about them, is it? This is what you want. That's why you didn't say anything to stop them!"

"I happen to agree with some of what they have to say, yes, but that... spectacle was not my idea. Do you not want to learn?"

"What exactly do you agree with?" I demand, ignoring his question.

"That you have not been living up to your potential. That your education is lacking, and I am concerned that your magical talent seems so difficult for you to control. I know you have potential, but you need to learn to harness it." He replies calmly.

"I'm not going to live my life based on what you think is important or what you think my 'potential' is! You don't even know me! You've been gone all my life, and now all you can think to do is try to... to turn me into *you!*"

"I'm trying to prepare you for the world and give you the best there is to offer." He rises slowly. He doesn't raise his voice, but it carries an edge of quiet anger. "I am your father; it is my duty to see to your upbringing."

"Like you did with Basil?! He hasn't even seen the world outside here! How can you prepare someone for the world when everything around them is so sterile and insulated?!" I demand.

"Our family has centuries of tradition and heritage to look to. Beyond these shores, there are those who would see us in ruin. Basil would actually be on a business trip now if I hadn't felt that you both would benefit from spending time together, but perhaps I should oversee your training instead."

I feel suddenly cold, looking at Basil. Did Dad just threaten to send him away...? I don't even want to consider how miserable I'd be here without him. The only other person close to my age that I've seen is Stathis, and my only experience with him was not exactly enjoyable. Besides, Basil's my best friend and half the reason I was so desperate to return to this place. I open my mouth, then close it, unable to form a reply.

The clock in his room ticks through the silence, sounding precisely like the one in the brandy room. For a moment, I'm transported back there. I shake my head.

This has been the longest day of my life, and the weight of it hits me suddenly, the anger and that pulsing hurt.

I turn away from my father, from his threats and assumptions and cruelty, turning my back on the entire castle as I do.

I walk out without another word. Dad doesn't follow me, and I don't expect him to. I return to the room I'd been given. It remains as clean and empty and hotel-like as the day I arrived.

I move slowly and carefully, not wanting to jostle the tears from my eyes. I breathe through my nose, trying to control my emotions along with my breath.

As my gaze sweeps across the too-tidy room, my eyes fix on the candles. It isn't night yet, but they've already been lit. Like someone's mocking me.

Unreasonable rage billows up within me, everything I've felt all day. Bitterness, betrayal, rage, desperation, fear... I channel it, reaching out again. "Enough!" I roar senselessly. Channeling all those emotions, I will the candle to be snuffed.

Two things happen at once.

The candle winks out with a pop, and something snaps inside me.

Dry ice cracks down my veins, flooding every pore with agony. My eyes burn, my vision goes red. Nothing exists but pain more intense than anything I've ever known. My ears ring as if deafened by a loud noise. I smell something metallic, and every muscle contracts at once.

I hit the floor

CHAPTER NINE

I jerk back into awareness in a panic, struggling, clawing back to reality as if escaping a nightmare.

My body aches, my eyes and throat burn. I force myself to relax and realize I've been screaming.

I become aware of Basil standing over me, his olive complexion turned moon-grey. I hear his voice distantly, like through water. "David! David, are you alright? What happened?"

I cough, unable to control my violent shaking. My muscles seem made of lead. Dazed, I mutter, clumsily seeking coherency. "C-candle...."

Basil's brow furrows. "What..?"

I lift a trembling hand to my cheek, feeling something wet. I inspect it.

Blood. That's why my eyes burn, what turned my vision red.

I bled from my eyes.

Horror holds Basil's tongue for a time, and he makes that strange grasping motion again, reaching, then holding himself back. He swallows, blinking rapidly as he takes me in. Finally, he kneels, bringing out a cloth handkerchief and dabbing gently at my cheeks.

"It.. it looks as if someone cursed you," I hear Basil say, his voice still distant but clearer than before.

I know better. I experienced it. That didn't come from the outside, and I can't fully explain *why* I know this, but I do. It wasn't something other. Snuffing out that candle had been *wrong*.

Basil is still talking. "Perhaps intending or happening to coincide with your lessons with the candle-"

"It's not a coincidence, Basil," I interrupt, my voice gruff and trembling almost as much as my body. "I can't do this. I... I don't want to become one of those things!" I'm ashamed to hear a note of hysteria in my voice.

"Please don't give up, David. Be strong. I... I don't want you to leave." Basil sounds strangely childlike, choking on his words. "I know you won't become one of the Corrupted."

"How can you know?! How can you risk it, when... when I could...." I shudder again, from cold or pain or spasms or some mix.

"Because I don't hate you," Basil answers quietly, looking pained.

His words hit me like a punch in the gut. "Wh-what?"

Basil turns away from me and swallows. "You... you're competition. You're older, your mother is..." He trails off, shaking his head. "Often, it feels as if you're Father's favorite. I know, logically, I should hate you... but I never could. You were my first real friend, but it's more than that. It started when we first met. It's why I was so instantly drawn to you to begin with. You *do* have magic, David."

I stare at him, barely aware of shaking my head. "I... I haven't done anything..." I protest helplessly.

"I know you aren't aware of it. Had I ever had a doubt in the matter, it's been made clear you have no idea what you're doing with how much you've struggled, even hurt yourself with magic. I wish I knew why." Basil purses his lips, sucking on his words. "You draw people to you, make them want to like you. You make it hard to be angry at you, to hurt you. When you smile, it makes people want to smile with you. I'm not being poetic; I'm being literal. I can feel it; I know it for what it is. You have exceptionally potent magic. They must sense it, too, despite what they say. It's part of what makes them angry, I think... not that they don't have other reasons...." He stops, running a hand through his hair.

I don't answer. I feel like I've been hollowed out, Basil's words echoing inside me. My life is reflected back at me, how carefree things always seemed to be, how quickly I made friends with each new school, and how easy it had always been to talk my way out of trouble and punishments until now. Even small things, Margaret's words, 'your tricks won't work on me.' I hadn't thought much of it at the time.

Is that why he hasn't even tried to defend me? Because he never really cared, it's just some… some sort of subconscious mind control? My limbs feel numb, my throat tightens, and I no longer know if it's tears or blood that stings my eyes. I can't think, can't breathe.

The only true friend I ever had, and he only likes me because of magic?

I cringe away from him. Basil doesn't fight me. I can't even look at him. Part of me welcomes the hardness and chill of the marble floor. The pain of the cold and the ache of my limbs feel suddenly welcome compared to the anguish in my heart.

Never in my life have I felt so alone.

I wake to the distant croaking of the ravens. A gentle breeze tugs at my hair. Despite the cold outside, I'm kept warm by the thick layers of blankets and a feathery down comforter bundled around me. The smell of the air is comforting. Firewood, the sweetness of flowers, ivy after a morning dew, and the slight but present saltiness of the sea. I open my eyes.

Where am I? It's smaller than my room, but brighter, full of windows, with an open balcony. A variety of bright, colorful flowers decorate the room. In a corner sits a fireplace, smaller and cozier than the one in my room, its light dancing off a delicately carved wardrobe sitting next to it. I find familiarity resting on a desk in front of a window. There are several familiar books, pictures of me, a photo of Mom and Dad, and Mom's laptop. This must be her room, or part of it. I'd only seen a small sitting room on my visit. I guess the bed's in a second room. I notice three doors, not counting the balcony, and I'm not sure where they might go, but I don't want to brave the cold to find out.

I close my eyes, snuggle deeper into the covers, and cautiously revisit the day before.

Does Mom only love me because I'm magically mind-controlling her too?

I shake my head. She's my mother. Of course she loves me; I don't need magic for that. It's there anyway, though, says a soft doubtful voice inside me, just like with Basil.

Can I learn to turn it off? And if I can... will Basil still like me? Or will he do what he considers logical and hate me? My heart squeezes, and I pull the blanket above my head, rubbing at my eyes. It doesn't matter. Whatever I'm doing is wrong, and I have to stop if I can. And even if he hates me after, he's still my brother. The thought isn't as comforting as it might have been had I not met the rest of my extended family.

I take a long, shuddering breath. I've been dressed in pajamas, and feel clean, which means someone undressed and bathed me. I hope it wasn't one of the staff. The idea of strangers touching me while I sleep makes me squirm.

I spot a glass and pitcher next to the bed. I suddenly realize how thirsty I am. I plunge into the cold long enough to pour myself some water.

One of the doors opens, and I look up.

"David? Are you awake?" Basil asks softly. He smiles when he sees me, "You're looking much better."

"Oh, yeah. Hey, Basil." I croak awkwardly. Dammit, I'm not used to awkward. "Well, it's hard not to be better than bleeding from the eyes." It's meant to be a joke, but speaking it out loud, it doesn't sound funny at all. He opens his mouth to speak, then shuts it again and sighs, shaking his head.

"Hungry?" He asks.

I'm about to refuse when my stomach grumbles a loud protest. "Um, 'parently," I admit, then frown. "Just how long was I sleeping?"

"A day. Shall I have them send something up? Or do you want to have another picnic?"

I shift. Right now, venturing out of the warm blankets, across the icy stone floors and all the way back to my room to get dressed seems like a horrible journey. On the other hand, I don't want to get crumbs on Mom's bed. Also, sleeping in my Mom's bed is weird… assuming that's where I am. "Where am I?" I ask, deciding to confirm it.

"Ms. Rose's quarters," Basil replies.

I wince, "that's what I thought. I dunno, being in Mom's bed at this age is just… embarrassing." I wonder if I'd be less embarrassed if I didn't run to her bed to hide from nightmares when I was a little kid. I wonder if the castle inspired some of those nightmares.

"It's unlikely she's used it," Basil adds.

I blanch. "That really doesn't help." I groan, blushing. I hop out, wincing at the cold. "I need to get changed."

He gestures to where a suit is folded neatly in the corner of the room. "It seems someone sent along a change of clothes for you." Amusement dances in his eyes, and the corners of his mouth twitch.

I glare for a moment at the clothes, then turn and walk past them. "Yeah, screw that. I'm not wearing a suit again in my life."

"David, don't be like that. What if we, I don't know, didn't button it up all the way…?"

"Never. Again." I hiss through my teeth. I pause, running a hand through my hair and glancing at him. "I… I'm not angry at you or anything, Basil. But I won't do that again. I'm done playing games; I'm done wearing a mask."

He looks taken aback. He scowls for a moment, then his face softens. "If you throw on a robe and I act as lookout, we can sneak you back to your quarters," he offers.

I laugh out loud. "Basil, I'm in pajamas, not naked. In fact, I'm less naked than the t-shirt and boxers, which we have already established doesn't count as naked at all. I'm really not worried. But thanks."

He makes a sour face, and his swarthy skin becomes a little rosier. He coughs and looks away. "Yes, well, we had best be going then." He glides to the door, peering out of it. "Coast is clear…"

"I can't even tell if you're serious anymore." I grin and push him out playfully. "Come on, let's just go." I pause in the middle of the hallway, glancing behind me. "Uh, should I… leave a note or something? Where *is* Mom?"

"She's speaking with father," Basil replies.

"Oh." A heavy weight settles in my stomach. I push it away. "Let's go. I really need to get some food."

Basil is anxious on my behalf, glancing around the halls, playing lookout. We reach my bedroom unseen, and he sighs heavily, leaning against the door to close it.

I bite my lip to hide my amusement, focusing on changing. Basil really does have a talent for cheering me up.

The combination of t-shirt, hoody, and jeans is comfortable, and I relax at once. "Let's eat."

"Picnic or room service?"

I hesitate, looking out the window. As much as I love the outdoors, I crave privacy. "Room service. I, um… wanted to talk to you."

"Why don't you tell me what you want, and I'll have them send it up."

"I don't suppose I could have a cheeseburger and fries?" I ask. Basil smiles. Crossing my room, he pulls a cord in a corner I thought was just another decorative tassel.

I blink. "What's that?

"It calls a servant to attend you… Forgive me; I hadn't considered you might not know."

"Um, yeah. Not exactly something I grew up with. Honestly, still not entirely comfortable with the whole thing…" I rub an arm.

"What's not to be comfortable with? It's their job. If they don't like working here, they can get jobs somewhere else, but frankly, it's considered a prestigious position and exceedingly well-paid. None of them would give it up. Just think of them like you would the staff of a hotel. Now, what did you want to talk about?"

"I… what you said yesterday… or whenever it was." I shift. "Look, I… I'm sorry, I don't know how or what I'm doing, but… if, if I'm doing something… I'll stop as soon as I find out. I promise." I swallow.

"I know," he looks at me expectantly. "Was there something else…?"

How can he brush this off so easily? "…are you sure?"

"Of course, you're new to your talent. I did the same thing as a child. I didn't know I did; it just happened. It will stop naturally once you learn control, because you want to use your energy when you want it, not all the time. I don't blame you. Besides, I can just brush it off."

Relief washes over me. If Basil can just brush it off, then all of this still counts. It's still real. I feel giddy and light-hearted and lift an eyebrow as I grin at him. "You mean I'm magically wetting the bed?" I ask playfully.

He gawks at me, then clears his throat and shakes his head. He looks at me again, and his composure cracks. He snorts out a grunt of a laugh, then covers his face and full-on guffaws.

"Yes!" he doubles over, holding his gut as he laughs. "A little old for it, aren't you, David?" His laughter turns into coughing, his face is red, and he wipes at the corners of his eyes. He sits and tries to calm himself but keeps chuckling.

"Man, calm down," I say, shaking my head as I watch him. "It wasn't even funny. All my awesome jokes and *that's* the one that cracks you? Never thought you'd be one for toilet humor..."

"I..." he flushes again and clears his throat, "I too would like to talk to you about what happened in your room, with the candles."

His words sober me instantly. I swallow, flopping down beside him and hugging my knees. "...can you really just brush it off?"

Before he can reply, there's a soft knock at the door.

"One moment," Basil calls. He stands, answering the door and speaking softly in Fyrnekh. I wait impatiently, tapping my hand against my legs.

"Sorry, where were we?" Basil asks as he returns.

"Mind control?" I offer.

"It isn't mind control, David. Believe me, I know that well. What you do is..." He trails off as if searching for a word, then seems to give up. "Never mind. If I couldn't handle my little brother accidentally charming me, I wouldn't be much of a Sorcerer, would I?"

"Older brother," I correct automatically, but I can't help but press. "So... I mean, it's not that? You still..." I trail off, flushing. Would he even know otherwise? And how many friends had I had that couldn't protect themselves from it? "You said.."

"Oh, well, strictly speaking, from an overly dramatic political standing, if I were to be especially villainous. But I'm not, and I don't."

I exhale slowly and run a hand through my hair. "So, what did you want to ask me about?" There's still doubt for everyone else I've ever known, sure. But not my brother, at least.

"Well, I thought we could discuss music, and women, and oh yes, you making yourself bleed from the eyes with magic!"

"Oh, I have plenty to say about women and the stupid misogynistic treatment of them in this castle," I mutter.

"You're being evasive."

"What the hell am I supposed to say?" I demand, squeezing my legs and giving him a helpless look. "I don't understand any of this, and every time I think of it, I think of those *things* below!"

"...Well, at least it proves that you do have talent; anyone with any magic sensitivity who comes in can feel the echo of what happened. It's not a big echo, but it's there."

"What are you talking about?!" I demand, "And isn't it a larger indication that I'm... I'm mutating or something?"

"You did it, you put the candles out, and you've been charming everyone. If you were going to mutate, you would have started already."

I study his eyes. "Can you really be sure about that?"

Basil doesn't meet my gaze. "Mostly..."

Great. I swallow. Well, it's my own fault for pressing. I could have just accepted it and felt safe. "But you think it's something else...?"

"That looked more like a curse; I thought someone attacked you. Are you sure you did it to yourself?"

I run a hand through my hair, draping an arm over one knee and letting the other dangle. Clouds shift over the sky, and the room fades from gold to gray to gold again. "It... was something I did. Something from inside. I... I know it." I say firmly. "Or I think I do." *Probably about as sure as you are I won't turn into a creepy mutant thing*, I think, but don't add that part.

"It's good to trust your instincts in matters like this. Do you know what you did? Were you trying to snuff the candles? Did you go through all the steps?"

"I've had the steps memorized for a week," I exclaim, then slump back. "I don't want to turn into a monster."

"You're not going to turn into a monster. If father sensed that you were beginning to change, he'd stop you from using magic. You'll be fine. The early stages are practically undetectable…" he freezes mid-sentence and stares at me for a moment, "…You are *not* going to become a monster!"

I swallow. A knock on the door rescues me from having to formulate a reply. Alfrèd enters carrying a silver tray. He removes the cloche dramatically, revealing thick bread, ground beef, cheese, and thick wedges of potatoes. My mouth waters. "Thank you, Alfrèd, you're amazing. Basil, you're the best brother in the world."

Alfrèd doesn't reply but looks pleased. Basil smiles, "I know."

"You have no idea how badly I've been wanting a burger," I say, flopping in front of the coffee table before Alfrèd can even put the tray down.

"Our chefs can make you anything you want. As long as they can understand what you're saying, of course."

"I'm learning Fyrnekh pretty fast, I think." I settle back and savor what has to be the best burger I've ever had.

I'm given a brief respite from spellcasting, and I intend to use it. Not for more tutoring, obviously. I have a much more productive activity in mind. After our last encounter, I like my uncles and cousins about as much as they like me.

I finger the Hydra key. It might not work, but it's identical to Basil's, which has to mean something. Everyone has secrets. I'm going to find theirs.

I don't really have a plan beyond that.

I wait until dinner, so I know they'll all be occupied. Skipping dinner isn't unusual for me without having bled from the eyes, so I'm not worried about suspicion.

I arm myself with the key and a lantern.

The most significant challenge turns out to be the dinner staff. Despite the calm way they glide to the table to present the food, they're rushing about frantically in the halls I'm trying to sneak through. I dodge them, hiding whenever they approach.

I arrive at the golden hydra that marks the door to the brandy room. I check the hall once, quickly, before darting inside. The fire isn't yet lit, and at first, I see nothing but silence and shadows. I leave the door open. It's risky, but I need enough light to see while I light the lantern. I scratch at a match and hear a whisper in my ear.

I jump, spinning around, but there's nothing but the heavy shadows that mute the room's colors. I glance at the still-open door, but no one's there. I hold my breath, listening. Nothing.

I swallow. Trying to suppress the trembling in my hands, I attempt once more. Once, twice… and at last, a brief blaze of flame. I press it into the lantern and turn the gas on. The flame flickers, and I swear I hear more whispering. The light reveals the room. Empty.

I softly close the door I entered by, then cross the room. I try the door; locked. Holding my breath, I try the golden hydra key. It clicks open, and I exhale loudly in relief. I grin triumphantly, slipping inside and closing the door before looking around.

The dark eyes of the portrait glare down at me. The shifting light of the flame gives the illusion that the painting breathes and changes expression. I shake my head. Just because I come from a family of sorcerers doesn't mean I should be paranoid.

I've already seen this room, anyway. I'm more curious about what's behind the door at the end of the room. Briefly, I feel guilty about not telling Basil my plan. Maybe he'd want to come too. But he probably already knows and might try to stop me or even let Dad know. I mean, he could have explored the caves below with me too, or told me, but he didn't. I love my brother, but he's too straight-laced to entrust my quest to.

Besides, I'm not entirely sure what my quest *is*. I just want to know more, and also, to show up those assholes. Maybe even unearth some sort of embarrassing secret.

I pass the now-empty lounge. The polished furniture glints in the flickering lantern light. I feel the weight of eyes on me in the darkness. I pause, glancing around uncertainly, then shake my head. I study the massive golden hydra and its seven snarling mouths. Seeing it this large, I recognize the objects held in some of their jaws; a bat, a key…

No, no getting distracted.

I glance behind me, even though I know they'll be just starting dinner now, probably still on the first or second course. I turn back, find the keyhole, and slip my own key inside. Holding my breath, I attempt to turn it.

Nothing. It won't budge at all. "Oh, come on!" I hiss. I jiggle it, press harder, and try different tactics I've used before on various stuck doors. It *has* to open. I can't just leave things like this-

The key clicks so suddenly that, for a moment, I think it's a hallucination. I stare, startled, at where the key now rests at a right angle and tentatively try the door. It creaks open. I grin.

There's a hallway full of unlit torches, with strange writing, elaborate symbols, and complex patterns carved into the walls. Some of the sigils glow as I approach, and I hesitate. Do they know I'm here now? I glance behind me. If I leave now, I can pretend I was never here, but I may never get a chance like this again.

...Yeah, forget that.

Instead of cowering and running, I plunge forward, determined to see and do as much as I can before and if they find me.

I touch one of the doors. My fingertips thrum, and a not-unpleasant tingling sensation runs up my arm.

My finger drifts along the door's surface, but this time, I can't find a keyhole. Dammit, it can't end this early! Maybe there's a trick to it? I recall the magic lock that Basil unlatched, but I still don't know how he did it. I frown, frustrated. I can't give up, not now. I look back at the main door, then scan the hall again. Some doors have keyholes; I could always try one of them. But my gut tells me that the most complicated magical protection hides the most enticing secrets.

I kick the door. I gain nothing but a hurt toe. I exhale upward, sending my hair waving over my forehead. Ok, I can figure this out, I just need time, and I have plenty of-

I hear the sound of a door being unlocked and swear internally.

I scan the room desperately. It's probably just one of the staff members preparing for their after-dinner brandy. Still, I don't want to be interrupted before I have a chance to do or see anything.

I randomly pick a door with a keyhole and slip the key in. It gets stuck. "Again?!" I hiss quietly. I hear the footsteps draw nearer. Crap, crap, crap.

The lock clicks open. I dart inside and swing it shut before I even look at what's inside, almost dropping my lantern.

Shelves and shelves of books line the walls, resembling the old tome that Basil's teaching me out of. Maybe there'll be something interesting in here-

I hear voices murmuring and hold my breath. They might see the candle from underneath the door if they get close enough. I'm not sure why they're even in this hall, but maybe there's a wine cellar down here or something. I mean, the path does have a subtle downward slope.

I can't be caught yet, not until I find something I can rub their faces in. I dart down the halls, moving behind bookshelves until I'm certain my lamplight won't be visible from the hallway.

I lean against a stone wall, surrounded by books, an unlit torch above me.

I sigh, sliding down. Well, who knows how long I'll have to wait here. Might as well read. Leaning against the rather uncomfortable bookshelf, I pull a book out at random. The paper crinkles when I open it, a musky smell escaping the ancient pages. To my surprise, it looks handwritten. I stare at it, squinting. It's in Fyrnekh, so it's already harder to read, but the calligraphy adds another layer of difficulty. Elaborate flourishes accent each painstakingly drawn letter, making it almost impossible for a non-native speaker, such as myself, to decipher.

I give up, slip it back and grab another book instead. The torch above me springs suddenly to life. I jerk and slap a hand over my mouth to cover my instinctive sound of surprise. I hold my breath and listen.

I don't hear footsteps, but I hear breathing at the door.

"I know you're in here, David." Dad's voice drifts from the doorway.

My heart clenches, but I stubbornly remain still and unbreathing. Footsteps echo against the stone, approaching my hiding spot.

They continue, and I turn off my lantern. The sound is quiet, but the footsteps pause when I do, then move more swiftly. Dammit. I fold my legs and sit stubbornly, determined not to apologize.

He rounds the bookshelf and looms over me, impossibly tall and straight. I remember Miss Rigo's threat about a corset. Maybe Dad was forced to wear one when he was a child. There's no way someone learned to stand that straight without help.

"What are you doing in here?" Dad asks. There's an odd tone to his voice I can't place, but he doesn't sound angry. "How did you get in here? I don't recall giving you permission to come here, let alone the key."

"It's the same key," I reply. "I figured that out. And you didn't tell me *not* to go in here. Besides, it was ok before." I say as if this is all just a misunderstanding and not inspired by pure spite.

Dad actually smiles. Something is definitely wrong. "Get up, David."

I stand slowly, uncertainly. "Shouldn't you be at dinner?"

"Yes, but then you got into somewhere you weren't meant to," Dad replies, still ominously calm. I swallow. This is so much more unsettling than anger.

Dad leads me out of the room, closing the door behind me, smiling the entire time. The torches along the hall are all blazing now. We enter the brandy room. The fire is crackling, and in front of it stand Leonid, Kolya, and a few other older men from the meeting. I freeze. Dad puts a hand on my shoulder, speaking with pride. "Will this suffice as a demonstration of my son's talents?"

"Not so much as it demonstrates his insolence and disobedience," snaps Kolya. "the boy is in more severe need of disciplining than any I've ever heard of. And how can we be certain you didn't simply let him in and lower the wards yourself?"

"You have proven overly attached," Leonid agrees. "And unable to oversee this matter with the clarity and distance it requires."

I hate it when people speak over me like I'm not there, but my attention is caught by a more significant realization. I stare at Kolya still, mind racing. Obviously, I did something magic coming in here, something that could be done by Dad as well. But that's not the only way Kolya's been fighting me; I just didn't realize it until now. "You already know I have magic," I say to Kolya.

Silence descends on the room as the men's attention turns to me. But I don't turn my attention away from Kolya, ecstatic to finally have a target for my rage.

"Impertinent brat! You think I would defend you?" Kolya's face goes red, expression torn between rage and scorn. I laugh, and he only looks angrier.

"No, but I don't need you to. We both know I've already proved you right?" I smirk at him, triumphant, vindicated. Basi's right; I use magic all the time. I just hadn't realized it. "How often did you have to keep trying to layer on spells to mind control Miss Rigo? Every day?"

The sharp gazes shift from me to Kolya.

"David, please explain. More clearly." Dad says, his voice full of deadly calm.

"Are you really going to entertain such baseless accusations?" Kolya demands. "Your favoritism goes too far!"

"What's wrong? Are you afraid he'll rip the truth from your mind?" I ask, purring. Kolya glowers at me, and I give Dad a wide-eyed, innocent look. "He mostly seemed focused on instructing her to favor *discipline* over learning any subjects. Oh, and he emphasized she should be teaching lessons with *pain*. When I overheard him instructing her, it pissed me off more than it should, more than just from the words, and I couldn't figure out why but I think I know; he was using magic, and I could fucking tell."

There's a crash of thunder strong enough to shake the stones of the castle. The candles, lanterns, and fireplace blaze to a greater intensity. Dad's hands slip off of my shoulders. He steps around me and approaches Kolya slowly.

"If it is baseless, then you will have no qualms if I question Miss Rigo. Immediately."

"What happened to ripping the answers from his mind? Isn't that what you do?" I ask. I swear I'm not a sadist, but payback can be so satisfying. The look of impotent fury Kolya gives me only makes it better.

"Surely dinner has already been disrupted enough by this charade," Kolya says, glancing around as if hoping to find some backing in the faces of the other men.

"Looking for someone to hide behind?" I can't help but snipe.

"That is enough, David! These are grave accusations. Do not distract from them with pettiness." I tense, mood souring. Of course, he lets all of that happen to me, but he dismisses the same words against Kolya. Dad continues, oblivious to my feelings, approaching Kolya until he stops directly in front of him. "I do not tolerate being lied to. Kolya, I am entertaining these very dire accusations. Did you mind control Miss Rigo, as my son says?"

Kolya stands very stiffly, hands clenching at his side. I can see the vein in his forehead pulse, but he doesn't try resisting the accusations this time. "You are too soft on him. The boy is undisciplined, and everyone knows it. Why bother with everything else when you fail to instill the essential obedience and deference into him?"

There is another ear-shaking crash of thunder.

"You are not the boy's father. I am! You have assaulted my blood. You have subverted my will and acted without my permission. You presume to know better than I? *I* lead the family! You have grossly overstepped your authority, Grand Uncle!" Dad says, his voice tinged with fury and something thick and dark. The room's mood has shifted; the scorn and hostility is focused on Kolya instead.

Leonid is the first to speak. "You have gone too far, Kolya." He glances back at the others, and several give nods. Most just scowl.

"The boy may be willful and undisciplined but can hardly be blamed for his lack of education if he was being sabotaged!" says one whose name I can't recall.

"He may be ignorant but has proven more than passing clever. Well done, lad." Says another, giving me a nod and an almost smile. This sets my hackles rising. My intention isn't to curry their favor and *certainly* not to be complimented like an obedient pet. I much prefer the blatant insults.

"As you say, he has provided an adequate demonstration," Leonid says; he rises to stare down at Kolya. "What of Kolya?"

"You speak to me about discipline, about obedience. You speak as if I'm blind. Do you think so little of me that you question my actions? Have you so little faith?!" Several people in the room shift uncomfortably.

Dad makes a disgusted sound and turns his back to them. He's facing me, and his face is devoid of warmth or kindness.

"I'll decide what to do about Kolya later." He pours himself a drink. "I'm well aware of my son's disposition. I know his mother. It is no surprise that she would raise him to be willful, proud, and defiant."

He looks at me and smiles, though I'm still rankled that he's doing the whole talking-about-me-like-I'm-not-here thing. "He is a wild thing, just like his mother. In time he will learn our ways."

Dad turns back to them and lifts his glass, then turns to the painting on the wall and does it once more before taking a deep drink. Apparently, this is some sort of signal.

They all visibly relax, taking their seats. Leonid remains standing. "Would it not be time then to begin considering an Arrangement? He is old enough."

"No doubt you have one of your granddaughters in mind, Uncle," Dad responds.

"Hardly. I said begin. Meaning I had not yet, till now, considered it. But we should." Leonid replies.

"That can wait. I'm in no hurry. Basil isn't even wed yet. And he remains my heir. That will not change." Several of them exchange looks.

I am starting to feel lost in the conversation again, which is incredibly frustrating as it's clearly *about* me, and also, *I'm right here.* I don't want to leave because I want to know precisely what plans and arrangements they wish to make involving me. I put effort into staying still, not wanting to draw attention with my movement that might lead to them censoring themselves or sending me away.

Not that I think any of them know how to censor themselves when it comes to being too polite to talk about me. Hypocrites.

"Besides. I'll need to speak with his mother. She should at least meet with any potential brides. It's her *right.*"

"I'm sorry," I can't stop myself. "Potential *brides?*" This has to be a joke. Especially in regards to me. Especially if he's talking about my *Uncle's granddaughters?* Who would be… related to me in some way which I don't know enough genealogy to be able to figure out, but *too much.*

Dad turns back to me, "Yes. Don't worry. That won't be for quite some time.

"Nope," I say, holding my hand up. "Amount of time doesn't matter.

This is not a thing that's happening, ever. What the actual *fuck*."

Dad's eyes narrow. He speaks slowly and purposefully, words laced with authority. "We will talk about this later."

"No, no, and hell no. That's not a thing that's up for discussion with *anyone*," I snap. I don't care how much authority Dad has. This is so beyond reasonable I can barely even process it.

"David…" he says, a warning edge to his voice.

"No, do *not* pretend there is anything reasonable about this. Who and *if* I marry is not a thing you get to control!" I say defiantly, fists clenching, ignoring the warning, glaring fiercely.

"As your father, I have a vested interest in such things. It is part of our culture."

"Being my father doesn't mean you get to pick who I fall in love with, if *anyone!* You don't even know me! Hell, you're just assuming I'm both straight and interested in sex at all!" This is definitely not how I imagined coming out to my dad but here we go, because I don't think I'm either.

"Marriage is not about love, David. It is about lineage. If you would calm down and listen, I am in no hurry to have you marry, but we will discuss it later. There is more to consider."

"Sure, *nothing* bad happens when you marry for lineage and politics instead of love. That's why you have a bastard son in the first place. How's the fact that you married a harpy instead of the woman you love working out for you?"

Dad slaps me. I… probably deserve it, a little. But he deserves every word I said just as much.

"Now you're trying to do the same thing to me," I say, voice cracking, tears gathering in my eyes despite myself. Dammit, I can't let him see me cry. "You're a terrible father!"

It's the second time I've accused a parent like that, but this time I truly believe my words. I can't bear to be in this suffocating room anymore, to be near him, near any of them. I turn, shoving roughly past the assholes that call themselves my relatives, and out the door.

"David, get back here; I'm not done with you!" Dad calls from behind me.

I slam the door as loud as I can in their face in answer. I reach the next door and slam that one too. A nearby kitchen worker jumps, staring with wide, startled eyes, but I don't take the time to apologize or explain. I just run.

I hate this place. I hate everyone in it. I hate my father for not caring. I hate myself for bringing us here. I hate my mother for just going along with everything so meekly when she's usually so damn strong. The anger burns and twists, a raging beast in my chest.

I dash to the nearest patio door. Apparently, most people are still at dinner, because beyond that first encounter, I don't run into another soul.

I open the door, panting. The sky is dark but still light enough that I can make out the edges of the garden. Unfortunately, on top of it being late, it's still bloated with dark clouds. The rain begins before I even step out, but I go out anyway.

Just like the first night. All I can seem to do is run away. I close my eyes, trying to banish the thought.

I don't care about the rain, the storm, the darkness. I savor it. I savor the wetness that blends with my tears and lets me pretend I'm not crying, the cold of it that numbs me and helps lessen my hurt, if only a little.

Pain spikes down my chest with each struggling breath. My legs burn with effort, and with the lashings of the roots and branches that claw at my clothes. I don't remember ever encountering so many before, but now the entire forest seems intent on strangling me. It's like the land itself is trying to punish me. Considering what Basil hinted at with magic, attunement, and the island, maybe it is.

My legs tremble, and I lean against the dark bark of one of the trees, trying to catch my breath through desperate panting and sobs. It's before sunset, but between the storm and thick foliage, it's as dark as night, and I can barely see a thing.

Movement catches my eye, and I lift my head to see.

The earth collapses under my feet. I've lived through a few earthquakes; they were nothing like this. Not just soil but stone is split in twain, creating a gaping maw. Abruptly there's nothing for me to stand on. I don't even have time to scream before I fall.

Chapter Ten

For the second time in a matter of days, I wake not knowing where I am. Only this time, agony wakes me. A sharp, constant pain radiates from my leg. I gasp, eyes pressing open, but I see nothing but darkness.

For pain is so overwhelming that for a long second, I can't make a sound. I manage a squeak, then a moan, tears pinching at my eyes. My whole body aches a little, but nothing compares to my leg.

The darkness is absolute. No matter how much my eyes widen or how long I give them to adjust, I can't see a thing. I focus on my other senses to try to make sense of my surroundings. The musky scent of lichen and mold clings to my nostrils. I feel dirty and dusty under all the aching, and I hear arhythmic water dripping onto stone and small puddles at several points in the room around me.

I shift and instantly regret it as pain lashes up my leg. I whimper pathetically and reach forward, touching my leg. I can feel moisture and stones. Please don't be blood. I have no idea where I am, and nor does anyone else. I struggle to think through the pain. The opening I fell through can't be far, can it?

I frown. How *did* I fall, anyway? Was there a landslide caused by the rain? I shake my head.

How doesn't help me. I wish I learned more magic, something useful... something like making light instead of putting it out.

I shift as much of my weight as possible to my uninjured leg. Even the slight movement jostles my leg and causes another stab of pain. I hiss, tears stinging my eyes. I shiver with cold and battle nausea.

I hear a deliberate scraping noise and freeze, listening. "H-hello?" I call, voice trembling even before its distorted by a cavernous echo.

Someone speaks Fyrnekh, slurring every word. I'm hit at once by repulsive recognition and panic. I know that accent. The approaching person must be one of the Corrupted.

I try to calm myself. Basil hadn't been concerned by them. And my bigotry is shameful, especially when they haven't done anything wrong.

There's a sudden bright light. I wince, raising my arm to block the intensity of it. My eyes adjust, and I realize that the bright flame is only a small lantern, its light licking hungrily at its cage.

It's held by a man in the priest robes the Corrupted seem to favor. His fingers curl and twist unnaturally around the lantern, looking more like an octopus than a hand. Between his hood and the dark, I can't see his face, but his eyes are yellow and luminous. They don't shine like a cat's eyes; it's closer to the large vacant glow of an angler fish.

The light does little to illuminate my surroundings. I can see the hint of a door past the man. Most of the room is uncarved stone, with stalactites and stalagmites surrounding the walls like teeth.

He's silent, staring at me with those vacant eyes. I clear my throat. "Um," I say, voice strained, and then in nervous Fyrnekh. "Hello?"

"You speak strangely," growls the cloaked one. "Are you truly Guthanderkaz?"

I make a face. "Not in spirit," I mutter in English.

"What was that?" The man barks sharply.

"Uh, yes. I mean, my father... yes." I say lamely. Dammit, it's hard enough to try speaking it when I'm not overwhelmed by pain. "I am happy to be seen." I say, in too much pain to think of the Fyrnekh word for 'found.'

"You won't be." Spittle sprays from his mouth as he speaks, color odd in the low candlelight.

"Sorry?" Is he threatening me? Did I mix up my words, or say something completely different from what I meant?

He says more, speech rapid and aggressive, which only makes him harder to understand. The only words I pick up are 'you,' 'secret,' and some form of the verb 'see.'

At the end of his speech, he dramatically rips back the hood of his robes with his free hand. Instead of a nose, he has a twisting tentacle. On one side, the skin is sagging and sloughing off his face; on the other, it's covered in scales and bubbles of flesh. Tendrils hang off his skin, writhing like tiny worms. Three curl from one nostril and several bulge from what's left of his strange lips. He isn't entirely hairless; several thin, white strands cling to his head and cheek, and somehow the effect is more disturbing than baldness would have been. I can't hide my horror and swallow the bile that rises in my throat.

"You see what I have given for a taste of power?!" He demands. He slurs his 's's, and now I see why, the grotesquely fascinating way the tendrils slipped around each other as he tries to manipulate them for speech. He says more, descending into a slew of words I don't recognize, though I don't know how much of my confusion is due to my lack of vocabulary and how much is because, the lip and tongue tendrils tremble violently with his anger, and he seems to have more trouble with the fine control needed to manipulate them.

He heaves in great breaths, liquid drooling down his tentacles, and seems to calm. He shakes his head slowly. "No more. I have you. You will suffer until you teach me."

It takes me half a second to process the key points of that statement, and I'm torn between anger, fear, and the mad desire to laugh at the sheer irony of it all. The Corrupted man couldn't have chosen a worse teacher for himself.

I sit up to answer, but my leg reminds me of its pain, and I crumple again with a whimper. I lay there panting, and then he moves forward with that slithering, scraping, dragging sound. I cringe, heart racing.

I silently plead that that unconscious power that makes people not want to hurt me kicks in right now. I turn my gaze up at him. I've never used it consciously, and I have no idea what I'm doing.

He glowers at me as furiously as before.

I lick my lips and decide to attempt reason. "Basil said it's something you're born with. Some people..." I trail off. I have no idea how to say "mutate" in Fyrnekh, so I substitute the English word and continue. "And others don't. It's not something you learn. And if it was-"

"*Silence!*" Roars the man before I can inform him of how terrible his choice is. I'm showered with his spittle. It's thick and mucusy, clinging to me in globules.

I can no longer hold back and double over, emptying my stomach. The movement sends more jolts of pain through my legs.

The man continues his rant, oblivious or uncaring. "Lies! All of your lies, Guthanderkaz, all of them, they do not fool me anymore. You *will* teach me!"

He reaches down and grabs me. I struggle weakly, but the jostling of my leg paralyzes me with agony, and I can't hold back a sob. His fingers twist and loop around me, gripping and groping at my clothes and flesh. Grunting, he hefts me and tosses me onto his back. To my horror, more tentacles curl from beneath his cloak to grab at me while he carries me.

We pass through a small room. I can barely focus through the white spots of pain. The room is unexpectedly manmade after the rocky room I'd been in a moment before. I spot uneven wooden siding and a simple bed before he pushes through another door, and then the walls expand outward. I see the tips of enormous stalactites, their mass disappearing into the dark.

He plunges downward, grunting and slurping with each breath. Each shuffling movement sends pain lancing through my leg. Agony extends time unnaturally until, finally, I'm thrown unceremoniously onto the ground.

For several ragged breaths, I can do nothing but shudder, my leg pulsing and hot. What's wrong with it? Is it broken, or something worse? I've never had a broken bone, and I have no experience to compare it to. For all I know, it's completely shattered. It certainly feels that way.

"You cry," He asks mockingly, following with words I don't know. "I have not even begun. If you are so weak, tell me now."

I force my eyes open. The lantern is no longer the only light. Radioactive green bathes my chin, and I snap my gaze down in alarm.

Esoteric patterns glow from where they've been carved into the floor. Twisting seals, a massive star, and a wide circle… a circle that I realize I'm in the center of. This can't be good.

"You see now, do you? What awaits you should my patience be tested?" Slurps the Corrupted triumphantly.

"Not… really." I cough.

"You are at my mercy. Do you not know this ritual? What it calls?"

"I already told you," I gasp, clutching my leg, wondering if I can crawl out of the circle in time. "I… I don't know anything. I just… started learning…" I trail off. How long had it been? A few days? I feel so dizzy it's hard to think…

"You told me nothing, nothing that has not already been said! Teach me the secrets. How? How do you do it? How do you-" and I don't understand again.

I tremble. I wonder why the man before me didn't stop before it became so bad. Somehow, asking him doesn't seem like a good idea. "Please don't do this. I can't help you. I don't know if anyone can, but I know it's not me," I say helplessly. I'm too exhausted and confused to speak Fyrnekh and speak in English instead.

The Corrupted's lip-tendrils flail about as he releases a senseless noise of rage, spittle flying. Luckily, I'm far enough back that the oily mess doesn't land on me this time. "Do not insult me with your pig's tongue! Speak the holy language!"

Indignation flares to life somewhere beneath the pain. Pig's tongue? "How can it be holy if you don't believe that crap?" I mutter.

"Silence! I said silence! This is your last chance, begin the lesson, reveal to me the secrets, or you will suffer!" He twitches in agitation. The strange lumps in his robes heave until there's no mistaking what stands before me for a human form.

Dread compels me to act. I ignore my pain as best I can and pull myself away from the circle. "I… have no idea…" I swallow. The effort of moving is difficult enough without adding speaking to it, "what-"

The man lets out another warbling scream of fury. "If you will not teach, then-" And another descent into words indecipherable to me. There's a distinct switch from ranting to chanting what is clearly some sort of invocation.

I scramble away from the circle desperately. The glow intensifies and starts to burn where it touches me. Adrenaline spikes through my veins, empowering me, and I tumble out of the circle right before the chanting peaks to a terrible height. A humming surrounds the room, and the earth begins to shake. The Corrupted stands, hands and tendrils lifted into the air, a mad grin on his writhing face, and then a corner of reality sucks inward.

It's a nightmare brought to life. I can't even say 'given physical form' because I don't think it actually conforms to the laws of physics. It's black and festering, a living, pulsing shadow with a thousand different eyes and mouths and teeth, all sticking out at random places with no sense of purpose or base in nature. There are teeth in the eyes and eyes in the veins and something more crawling below that I don't have words to describe. Somehow, multiple parts occupy the same space without touching at all.

Ooze- or is that saliva?- drips from its form as it slowly surrounds us both. It doesn't crawl or even drift. Wherever you aren't looking, it's there, looming. I can *feel* its hunger.

I stare, a scream frozen in my throat.

Sound emanates from it, echoing through my bones, through my mind, sending every rational part of me screaming in denial.

I thought the Corrupted a monster. How wrong I was.

Oily ooze drips in front of me. It lands on a rock and bubbles and sizzles.

I stare upwards and into an endless array of sharp-toothed mouths that spin backward into infinity, like a face caught between two mirrors.

Instinct takes over. My will to live merges with everything I feel; anger, repulsion, fear, pain, denial. My emotions harden inside me, and I feel the tingling of magic, that wellspring Basil taught me about. I shout blindly, not thinking of what to say. "Stop," maybe, or "no." I know it's brief, and simple, and it conveys exactly what my desire is at that moment.

The monster stops. The mouths erupt into eyes, and I shudder under the unfathomable gaze that regards me. Behind me, I hear another wail of anger. Yet between the two? I'd rather keep the crazy once-and-almost human to my back then… whatever this creature is. I swallow. Do I have to say more? Do more? I'm not even sure what I did.

Weirdly, though? I don't have a headache, and I'm not fatigued. My heart hammers in my chest and my palms are sweating, but I think that has less to do with my casting and more to do with the fact that I can't see anything except… whatever that thing even is.

"With a word, a single word, you Command-" he descends into garbling. Again, I have no idea how much is my lack of understanding and how much is his bastardization of Fyrnekh.

I swallow and shift my weight, but I don't take my eyes off the abyss that gazes at me. I promise myself that if, no, when I make my way out of this, I'll laugh at the surreality of the whole thing, and it definitely, definitely will not be that insane madman laugh I've seen in so many movies. Hopefully.

"Fine, *fine!* If it is in the blood, I will take it! I will take the power of the blood with your blood!" Slurs the Corrupted man, his words fading back into coherency.

I don't want to turn my eyes away from the thing, but the Corrupted's rant about taking my blood is too alarming to ignore. I snap my head to stare at the Corrupted. He's closer than I remember, his vacant angler fish eyes fixated on me. In one hand, he holds a curved dagger. It's gold, with a strangely oily sheen. The blade has a jaggedness that doesn't look intentional, like it's been ground against rocks.

I take a step back and feel something brush against me almost tenderly. My gaze darts briefly behind me. The creature is there, it hasn't moved, but it quivers, as if eager, waiting for me to go closer.

I scan the room helplessly, but the mass, or whatever you call it, of sprawling teeth and tentacles is curved all around me. The only path of escape I can see is where the Corrupted approaches, with a knife in hand and a greedy smile.

My heart hammers in my ears. I'm colder and more terrified than I've ever been in my life. My very short life, which I don't want to end.

I watch the approaching madman, helpless. A glimmer past and above him catches my eyes. A desperate hope wells inside me. Yes, it might just be another psychopathic Corrupted, but there's a chance… "H-" I try to call for help, but the Corrupted grabs me, slamming me to the ground, the slimy tendrils covering his limbs wrapping around me, one of them covering my mouth.

I squirm, trying to speak, eyes wide. The Corrupted man looms above me. Behind him, I see the creature bubble and begin to grow again, filling the room like spilled water, watching us. The Corrupted sneers at me. The gold of his dagger winks a promise in the shrinking lantern light. *Help,* I think desperately. But I can't form the words; I can't do anything.

The world seems to slow as I watch the blade descend, watch my death come to meet me. My eyes squeeze closed on instinct, and a scream fills my ears and mind.

A scream that isn't mine.

I'm released abruptly. I open my eyes to see the Corrupted writhing before me, shrieking in a way no human should be capable of, as black fire erupts from his bones and sears a hole in his chest, burning him from the inside out. Towering above him, eyes merciless, stands Dad. There must be a lantern behind him because I can barely see past the silhouetting flame.

Joy, relief, and fear war inside me… until I see the summoned monster flow towards Dad.

A sound like piercing metal tears through the room, sending my bones vibrating and my ears burning. My mind reels under the force of it.

The fire behind Dad moves. I realize it's the shape of a person. A fiery person, holding a sword.

The flaming figure leaps forward, and the fiery sword elongates as they swing until it fills the entire space, sweeping across the monster. The endless shadows writhe, and another cry shudders through me as gold flames spread over its form. This time, it can't flow away fast enough to outpace the fire.

I see Dad lift his head, looking completely undisturbed, watching as flame consumes shadow.

The flame around the figure fades to a dull glow, and I tremble, confused, doubting my own perception, as I recognize, "…Mom?"

My throat aches, as does my leg. "Dad..?"

Both look at me. I realize with a sudden shock that they're both crying.

"David!" they cry close enough together that their voices almost harmonize, and they rush to my side.

"Can you move your leg?" Dad asks. His voice echoes strangely in my ears, and I try to focus on it. My vision grows blurrier, though I don't know if it's from my weakness or my tears. I've never been more relieved nor as happy to see anyone. I reach up towards him. I'm not sure I have the strength to speak.

"H-hurts…" I whimper with effort.

"David…" It's Mom's voice, sounding pained. I feel her hand brushing my hair. It feels so warm, and I feel so cold. I don't know how much of my shivering is due to the temperature and how much is from weakness and horror. She repeats my name over and over as if in prayer.

"Come, let's get you back home," Dad says, slipping his arms under my body with great care. His touch spreads a chill numbness through me, and I sob with relief. I clutch at him like a child and don't even care. I don't care that he can see me crying; I don't care about any of it.

He carries me like I weigh nothing and navigates the strange stony maze with familiarity and ease. Mom holds my hand, still radiant, lighting the way. I listen to their steps echoing in the caves all around us. Rain joins the sound of footsteps, and I can smell the sea. We emerge from the earth at last, exiting through the same gate Basil and I descend every time we study magic. The castle waits ahead of us, casting warm light in all directions, every window lit, with the shutters open. I can vaguely see figures holding lanterns wandering the grounds.

The grey sky and bleak fortress have never seemed so safe and comforting.

The light from Mom fades completely. "Mom… you're… magic?"

Mom frowns at me, brows drawing together. "Please don't speak of it here, David. Now rest; we'll discuss it later, after the doctor sees to you."

I don't want to see what's been done to my leg, but I can't help but look.

I'm covered in blood, to the point I can't see any of it. Most of that pant leg has been ripped away, and the surface beneath the skin doesn't look as flat as it should. Moreover, there's a blackness to it that terrifies me. "What…?" My eyes widen as I stare, denying what I see. Will I even be able to walk again…?

Dad follows my gaze. "You will be fine, David." He assures softly. The sound of spoken English is strangely comforting. It helps make the world feel real and whole again.

I'm distantly aware of people staring at us. They seem so pitiful now in their nice suits and pretty dresses that I can't imagine them ever being able to hurt me. Dad says something to them, and they rush out of the way.

I don't recognize the room I'm brought to. There's a large bed, but it's free of the usual excessive decorations or furniture, and the air stings with that sterile hospital smell. Dad lays me carefully down. I hope whoever owns this room doesn't mind their bed being dyed black and red.

Someone hangs a bag of plasma next to the bed, and another man I don't recognize enters the room. Both my parents step aside. I assume he's the doctor. The doctor slips something over my mouth and nose, and breathing at once becomes more effortless and makes my thoughts even murkier. I think the doctor is talking, but I can't hear what he's saying, and everything is blurring into strange dreams.

The day is painfully bright. My leg aches, but it's a dull, distant throbbing, not the mind-searing pain from before. I shift and look around the room. I'm still on the white bed, though at some point, it and I appear to have been cleaned, and my clothing has again been replaced.

I swallow; my mouth and throat are dry. I grope weakly at the dresser, hoping to find some water.

"David?" Mom calls. I turn as she enters my field of view. "What is it, David?"

"Thirsty," I croak. The very act of speaking is painful.

Mom pours a glass of water and holds it for me to drink. I blush, embarrassed at my own helplessness, but I'm too thirsty to complain and too weak to hold the glass myself.

I drink deeply, but Mom pulls the glass away before my thirst feels even close to quenched. "Not too fast," she chides gently. "Wait a bit before drinking more.

I watch her. She sits in a chair beside the bed, eyes gentle as she watches me. Part of me feels like I'm a kid with a fever again, but I push it aside. There are things I need to say.

"You're not going to tell me anything, are you?" I ask.

Mom looks startled. "What are you talking about, David?"

"You never do." I turn away from her. "You still haven't said anything about this place, or why you left, or… or anything. You're not going to tell me about the magic either, are you?"

Mom is silent. I guess that's my answer. I close my eyes.

I've started to drift asleep when her voice startles me awake.

"I'm sorry, David. I don't suppose it's enough to tell you I have my reasons." Mom says. I snort, and she sighs. "I… perhaps I will, someday. You deserve it, but… what happened that night…" She trails off.

Despite myself, I turn back to look at her, curious. She stares out the window.

"I don't trust this place, David. For all I love your father, I want to protect you from it in any way I can… and from the people here who would use you. But it seems like it's too late for that now." She hesitates, then turns back, finally meeting my eyes. "I do have magic, David. Magic that is very different from your father's. I… I think that may be why you're having so much trouble."

I stare. Mom frowns as she studies my face, continuing. "Your father spoke to me about it, but I told him I had no intention of teaching you just so you could be used as a tool. But…" She stops and looks at her hands. "You need to be able to protect yourself. No, I should have told you after you hurt yourself."

"Hurt myself?" I repeat. "Are you talking about the thing with the candle?"

She closes her eyes tightly, takes a long, shuddering breath, and nods. "I never imagined you would…" Her voice fades once more, and she sadly opens her eyes to gaze into mine. "I'm so sorry, David."

I just stare. All that pain, all that terror that I'll warp into some disturbed, insane monster, and she knew what was going on?! "What happened, then? Why did that happen? Why did it hurt every time I cast the spell?! I thought… I thought I was going to-" my voice breaks, and I swallow, blinking back tears.

"As I said, our magic is different. No rituals, no enchantments, no channeling or symbols. Will, yes. But it's done instinctively, a natural response to our whims and emotion. And what is natural for me, *part* of me, and so a part of you, is light and flame. You saw a glimpse of it in the cave. That's part of what magic is for me, and for you as well.

Unfortunately, for you, it's only half. You used a spell that, at its most primitive level, is designed to extinguish light. When you used it, you didn't just attack that candle; you attacked a part of yourself."

I struggle to process her words and compare them with what Basil's already taught me. "I... I'm not sure I really get it." I admit.

"No. Our magic works by different rules. I'm not sure how that will affect you in the long run. As I said," She said, staring at me regretfully, "I had hoped to protect you from it. From them."

"From Basil?" I challenge, angered by her words, her interference.

"No," She smiles. Her eyes are sad but her dimples press softly against her cheeks. "You were inseparable as children, you know. Viktor's father- no, never mind." She shakes her head. "You two are brothers, despite whatever difference of blood there may be. No, it's not Basil I wish to protect you from, but from what I've heard, you've already met them. And you'll never meet the one who was the most dangerous, thank God."

I bite my tongue, not wanting to snap at her. She's being frustratingly vague, but at least she's saying *something*.

"It... isn't easy." Mom adds. "I don't like thinking I've been wrong about what's best for you. I'm glad you had a chance to live outside this castle. I think the more you stay here, the more grateful you'll be as well. But you're stubborn, I know that. You get it from.... well, from both of us, I suppose." She smiles sadly. "Which certainly can't help. And if you learn, I think you need to learn both ways... the magic of your father and... mine."

Is Mom actually offering what I think she is? "You mean you're actually going to be consistently telling me things?"

Mom frowns, but I don't care. It is unusual, after all. Especially things like this. Mom sighs. "...I will be training you, yes. But I don't want you telling anyone about this-"

"I'm telling Basil." I interrupt. Mom stares, and before she can protest, I add, "you owe me that much. Anyway, you already told me, and I'm telling him whether you teach me or not. He's stood by me all this time. You obviously told Dad."

To my surprise, Mom nods. "You're right. I think it will be alright to tell him. Just… make sure he knows to keep it secret. Make him promise. It's important, David. It's important that your extended family not know about you… or me."

I squirm. I feel restless, but the numbness is fading away, and the pain is returning in its place, sharper now. I try to ignore it. "I'll tell him. Um. Will… my leg be okay?" It doesn't feel like it's been amputated, at least.

"You'll be out for a few months. I'm afraid you won't be able to do as much running around as you enjoyed. But you'll be fine."

I stare at her with horror, imagining being stuck in bed for months, in this place, with no internet and no one to talk to. Mom frowns.

"Don't fuss, David. You were worried, and now you're upset when I tell you it will be fine?"

"But," I protest helplessly. "*Months?*"

"I'll buy some books for you. And you'll have your father, brother, and I to train you. I'm sure that will occupy you as well." She pauses. "Your father wanted your teacher to come to tutor you-"

I bolt upright. "No!"

Mom laughs at my panic. "I thought you might feel that way. I suggested it would be easier on both of you if Basil perhaps helped tutor you instead. I think he'd be willing."

I sigh in relief and flop back on the bed. Lessons will be fine if it's Basil. I hope. At the least, I won't have much trouble distracting him if things become unbearably dull. Still… "Am I really going to be stuck in bed this whole time?" I ask, craning my neck at her.

"You can move around in crutches… actually, we should get you back to your own room as soon as you're ready. You'll be more comfortable there…" Mom hesitates, then murmurs, "and safer."

The top floor suite she's referring to still doesn't feel like *my* room. I guess it's time for me to start changing that. I smile to myself and stretch. "Sounds good. At least I'll be able to walk around some, even if it's not far."

Hopefully, I'll be able to get to the garden every day. I think I'll go stir-crazy if I can't go outside.

There's a knock at the door, and we both turn to look. "It's alright," says Mom, "I've spoken to him. You can come in now."

Dad and Basil step inside. I'm relieved to see no sign of Margaret. I smile at Basil. If this is what it takes to get my family together, I might have to face a horrific abomination and get my leg mutilated again. My smile fades a bit as I turn my attention to Dad, remembering our last conversation. "Hey." Is all I can manage for greeting.

"David," Dad nods, expression unreadable. It's hard to mesh his stony expression with his tear-streaked face the night before. I wonder if I'll ever see him cry again. Basil says nothing, though he gives me a small smile. His gaze darts between Dad and me.

"Dad," I respond. I'm tempted to say 'father' like Basil always does, just to see how he'd react... but he *did* just save my life. He deserves to be called Dad. ....then again... I look away. Why did he even save me? Was it even about me at all?

Mom stands. "I should leave you two to talk."

Dad nods and smiles softly at her. "Don't go too far. Basil, why don't you escort her?"

"Yes, Father," Basil opens the door for Mom, giving a little bow and gesturing formally. "Shall we walk in the garden, Miss Rose?"

"I'd rather stay a bit closer than-" the door shuts, abruptly cutting off Mom's words. I adjust my position uncomfortably, looking anywhere but at Dad. He walks over to the window and clasps his hands behind his back.

"You shouldn't run off like that. Storms are dangerous, and so is the dark. Don't run off alone again."

"Dad," I say, "I don't think the weather would have made much difference as far as me being attacked by a crazy person."

"Then you should take a servant when you go exploring."

"No." There's no way I'll give up what little freedom and alone time I have. "Not happening."

"Until you learn to properly defend yourself, you need to be accompanied. Take Basil." Dad says firmly.

I consider this. I do enjoy Basil's company, sure. But I know sometimes I'll want my own privacy. "Maybe."

"Perhaps it's time you began learning self-defense. Past time most like." Dad muses, partially to himself.

"Um, I wouldn't mind learning some, but I don't think that's gonna happen for a while." I gesture to my leg with a nod of my head.

"No, of course not. Unfortunately, martial arts theory can only take you so far. Once you can move about again, I want you to carry a whistle and a can of mace. When you've trained enough, you can have a knife, then a gun."

I brighten, ignoring the comment about the knife, gun, mace, and all that stupid crap. "I get to learn martial arts?"

"Of course. I want you to be prepared for anything. You can pick any style, though I recommend something more functional than showy. Hmm." He rubs his chin, "Basil can teach you, at least in the beginning."

"I want to learn kung fu." I say immediately. Kung fu is definitely the cool one. Also, well… I doubt he'll get the reference, but I know it, and that's good enough for now. My smile fades, and I stare at him for a long moment. "… you're not marrying me off to anyone."

"Marrying you off? You make it sound like it would be hard or burdensome not to. David, you'll be able to have any woman you want. You're my son, you're royalty, you're a prince."

"Like you could have anyone you wanted?" I challenge.

"I am not my grandfather."

"Then why are you trying to decide who we should marry for us? You said Basil, too. You're trying to do the same thing to him, aren't you? Only Basil will just go along with it because he just goes along with whatever you tell him, and he'll be miserable and never know better, and it will be all your fault!" He turns and looks at me, and there's genuine hurt on his face before anger clouds it over.

"Change comes slowly…" He almost growls, "…and Basil is my Heir–"

I interrupt, cutting off his tirade. "So that gives you the right to choose your happiness over his?"

"I'm his father; it's my right to decide his path. Once I'm gone, and he's in charge, he can make whatever decisions he wants."

"Because that worked out great for you," I say sarcastically. "I don't believe this. You don't even care about us at all, do you!? You just see us as… little dolls to send wherever is most convenient to you!" Not the best analogy ever, but I'm too exhausted and upset to be witty.

"You and your mother are the best things that happened to me, but being a leader means you have to set aside your happiness and do what is best. I don't just lead our family, I guide our nation, and Basil will after me, and his son after him."

"And somehow, that all equates to him having to marry whoever the hell you think is best. Fuck you, Dad. I didn't even know you, Mom has been miserable for years, and you are honestly trying to justify doing the same thing to Basil?!" I say, disgust and hurt straining at my throat.

"Your mother ran from here, and there was nothing I could do to stop her or to find you. I spent all the resources I could trying to find you, but she did not want to be found. If I could, I would have had you here your whole life, but things didn't turn out that way, and lamenting it and casting blame won't return to us lost time."

"Like being here makes things better?" I snap. "With Margaret!? With everyone treating her like crap?! All you're thinking about is yourself, about what you want!"

"Are you saying you don't want to be here?"

I clench the blanket in my fist, glaring fiercely at him, then away. "...honestly, I don't know. Everyone here's a complete asshole. You and Basil are the only things that make it worth it, and right now, you're acting as much of an ass as they are. You don't even care about us, do you? Not really."

"Of course I care," he says, moving next to the bed to stand over me, "If I didn't care, I wouldn't have brought you here. I wouldn't be so angry with you all the time. Angry with myself for not being there for you all these years, and I wouldn't be fighting my Uncles so hard to make sure you got everything you deserve."

"What exactly do you think I deserve? Clearly, it's not happiness," I say quietly.

"Only joy and endless days of happiness..." He says darkly, "...but such things are always fleeting. The world is a dark and terrible place, David. You deserve to be safe. You deserve fine things. The finest of everything. You deserve access to the wealth of the world's knowledge and our family's ancient power. But when you are as powerful as I am, allies and enemies are the same thing. My methods, our methods, have kept our family safe for hundreds of years, through invasions, conquests, crusades, rebellions, revolutions, and revelations. Basil will marry. And his Mother and I will have a considerable say in the matter. His alliance with his wife's family will make the family stronger. Safer. Sometimes duty is about sacrifice."

"I thought the family motto was 'power, family, reputation,' or that's what Basil said it meant. Seems more like Pessimism, Bargaining, and Sacrifice. Not even self-sacrifice, either. You're putting Basil up on the altar." I say, glaring.

"I do not yet have enough power to conquer the world, David. Political power can be difficult to maintain."

He attempts to say more, but I interrupt, "that's bullshit, Dad. No one secures political power through marriage anymore. It's not the god damn middle ages."

"You're being childish. I'm not asking you to run the country. Or marry someone you've never met and immediately begin fathering a horde of children. You will attend your lessons. You will learn etiquette. At some point, you will smile at a pretty girl-"

"No I won't," I interrupt again.

"Do not interrupt me!"

"Stop saying bullshit, and I won't have reason to," I say, uncowed.

"Don't swear at me, young man!"

"Or what?" I scoff.

"You're grounded!" He snarls and turns to storm out.

"I have a broken leg!" I yell back. "Where the fuck am I going to go?!"

"Don't you curse at me, young man, or I'll make you wish you were back down in the pit with the monsters!" he whirls and shouts. His face is an unrecognizable mask of twisted anger. His words chill me. "You are not too old for me to put you over my knee. Keep acting like a child, and I and everyone else will keep treating you like one!"

I swallow hard; images of the monster, of how close I came to death, or something worse, haunt my vision for a moment, blocking out my sight. I'm ashamed to realize I'm trembling, and I can't seem to stop it, and I don't seem to be controlling my own breathing, and part of me is still back there staring at that endless impossible darkness.

I blink back the tears that press against my eyes. Dad really doesn't care at all. The realization saps my strength and any will to fight. I turn away from Dad, leg pulsing with pain, feeling weak. "Just go away," I mumble, half into the pillow. I'd been waiting and hoping my entire life, and for what? There was a moment last night when I truly believed he cared, but it wasn't me he cried for. It was never me, just the potential I represent.

I laugh bitterly even as I cry, until I'm not sure which I'm doing. It's almost a fairytale ending. I discovered I'm magical royalty. Only I've never read a story where that means that the family you wanted, the only part you care about, doesn't give a crap about you. That all you get for your efforts and dreams is some twisted monkey's paw distortion of what you really wanted.

I'd been so sure he loved me.

I really am a complete idiot, aren't I?

That's why I like stories better. They always have good endings. Even when things go wrong, there's some form of catharsis. After all the crap I've been through, I deserve a good ending.

I hear Dad straighten his suit, hear the sound of his footsteps walk down the hall.

"David?" Mom calls softly.

"Go away," I mumble, burying my face in my pillow.

A moment of silence, and then Mom replies, sounding angry. "I'm going to go speak with your father. Someone should be bringing you food soon…" She pauses, then moves my pillow aside to kiss my forehead. "I love you."

I just keep hugging the pillow, leaving only a small hole to breathe out of.

"David?" Basil asks softly, "…can I get you anything?"

I swallow, flushing, and don't turn to look at him. "… Dad's an asshole."

"He's just upset. Uncle Leonid has been hounding him since you got here. Mother too. Everyone stood with him before, and now it seems they are all against him. You know, I've never heard him yell like that before…"

"That's because you blindly do whatever he says," I mutter. "Which is all he cares about."

"Shut-just stop! I know you're angry at him, but you don't need to take it out on me! Of course he wants you to do what he says, Father is a king, and he's doing everything the way *his* father did. You may not have a sense of pride about your lineage, but we do. *I* do! And every time you speak against it, you insult us, and it hurts! But I didn't come here to argue with you; I came to spend time with you, and honestly, you look like you've been kicked enough today. Now, do you want to do something to get your mind off this, or shall I go and let you wallow in misery alone?"

"I'm a bastard, Basil, remember?" I ask bitterly. "What do I have to be proud about? Why would I care anything about people who do nothing but treat my mother and me like shit?"

"*I* don't treat you like shit…" Basil protests.

"Yeah, and you're the only one," I say. "In this entire castle. And now you're angry at me for being upset. Because I'm treated like shit." I close my eyes. The familiar ache of loneliness has returned. "There's no one else here that isn't related to us except the staff, and they're constantly acting weird. Doesn't that bother you?"

"… I'm sorry, David…I don't want to fight with you, and I don't want you to leave." Basil says, sounding lost. I hear the chair creak quietly as he sits beside the bed. "I don't find the servants weird."

I shake my head. "Yeah, I'm sure they're great at their jobs. But it's not like you can really have a real conversation with them. There's the whole propriety bullshit, not to mention the obvious power imbalance. Besides, I doubt they'd appreciate the interruption, they're too busy trying to do their job. It'd just be awkward all around."

"You could probably make it work with magic. Disguise yourself and charm them to not think about the fact that they don't know you. Then you're just another person…"

I turn to stare at Basil, not sure I heard right. "Mind control? *That's* your idea of how to have a normal conversation with someone? By *mind controlling* them!?"

"No, not mind control! Just... ... okay, fine, shut up." he folds his arms and looks away, flushing, unable to deny the absurdity of his claim.

I watch him, frowning. "Basil, have you ever spent any time with kids your age that weren't family?"

"...No..." he sighs.

"That's exactly what I'm talking about," I say, sitting up and ignoring the shock of pain up my leg. "It's not even about pride for your lineage; it's about human dignity. Do you honestly think this place is paradise just because you get nice food whenever you want it? We're basically locked up in a cage while some twisted old bastards try to dictate our entire lives for us!"

"Who know how to make millions every year even though our country is tiny! Our people have great education, are never cold, hungry, or without medicine. Fyrnlendh is a great place. You just haven't gotten to see that yet..."

"They just have a slight chance of dabbling with strange magic and turning into mutated, psychopathic crazy people," I mutter. "And that's also based on the assumption that none of these things would happen without it. You can have a happy populace without the requisite of magical nepotism. Besides, none of that changes things for *us*."

"Fine, everything is terrible, and there's no point, let's all get drunk and not go to work anymore. We can play the viola as we watch the world burn around us..." he throws his hands up in the air and stands, drifting to a counter and searching for something before giving up.

"Or, y'know, instead of being overly dramatic Nietzsche-spouting followers of the joker, we could go out and do things," I suggest. "When my leg gets better, we should take a trip. Let you really see the world. Go to new places, do new things, get some good burgers, Climb Mount Everest, whatever! Live life to its fullest."

"Okay, I think we can swing that; if I make it a business trip..." Basil says, looking thoughtful, "How do you feel about visiting Moscow? Or Rome?"

"Not a business trip," I say firmly. "Basil, when was the last time you took time off just to have fun? Do you even have summer break here, or is it just work to the bone, every day, your entire life, without respite?"

"I take as much time as I need whenever I need it. I had a day off...A month before you got here. I spent half the day reading," he says with utter confidence, as if he had just won this argument.

"...you *do* know why Saturday and Sunday are called 'the weekend,' right? And, y'know, about Summer vacation, and the smaller ones, Christmas, spring break, I know you wouldn't have Thanksgiving, but really that's just like the herald of Christmas at this point..."

"What's the weekend?" he asks, scowling, "Never mind, I get plenty of breaks. I get a massage every day."

"If you don't have weekends in Fyrnlendh, it sure as fuck isn't the utopia you paint it as. The weekend is the day no one works every week, or days, usually. That's why Monday through Friday are called 'business days.' If you order something, they'll list the business days for shipping, which basically just excludes Saturday and Sunday. Because people need breaks." I shake my head. "You realize American kids get the entire summer off school? Not just us, either. Most of Europe has months or more breaks between the school year. And you're really, really due for yours."

"That doesn't sound very productive. I guess I could call it a sabbatical..." Basil says, frowning.

"Call it what it is," I say, leaning back. "A vacation. If you like, a celebration for reuniting with your long lost brother. We deserve one, right?"

"That we do. So, you don't work...at all? What do you do with the day?" Basil asks.

I don't know whether to laugh or cry. "I... I don't want to fight by pointing out how messed up it is that you literally cannot think of anything to do besides work at this point. There's so much *to* do. But I guess step one will be finding things you enjoy. Finding your favorites, foods, songs, movies, places, everything. Find out what's fun for you. As soon as my leg's better, we'll go. You promise?"

"I'll make arrangements; I'm fairly certain I'll be able to convince father."

The smile slides from my face again at the mention of Dad, and I glare at my hands. "I'm not sure about that, but good luck trying." I glance at him and try to push aside my unhappiness. "Hey, Mom said she talked to you about potentially tutoring me while my leg's hurt. Are you going to?" I bite my lip, staring hopefully at him. He grins.

"I don't know; I'm going to be awfully busy for the next couple of months getting things done so we can go on our vacation…"

I droop. "Oh, come on, Basil. You've worked hard enough; you deserve a vacation." I say, then realize how selfish I'm being. He did work hard, and now I'm asking him to work more for my sake. "Nevermind, then. But I still don't think you should have to work so hard. You've earned, like, ten years of vacation by now. And I'd still like to go with you."

"Wow, you really are out of it. I was kidding; of course I'll tutor you. Do you think I'd give up the opportunity to make you do math problems for hours?" Basil's grin turns wicked.

"Ahaha, you think I'm gonna be doing math problems for hours…"

"You'll do it, or you'll get no other form of entertainment. No fun 'til your work is done!" Basil wags a finger at me, grinning sadistically.

I smirk at him and, as a retort, grab a pillow and smack him with it. He may act arrogant now, but I'm confident I can distract him when necessary.

"Hey, careful of your leg, don't make me bind you to the bed."

I pause, pillow poised, and peer down. "Oh… right." I lower the pillow. The unpleasant pulsing in my leg is definitely worse; I've just been distracted enough to ignore it. "Dammit. This sucks."

"Do you want some morphine?"

I laugh. "I really hope you're kidding. I'll be okay. It's easy to ignore. I'm just going to go a bit crazy having to sit still all the time."

"We can put you in a wheelchair, and I'll roll you around like an old man…"

"Hell no," I said, shaking my head violently. "I'll be fine with crutches, thanks. Besides, being in a wheelchair would just be more sitting. That's exactly the definition of sitting still. Where are the crutches, anyway? I should try it out, maybe attempt to head back to my room."

"I don't know. I'll send for them if you're sure you're up for it." He crosses the room and gives two gentle tugs on what I've inwardly dubbed the servant summoner.

I squirm impatiently, then flop back, huffing. "I hope Mom and Dad aren't fighting again," I murmur out loud. My feelings are so complicated. I'm angry at Dad, and I don't regret fighting with him at all. But... I don't want Mom to be.

"... I'm sure they're fine. Your mother is a lot braver than I gave her credit for, but I'm surprised Father let her down into the caves." Basil says. I bolt up again.

"That's right! I forgot to tell you! I mean, not that it's been that long, I only just now found out..." I trail off and shake my head, staring at him with bright eyes. "Mom's- oh, right, first, you have to promise not to tell anyone except Dad, I guess because he knows."

"What? Tell Father what?"

"No, don't tell... I mean, don't tell anyone, but-" I stop and throw my arms up in exaggerated exasperation. "Just promise already!"

"I promise. What is it?"

I grin, happy to see him actually excited about something. "Mom's magic! It's a different type of magic or something. And it has something to do with why I kept messing up that spell. But she says she's going to teach me with you guys now, or as well as, or something, so it shouldn't happen again, and I'll definitely be able to learn now!"

"Wait, what? She's magic, but a different kind? What kind?" Basil asks, confused.

"Something to do with turning into a fiery inferno with a magic sword that blows up giant evil abominations?" I shrug. "It looks rad."

"...why don't you tell me everything that happened from the beginning?" Basil suggests looking even more confused.

"I guess... You probably know I ran out," I begin, and explain as best I can remember what followed. I do leave out the crying; not about to tell *that* to my younger brother. Also, detailing the creature that was summoned proves difficult. It's hard to quantify in words, and mostly I try to focus on what it was made up of, how it moved, and how it didn't. But I detail what Mom looked like, as best as I can remember, and the effects of Dad's spell. How thoroughly the white and gold fire obliterated the monstrosity, I also dwell on, but I think that's mostly to reassure myself.

There's a knock, and a man enters, bowing. I remain silent as Basil requests crutches and some brandy and resume my retelling.

"I've never heard of anyone doing anything like that. Do you know where she learned to do it?" Basil asks, leaning back in his chair again.

"She said something about the fact that our magic is very... instinctual? Or something. She said it's centered around light and fire, which is why the candle spell backfired. Because when I used it, my magic sort of... attacked itself." I explain, trying to remember the details. "All that trouble and panic, all because I happened to start with putting out a candle."

"Okay, how about trying to light a candle?" Asks Basil, looking thoughtful.

"Uh, well, Mom hasn't actually taught me anything yet. And... last time you gave me a spell to use because incantations are how you shape magic, and all that... so... um... Do you have a candle-lighting spell? I mean, I assume so," I add, looking thoughtful. "There's been a lot of dramatically lit torches... ... that's why there's no electricity here, huh? Because you can't dramatically turn the power on with magic?"

"I think it has more to do with tradition than drama, but sure, I can teach you a candle-lighting spell; it's basically the opposite of the snuff spell..." Basil proceeds to explain the construction of the spell. He teaches me a relevant chant and makes me repeat it several times before letting me try casting it.

He brings over a candlestick, setting it down on a nearby dresser. Before I can begin, two men enter, one bearing crutches, the other with a golden tray holding two glasses and a jar of brandy.

I fidget while they take the time to pour us each a glass, set it down, and bow. Basil dismisses them, and I turn my attention to the candle. "Okay," I say, holding a hand up. "Here it goes."

I close my eyes, bearing in mind not just the quick lesson Basil gave me, but memories of the candle-snuffing spell I now know was correctly cast. It isn't just will, but emotions, so I add some of those. This time, it's happier emotions: I'm eager, excited, and, well, maybe want to show off in front of Basil, just a bit. I suck in a breath, feel for the energy to cast, and pull at my will, that tingling inside that has to be my magic, shaping it out as I breathe.

The candle erupts into a fireball, setting the curtains and a nearby plant alight. I yelp in surprise, scrambling back.

Basil's eyes go huge, and he quickly chants a spell. Shadows wrap around the fire, dispelling it.

We both stare at the melted pile of wax where the candle was moments before. Even the gold candleholder is now distorted, bent oddly and half caved in, fused to the dresser it had been set on. After a long silence, Basil closes his mouth and clears his throat.

"I think you should do that the next time Uncle Leonid suggests that you don't have a place here. Probably make him fluster himself into unconsciousness."

I grin at him and reach up to ruffle his hair playfully. "Awe, Basil! You always know just what to say."

He ruffles my hair back. "That's what big brothers are for."

As desperate as I am to return to my own room, the journey is unexpectedly challenging. Not only am I weak, not only do the crutches dig uncomfortably into my armpit, but every little movement I make sends bolts of agony shooting through my leg. I'll accidentally brush it against something or unconsciously put the slightest weight on it, and it's enough to bring tears to my eyes.

I push through it anyway, desperate. Or, I intend to. The doctor catches me and forbids me from attempting again for another week. He leaves the room muttering in Fyrnekh, and I can do nothing but scowl after him.

An entire week of being stuck in one room, unable to move. Not even *my* room, at that. Which, even if it doesn't feel mine in the same way, is private and on the upper floor.

"I can still have them bring the wheelchair," Basil suggests when I complain, more serious than when he initially brought it up.

"Hell no," I shake my head vehemently. "I'm not going to be wheeled around. I'll just feel *more* helpless, and I doubt it's really going to hurt any less. It's not like whoever's pushing will know when they move too fast or bump my leg."

"I only wished to help," Basil says, frowning. "And you're swearing again."

"I think I've earned the right to swear, considering the circumstances," I grumble, folding my arms.

"If you consider this to be the worst of times, then it is the perfect time to practice not to," counters Basil smoothly. "I'll help you with it and punish you every time you do."

"How? By poking my leg?" I snap.

Basil's eyes widen, and he looks hurt. "Poke…? No! I'd never hurt you like that, David." He answers with quiet sincerity.

I sigh and rub my head. "I know, I know. Sorry. I know you were just playing around. I guess pain makes me grumpy." I smile ruefully. "How about some distraction?"

Basil nods, sitting down. "We can begin your tutoring." He states.

I groan and flop back, covering my head with a pillow.

"David, you still must continue your education."

I grunt in response.

I hear Basil let out a breath. There's a pause, and he adds. "David, perhaps… if you do well with me, I can take over your classes even after you've recovered."

I peek out suspiciously from the pillow. "…you mean it?"

Basil hesitates, then nods with more confidence. "Yes, I think Father would agree to it. But you'd have to make more progress with me than Miss Rigo, and that means you have to actually work. So, let us start."

I consider this before sighing and reluctantly crawling back up and rearranging the pillows. "Fine, fine. Learning more than I did from Miss Rigo is hardly a high bar. But we have to have breaks to do something fun. Speaking of which, I'm gonna need my music."

Basil smiles. "Perhaps, when you're better, you can take some music classes too."

My breath catches, and I look at him. "Do you think so?" Excitement bubbles up, blotting out the pain.

Basil looks surprised. "Of course. Father *wants* you to educate yourself. I'm surprised you haven't already studied it. You speak as if you have when you talk of your music and what you admire about it."

"That's mostly stuff I've taught myself. Most of the schools I went to… didn't really have the best music programs."

Maybe that's unfair of me. There were excellent musicians at some of the schools I attended, and the classes were designed to be attended for years at a time rather than a few months. Of course, that's only true for the schools that allowed me to take a music class without being able to play any instrument before starting, which was not that many.

"I'll speak to father about it," Basil promises, smiling.

"Oh, have you asked him about the vacation?" I ask hopefully.

"Not yet," Basil says. "I'm sorry, it slipped my mind. I'll be sure to bring it up soon, perhaps after dinner."

I shake my head. "If there's any good point about this leg thing, at least I'm missing dinner."

"You already missed most of the dinners," Basil points out.

"Maybe. But I have an excuse this time."

Basil shakes his head. "Enough distraction. Let's begin. I hear you have trouble with math, so we'll start there."

I groan.

"There's a lot of math in music," Basil prods. "The Fibonacci sequence, to begin with, and mathematics shape scales a lot. Not to mention that chords are designed around the frequency by which the strings vibrate. What if we approach it from that direction, into something tangible?"

I look at Basil, intrigued despite myself. "That could be interesting," I admit.

Basil smiles and presents me with the best mathematics-related lecture I've ever had. It's so fascinating; I actually ask him to stop and get me some paper so I can take notes because *I* want them.

"I knew you'd be a great teacher!" I say happily at the end. I still have a bit of a math headache, and the concepts are still a bit overwhelming, but they're interesting and I actually have reason to review them later.

Basil blushes. "I think Father will be happy with your progress."

I remember my last conversation with Dad, and my mood darkens.

"Who cares what he thinks," I mutter unhappily. Basil purses his lips but doesn't press.

"...but if he does want it, maybe you can sell tutoring me as part of our vacation plan," I add in a stroke of genius. "Immersion is supposed to be the best teacher for language, plus I know history will stick with me more if it's taught in the actual places."

"That isn't a terrible idea," Basil admits thoughtfully.

I frown. "But, if we do, it might not be a real vacation for you."

"Oh, no, it would," Basil says, smirking.

I stare blankly for a moment. "...you really like to be in a position where you can boss me around, don't you."

Basil flushes and clears his throat. "Let's try another subject." He suggests. I snort. I definitely hit the nail on the head there, but I let it go.

Mom stops by after Basil leaves for lunch, setting some sandwiches and cookies next to my bed before sitting in a chair across from me, scooting it into the small patch of sunlight that made its way through Fyrnlendh's stubborn fog.

I pick up one of the cookies. They're different from the food I've had here. They're non-uniform, imperfect, warm, and smell tantalizingly familiar. "Did you... make these?" I ask, barely believing it.

Mom smiles. "Sometimes I just want to cook something myself. The kitchen staff doesn't love me for it, but one of the head chefs was kind enough to set aside a little area for me to use last time I came here and agreed to do the same this trip."

I open my mouth wide, ready to shove the cookie in, but Mom plucks it from my hand.

"Not until you eat your sandwich." Mom chides. I huff, and she adds. "You'll like it; it's the freshest tuna melt you've ever had. The tuna was caught and prepared today."

My stomach rumbles approvingly. I love Tuna Melt sandwiches. "Thanks, Mom."

Mom nods. "I'd also like to begin some of your... other magic lessons today."

I pause mid-chew, staring at her intently. Excitement makes it difficult to focus on eating.

"I'm not teaching you anything until you finish your sandwich," Mom says firmly and sighs. "And it's going to be very simple to start. I've spoken to your father about arranging a spot for it. Still, I want to go over things enough that I don't have to worry about you accidentally hurting yourself again."

I obediently bite into my sandwich, which is as impressive as Mom advertised. "Hey, Mom?" I ask after swallowing my first bite.

"Yes, sweetie?"

"Can I order some stuff for my room? Like, decor that actually suits me." I ask.

Mom smiles softly. "That sounds like a good idea. I'll try to get you internet access to make a wishlist, but don't expect everything you ask for."

I nod eagerly, grinning, and tear into the sandwich.

I start licking some tuna juice off my finger when I finish, but Mom gives me a wet wipe and a pointed look. I sigh dramatically.

"It's wasteful not to savor all of it," I protest, but reluctantly clean myself with the wipe.

"I think you savored it plenty," Mom says, picking up my spotless plate and eyeing it.

"I wonder what the reaction would be if I did that at one of the dinners," I muse. Mom lets out a snort and then clears her throat, coughing a bit, fighting to keep her expression neutral. She ends up with a straight lip and intense dimples.

"Don't try it," Mom says firmly, meeting my gaze.

"You know it would be funny." I push.

"I'm not going to encourage you to have bad manners just because it crosses a point where they'd be in agreement, too," Mom says firmly. "Do. Not."

I sigh. "Fine." She's no fun.

Mom offers me the plate of cookies and some milk. "You can eat while I begin."

I take a bite and close my eyes. It's delicious. It tastes like the best moments of my childhood. There isn't the extravagant overcomplication of most meals I've had here, just a simple, delicious chocolate chip cookie.

"As I said, our magic is more based on whim and emotion, so you won't need to recite any incantations. For the first lesson, I want to start with the ability I believe will protect you most."

I open my eyes and swallow quickly. "Does that mean you're going to teach me to turn into fire?"

Mom smirks at me. "Not to start, and that isn't what will keep you most safe. Seeing will."

I droop. "Seeing?" That doesn't sound nearly as cool.

"I know your father has his own ways of sensing magic, and I don't know how the two will blend. But having an awareness of dangers around you, of potential monsters, and of magic when it is cast around or on you, and knowing what it means is the best thing you can do." Mom explains firmly. "It may not sound exciting, but it's essential, and you'll be grateful for it."

I consider this. It isn't as cool, but I can't argue that it sounds handy. "How do you know it's different from Dad's?"

"Partially from speaking with him, partially from, well, Seeing, as I said. He senses magic, which I can too, but he can't see spells the way I can and the way I hope you can learn to." Mom folds her legs and places her hands on top of them. "When you encountered that thing in the cave, if you can remember any point where you know magic has been cast around you, have you noticed any feelings associated with it?"

I frown, setting the cookie I was nibbling back on the plate. I still feel sick thinking about what happened. Still... "Cold and disgusted, I think. Around... around the Corrupted. And I think I saw Kolya mind controlling someone, and it really pissed me off."

Mom's eyes flash at that, and she straightens. She bites her lip like she's trying to hold in a reply. "Those are certainly your instincts. As I mentioned, emotions are tied to them, so remember to trust your gut. But that's only one part of it. You need to use Sight to understand beyond that."

"How do I do that?" I ask, studying her face, hoping to get my mind away from the caves so I can actually enjoy the cookies.

Mom sighs. "It's second nature for me, but you might need more practice. It might help if you unfocus your eyes while you're still learning how things work." She cups her hands together, and her fingers turn red, edges rimmed with gold, as she assumably holds light or flame or something inside them. "Try to stare at my hands while you do. Your intuition should guide you, as well as your natural sense of magic. If you feel any emotion, use that to help channel. It may even be that the emotion you feel is related to the type of spell. Draw on your magic as normal, but focus on what you see and sense and your desire to understand more."

"Curiosity, then," I ask.

Mom smiles. "Yes. Curiosity is perfect."

Well, that makes things easier, at least. Curiosity's never been something I've had in short supply. I stare at Mom's hands intently, letting my gaze go off focus. I draw from the well of power and channel my curiosity.

At first, nothing happens, and I'm worried it will be the candle-snuffing spell all over again, but I push that thought aside. Fear isn't going to help me here.

I focus, on my emotions, on the magic, and on a sense of magic I can feel subtly from her palms. And as I do, slowly, it takes shape.

The light intensifies until it looks like her hands are cupping a miniature sun. Glimmering veins of light and flame flow through her body, to the sun, and around her body, radiating subtly outward in tiny sparks. Behind her, tendrils of shadows creep along the walls, curling. A tendril of shadow reaches towards her, and Mom turns and looks at it as well.

She frowns, and her light flares a little brighter for a moment and it fades.

I blink and lose that focused state I'd managed to meditate into.

Mom drops her hands back on her lap and smiles a little tightly at me. "Well, it seems you've figured it out."

"For a moment," I say, frowning. "What was that? Did someone just try to cast a spell at you?"

Mom tilts her head, then shakes it. "No, that wasn't any sort of active spell. That's just the castle."

"The… castle?" I repeat, goosebumps prickling my skin.

"It's always been like this," Mom says softly. She shakes her head and smiles at me. "That's enough for now. Eat your cookies; you're still recovering and shouldn't push yourself."

I swallow and nod. Even if I wanted to continue, I'm too creeped out to focus on curiosity at the moment anyway.

I have Basil and Mom's lessons, reading, and listening to the music made by my math problems on the laptop Basil lent me. You'd think all that would keep me distracted, but time crawls by like the final hours before Christmas.

The balcony is usually left open to keep the room from getting stuffy. Wind lures me, salted by fog and sweetened by the flowers around the room, and the distant calls of ravens are maddeningly tempting. I want to run, to explore. I want to go to the ocean or endure sitting in a car for a couple hours to experience the culture of a Fyrnekh city for the first time.

I keep trying to sneak out of bed and start moving, seeing how long I can endure the pain in my leg, until the doctor orders my crutches removed.

Today is worse than usual. Basil abandoned me to catch up on some of the work he's behind on, and Mom's with Margaret, so she's avoiding me for my own sake. I still don't know how Mom can stand to be around her. Why does she like her?

A single rap against the door startles me. I straighten hopefully. Maybe one of them is done early.

"Yeah?" I call.

The door opens, and Dad steps in. "That is hardly the proper response to a knock," he grunts.

I stare at him, then pick up one of my books, open it, and glare at a random page. "Busy."

"You're holding it upside down," Dad says.

I snort through my nose and slam the book down onto my stomach. "What do you want?"

"To begin with, civility," Dad says. His shadow falls over me, but I refuse to look at him.

"And I want a father who cares about me. I guess we'll both have to learn to do without." I snap, cheeks stinging at the memory of our last exchange.

"I will not spoil you, David. You've been coddled too much as it is."

I bark out a laugh. "You have a funny idea of 'coddling,'" I fold my arms and stare to the side. My eyes fall on one of the photos Mom brought to keep me comfortable until I can return to my own room. It depicts younger versions of my parents, taken at an amusement park. It's hard to think of Dad at an amusement park and stranger still to see him smiling. "...you just want to make me as miserable as you are, don't you?"

I hear Dad sit down and steal a glance at him. He's rubbing his temple, eyes closed, scowling. Neither of us say a word for a long time. When he opens his eyes again, I look away quickly, staring down and tugging at the blanket.

"...I want you to never be defenseless if you ever get attacked by another psychopath. I want you to be as eloquent as you are intelligent. I want you to be as knowledgeable as you are passionate. I want all the world for you, everything I didn't have growing up. The things that your mother showed me, amusement parks, dates, graphic novels, love. But most of all, I want you to be safe. I know how to do that; I don't know how to make you happy...." he trails off.

I swallow the lump in my throat, which is tightened by the words. My hands tremble where they grip the comforter, and I feel strangely warm. "You want me to love, but you still want to arrange a marriage for me? For Basil?"

"I have no illusions about ever making you do anything you truly don't want to, David. But, if I find a girl I think you may like, I'll introduce you, and who knows."

I eye Dad suspiciously. Will I ever trust him enough to tell him every reason why I'm repulsed by the idea? "If that's the case, why did you bring it up again? Also, it's still creepy to talk about marrying me to people who are related to me."

"Everyone is related somehow, David." He shakes his head, "It's not going to be for a long time anyway."

I make a face. "Not like that, they're not," I say, shaking my head to erase the thought. I stare at my hands. I'm furious at him, at how much it seems like he's turned into his own father. How he's just perpetuating the same cycles of pain. But I don't want to fight or think about it. And I'm not unmoved by his words that aren't about marriage. "...so has Basil talked to you yet?"

"The vacation? Yes, he mentioned it."

I squirm and wince when the excited movements cause pain to shoot through my leg again. "And?" I press.

"You can go, but not till after the family reunion."

I blink. "Reunion?".

"Yes, the whole family will be here in a few months; he can't leave till after."

I frown. "Why didn't you mention this reunion thing before?"

Dad looks at me, and I feel my ears burn. Right. The argument. I flip absently through the book.

"It's... more than just a friendly family gathering," Dad adds after a pause.

I roll my eyes. "Of course it is. Nothing this family does is normal."

He scowls. "David…"

"So what is it if it's something even you admit isn't normal?" I ask.

He glares at me for a long moment before resuming. "It's related to magic, of course. Ours is the most magically powerful family, no, force in the world-"

"That you know of." I interrupt.

His lip quirks upward in a half smile. "That we know of." He agrees. "Your mother was a first for me, and I never told anyone else in the family about her. But I digress. Our family is powerful, and as you've seen firsthand, power can attract jealousy, for all I tried to protect you from it."

I grip my shoulders and nod. Dad continues.

"You already know the benefits of preparing magic on a small scale." He pauses again, waiting for another nod. "The reunion is where we cast spells on a larger scale. Spells of power, protection, and prosperity."

I wonder if the alliteration is intentional. I can't help but appreciate it.

"There are many complicated rituals that will be cast during the reunion, the largest and most important being the one that takes place during the Winter Solstice, the longest night of the year. For this, we draw in all magic using members of the family, even those who live outside Fyrnlendh. More details will be covered in your education, but I will be asking Basil to focus on your Fyrnekh and magic for the time being." Dad folds his hands behind his back and looks at me. "If you want to go on your vacation with Basil, you must participate in that ritual. I expect great contributions, ones that the family cannot ignore. Do so, and I shall fully fund a month's vacation for both of you, wherever you would like to go, through whatever means."

I meet Dad's eyes. "Three months. Basil's earned way more than one."

Dad's lip quirks at the corner. "Two."

"Three, and I study and learn as we travel."

"I've been told that was part of the plan already," Dad says, lifting his eyebrows.

"Not if it's only one month."

Dad chuckles, looking surprisingly pleased. "Very well, but remember" He points a finger at me. "This hinges on your performance at the reunion. Make me proud."

I'm beginning to hate those words, but I nod. At least I have something to look forward to. Dad leaves, and I stare into the Fyrnlendh fog, imagining all the places I'll show Basil. So much has happened so quickly, and this place still doesn't feel like the home I longed for. But my family is a little bigger. Most important of all, I have something to fight for. I promise myself I'm not going to bend myself for anyone anymore.

For the first time in an eternity, I can look to the future and have something to look forward to.

END OF BOOK ONE

About the Author

C.T. BRYCE is the pen name for the writing partnership of two authors who are also partners in life. They have been creating stories together for years and have decided to share them with the world. This is their debut novel and the first in the Guthanderkaz series. They currently reside in Santa Cruz, California.

They love cats, foggy days, the songs of corvids and all things gothic.

keep updated on the next book at
www.guthanderkaz.com